FIRE FALL

JD Glass

2024

Bywater Books

Print ISBN: 978-1-61294-295-7

Bywater Books First Edition: September 2024

Printed in the United States of America on acid-free paper.

Cover designer: TreeHouse Studio

Bywater Books
PO Box 3671
Ann Arbor MI 48106-3671

www.bywaterbooks.com

Prologue

Last Night

THERE ARE TIMES when I really hate sleeping.

When those times come around, there's this moment where I feel like I'm falling, and I jerk myself up and out of it because falling is the *worst* thing—ever.

According to some very well-respected research on the topic, it's the first fear we learn as infants, and it really shouldn't be a surprise as to why. There you are, helpless and unable to do anything other than hope to everything that you know—and let's face it, as a baby you truly know *nothing*—that someone or something catches you before you get hurt—or worse.

Then as you get older, grow control over your limbs and the landscape, you become aware—aware of what can hurt you, aware of what can happen when you fall.

Like most, I grew past it, able to ignore it, even learned how to work with it. And then . . .

I fell, once.

I fell out of the sky, under stars I couldn't see, through smoke that blew and billowed, choking me and all that lived with the rage of the fire that powered it, pulling my life from me to feed its own, each of us desperate to stay alive by extinguishing the other.

I fell into a black so complete that even though I felt the movement of my body, the weight of my gear upon me, the twist of the cords that would direct motion instead fighting my hands, in that moment words, directions like *up* or *right* or *left*, had no meaning, and all I knew was that I . . . was . . . going . . .

Down.

Down into the unknown.

Down into the black.

Down into the choke I couldn't see, to the heat that roared in the ever-closing distance, a heat that crackled and rumbled and screamed "I'll get you, my pretty!" because its desire to survive weighed directly against mine.

And I fell down into a pain so complete that the roar and the choke and the growing heat exploded into the brightest white, was the sum total of the entire universe before it disappeared, taking me with it.

I really hate falling.

And sometimes I really hate falling into sleep.

"I've got you. You're okay. It's me—I've got you."

I wake, just for a few moments, but this time it's all okay and I know she's right, because I can feel her pressed against my back, her arm wrapped tightly about my shoulder and over my chest, pulling me even closer into her as her fingers twine through mine, and her breath is the sweetest breeze over my shoulder.

"I love you," I murmur, overjoyed even in my exhaustion that she is so close, and I hold her hand even tighter, because I mean what I say with everything that's in me, that I'm made of, as I snug myself even closer to feel every precious inch of her against me that I possibly can.

She's the one, *my* one, the center and sum and meaning of my even being alive at this very moment, and this time, because I know she's here, she's with me, and we are *both* okay, I don't fall—I land.

Safe.

Chapter 1

More Than One Yesterday Ago

Bennie: Hey! So you didn't tell me how it went the other day—I'm guessing it went well?

Trish: Well is a word—if you count surviving the last jump without any incident!

Bennie: We didn't hear about anything out here.

Trish: That's because we got it under control—the ground crew cut a LOT of line, and caught a weather break, so we got clear super-quick!

Bennie: I'm glad for that but I meant your date. You were supposed to have one of those.

Trish: Was I?

Bennie: Uh, yeah!

Trish: I guess I forgot! There was a fire to go to, ya know . . .

Trish: And didn't you have something similar going on?

Bennie: Who, me?

Trish: Uh, yeah!

Bennie: I have no idea what you're texting about.

Trish: Uh-huh.

Bennie: Look, how about the next time I'm out there or you're out here, we just talk about this instead of texting bad jokes?

Trish: When's the last time we did that?

Bennie: Fire last summer out over the Alamos Ridge.

Trish: Maybe we should grab a coffee without a fire?

Bennie: Wait a minute . . . I'm thinking about this! What would it be like to actually chat and NOT smell like smoke?

Trish: I DON'T REMEMBER ANYMORE!!!

Bennie: Ok—let's find out, then!

Trish: Done deal—I'll go to NYC, or you come out thisaway?

Bennie: Either/or is good. I'm off tomorrow in the a.m. Seriously—let's look at the calendar and figure it out?

Trish: Better yet—we'll synchronize our calendars!

Bennie: Lol! Love it—and it sounds like the beginnings of a plan.

Trish: Go to sleep—it's already late for you!

Bennie: Or is it just very early?

Trish: G'night (or good

morning. Or whatever.)

Bennie: Good whatever to
you, too!

So of course, the call came in at what-the-fuck o'clock.

"Your phone is ringing," sing-songed a voice I really liked—even loved—but honestly, I didn't want to hear *any*thing but my dreams after working not one, not two, but actually three twelve-plus-hour shifts in a row—and those right after I'd already worked two ten-hour days.

"It's just a nightmare," I mumbled back at my cousin Linda as I tried to bury my head under my pillow. Sleep felt so damn good, and my chest and shoulders were sore with the fullness of the need for it . . .

"It's your *bat* phone," Linda said, and I could feel her move around the bed we shared in this small apartment as she spoke. "Here."

She dropped it on the pillow over my head. It landed with a soft thump.

Fuck.

The bat phone.

So named because, like the comic book hero who saw a signal in the sky when the city needed him, this phone rang when help was needed—my help, specifically.

It felt like my whole body groaned as I sighed out heavily. "Thanks for not dropping it on my head," I ground out to her, then grabbed the phone.

"Only because you're gonna need it," she answered, "and I can't risk hurting a pretty face that looks so much like mine."

"Little favors," I said as I rolled my eyes, because with Linda, it was always spice—you just never knew how much sweet, salt, or heat, you would get. "But I am sorry this woke you."

"Eh, you know I know it's an emergency, right?"

"Thanks," I said again; she finally hit the right button.

"It's Grego," I answered, giving my last name, knowing that whoever it was already knew that—they were calling me, after all.

"Grego, this is Coordinating Officer Ryan. We've got a request to send support to a sustained fire situation in California. Are you available for immediate pickup and transport?"

I winced at the crispness of the voice in my ear and held the phone just slightly away from my offended head.

"I'll need about half an hour to be ready," I answered, already mentally cataloguing what I needed and where everything was.

"I'll make you coffee," Linda stage-whispered to me as I swung my legs out from under my oh-so-warm and comfortable blankets to stand.

"No—you'll wake Nana!" I stage-whispered back as I felt for then grabbed the right uniform out of the closet, then followed her through the open door to make my way down the hall to the bathroom to wash up before I got ready in the room we called the studio.

Nana, our grandmother, was, as per her current usual, sleeping in the living room on the sofa instead of what was supposed to be her room, a habit she'd developed since she'd recently been ill. Yes, she was much better now, thankfully, but I didn't want to wake her before I had to. Still, though, I needed to hear everything Coordinating Officer Ryan was telling me.

"Twenty-five minutes, Grego, gear check and all. You good with that?" he both ordered and asked while I spit and rinsed.

"Yes, sir, twenty-five minutes!" I agreed with fresh minty breath. I twisted my hair up into a ponytail. I hurried down the hallway towards the studio where the rest of my gear waited, tucking my shirt into my waistband on the way. I passed Linda, who stuck her tongue out at me, and I rolled my eyes back at her. "Chute was already examined last jump," I assured into the phone as I snapped the light on.

"Good. See you in the air." Ryan clicked off and I did the same.

Technically, the studio was supposed to be Nana's bedroom, and while there *was* a single bed in there, it was a daybed that now almost never got used as anything other than a sofa or, more usually, a resting place for bolts of cloth that Nana made beautiful clothes with. It doubled as a safe place to temporarily lay half-finished constructions.

I carefully wove my way around the dress form and its draped pieces, not wanting to disturb my grandmother's carefully pinned work. I glanced around at the shelves that held Nana's collection of saints and the bookcase with her ever-growing Italian *Vogue* collection ("American *Vogue* is great for knowing what happened in Europe five months ago—and some of it is very watered down from true art," Nana had told me once) while I reached into the closet for my gear. I made a note in my head to go to her favorite international newsstand in Manhattan to pick up the newest one for her.

Besides, that meant I could make a stop at my favorite comic bookstore, JHU, on the way back. Momentarily happy with my future-future plans, I slid my feet into my boots, then grabbed my personal gear bag. I opened it to double-check that I'd have everything I needed for emergency rescue work.

I had everything on my required list, my personal necessities, and a few extras—just in case. I took a breath, then nodded. I glanced at the drawing board against the wall—my part of the studio—which held the latest project I'd been working on.

Aw man. I sighed regretfully.

I'd have to text my friend and creative partner, Jean, when I had a moment, to let her know that I might be delayed in getting those panels and pages of our comic done. But, as I continued to pack my personals into a separate compartment in my gear bag, I made sure to include the things that might make the difference between unrelieved trauma and at least a small oasis of sanity, not only small yet helpful creature comforts, but some really inexpensive mechanical pencils, to go along with a small four-by-five drawing pad I had already tucked into my inside chest pocket.

Common sense meant I never carried pencils or pens directly on me because, basically, they could become little spears during a landing impact. These particular ones were the disposable variety because I didn't want them to get wrecked or, worse, lost. But . . .

If there was downtime, and sooner or later there would be, it meant that I would find a moment to sketch. It kept me calm, it kept me mindful, and it also meant that, no matter what, I was still making progress on my project, which was always a feel-good for me. That, and sometimes I doodled little things about the crew I worked with. Everyone I worked with knew I did it. Sometimes it made folks laugh when I shared funnier sketches.

God, I don't think there was anyone I worked crew with who didn't have something I drew with them in it . . .

Christ—I had to move and get out. My gear bag complete, I slung it over my shoulder. Just behind where it had lain was my chute. As I'd already assured my coordinating officer, it had already been checked in minute detail before I'd repacked it. Okay, well, actually, I'd checked it, then Nana had reviewed it, too.

That part—the piece of equipment that not just my job but my actual life depended on—I already knew was good to go.

I ran my thumb under the strap resting on my shoulder, then glanced around for the phone charger.

"Here," Linda said from the door. She grinned and held one out to me.

"*Gracias, querida,*" I told her as I tucked it into a flap on my bag, then reached out to give her a hug. "Thank you so much for all you've been doing around home these last few weeks. I honestly don't know what we'd do without you," I told her as we held each other.

"You'd miss me, of course—and my fabulous cooking!"

I couldn't help but chuckle. "All true," I agreed, and squeezed her to me. I sighed as the reality of what was about to happen and the needs it would create filled my mind. "This might take at least a week—maybe longer, since they're calling in my unit, but hopefully not more than that. You'll be able to balance work and classes with that?"

"Ah, *querida*," Linda said against my cheek. "There's been so many crazy emergencies this week—so yeah, you've worked extra hours, Nana's been sick—of course I'm gonna help! And besides," she said as she tugged on my ponytail, "she's my Nana, and this is my home, too! My cousin is a hero, my Nana is a wonderful and tireless artist, and you let me cook whatever I want—so I'm a lucky girl!"

"I'm the lucky one," I countered as I released her. "I have an amazing family." I glanced towards the living room, where Nana was supposedly sleeping on the sofa. Although I really wished she'd sleep in the bed, I understood. Still, it had been several years since we'd moved into this two-bedroom apartment, and since Linda had only recently moved in to be closer to both work and school, Nana insisted that the studio be purely a room we could each work in.

I sighed quietly as I glanced around.

As pretty as this space was, it was too small.

What I hoped was that between the three of us and the extra money that working this job pulled in, maybe sooner rather than later we'd be able to afford a larger place . . .

Linda's gaze traveled with mine. "Should I tell her when she wakes or . . ."

I touched Linda's shoulder. "I'll do it," I said, then sighed again, inwardly this time. "Otherwise she'll get mad that I didn't, and then worry even more than she already does. Besides," I said, and grinned at her, "you know she's already awake."

There wasn't any need, nor did I want to say the obvious: every day, every call, every mission—especially ones like this, the emergency multiple-agency responses—was a risk: a risk of getting injured, a risk of being scarred, and even possibly the risk of death to not only to those affected by the event directly but also to the rescuers, like me.

Linda smiled even as she rolled her eyes and nodded. "You need coffee," she told me as she gave a quick pat to my shoulder.

"I need coffee," I agreed.

"That's what I said," Linda reminded me, then moved to the kitchen.

I took a deep breath as I resettled my bag over my shoulder, then squared myself. I walked into the semi-darkened living room. The light on the table just next to the sofa softly lit a resin statue of the Sacred Heart of Jesus, symbolic of love and compassion for all of humanity. Next to that, my grandmother had placed a figure of Saint Joseph holding a child, because he was the patron saint of fathers, immigrants, and workers of all sorts. And completing her holy tableau, behind both figures stood a third: Saint Michael the Archangel himself, sword raised in protection. He was considered to be the patron of people like me: paramedics, police, emergency medical technicians, and firefighters.

Still, though, even with the visible shrine on top, under the table itself were several years' worth of *Architectural Digest*, because "form and function must both always be considered," Nana always said.

Considering how carefully she inspected and repaired my parachutes, as well as how necessary it was, I not only agreed, I was grateful for her exacting standards and discerning eye.

I knew, even as I crouched down by Nana's head on the sofa, that she wasn't sleeping, and she confirmed that when she raised herself to a seated position.

"*Otra vez, mi vida?*" she asked, her eyes gleaming at me

as her hands reached out for mine. "You just came back from work—you haven't even really slept!"

I took the hands she offered me and kissed each one, soft and fragile-seeming in my careful grip. "Again, yes," I confirmed. "And yes, I know. They need me. I'll catch some sleep on the flight out."

Nana's fingers tightened over my hands. "You'll be careful— you'll be *safe*"—she pulled me in to kiss the crown of my head— "and you'll come home soon."

I released her hands, only so I could put my arms around her and hug her. "Yes, Nana," I agreed, although none of what she'd said was a request: they were commands both to me and the Universe. I knew I would do my utmost to obey—and given the force of my Nana's will, I was pretty certain the Universe would, too. "I will—all of that."

Nana cradled my head to her chest, and I could hear her heartbeat, strong and steady under my ear, along with her words. "Take my blessing," she murmured into my hair, and I could feel her shift. I knew she was reaching for the holy water she kept in a small plastic bottle, she always had it close to hand.

"Gracious St. Joseph," she began as she performed the sign of the cross on my head, "protect my Bennadette from all evil as you did the Holy Family. Kindly keep us ever united, ever fervent in imitation of virtue, and always faithful in devotion to you. Amen."

"Amen," I repeated. "*Gracias, mi Nana adorada*," I said after she gave me another kiss on my head, then I stood. "*Yo te amo*."

Nana gave me a warm smile in the low light. "*Yo te amo más*." I couldn't help but smile back because she always told me she loved me more. "And bring me a new sketch," she reminded me.

"Yes, Nana," I promised as the feeling of how much I loved her suffused me, and the impulse to hug her again made me do exactly that until Linda came in, announced by an aroma that could only mean—

"Coffee!" she announced, handing me a mug steaming with the wonderful stuff.

"*Gracias, querida*," I said. I raised the mug to my face and inhaled deeply.

And of course, just as I was about to take a sip, my phone went off in my pocket, letting me know the anticipated car had arrived.

But still, the coffee was fresh and hot and made with all my cousin's love and not insignificant skill—and who knew how many days it might be before I could get another? The car wasn't going to leave without me.

I took a healthy sip then swallowed.

"I've gotta go," I said with real regret as I handed the still warm and barely touched mug to Linda.

"Be careful—be safe, *querida*," Linda said as she wrapped an arm around me.

"Of course," I promised as I quickly hugged her back.

She released me only so I could quickly jog over and give my grandmother another hug. "I love you—I'll be back soon."

"I love you—and be safe," she said to me, and traced the sign of the cross on my forehead.

I gave her one last kiss, quickly gave another to my cousin as I rushed to the door, then with one last hoist of my bag over my shoulder, I squared myself and walked out to face whatever was next.

It's fast, the transition from one head state to another, from location to location—at least, when you know you have a job to do and with it, the means to get there. And for this particular rescue organization, well, that trip went even faster, since transport was under contract and paid for by various entities, both public and private.

I'd done my time as a New York City emergency medical technician for a few years, and while I could have gone for a promotion and become a firefighter proper, that bothered me—I enjoyed and was good at rescue, but I didn't want to be removed from the medical aspect of it entirely; after all, that's why I'd become an EMT.

I honestly couldn't say if what had prompted me in this career direction was the massive tragedy that was the attack on American soil that took over three thousand lives on a seemingly perfect early autumn day, or the Indian Ocean earthquake with its subsequent tsunami that killed over ten times that, or what it was, but I did know this: I had to do *something*.

So when the letter came in, noting that I was a highly decorated EMT, and asking me to consider joining a global medical and rescue response team, I jumped at the opportunity—literally. And the next thing I knew, I was asking for and being granted time off from the city so I could train with an elite crew—all of whom had been recruited at the same time I'd been.

Together, we all learned how to jump out of a (hopefully) perfectly good plane, proper aircraft-exiting procedures, the ins-and-outs of parachute maneuvering, and crazy things that would keep us intact, such as parachute-landing rolls, let-down procedures, and tree climbing. After fifteen training jumps, I successfully completed the program and was made available for fire as well as other rescue assignments.

This meant that when disaster struck anywhere—and I do mean *anywhere*—I got a phone call on a dedicated line that they provided me with, and if I was available, they'd send transport of whatever kind so I could hightail it to wherever I was needed. It could be anything: earthquakes in Central America, tsunamis in Asia, massive wildfires in the domestic United States and Canada.

So. Many. Wildfires.

Aid, rescue, assistance in its various forms—these things were all of critical importance, and it was weird to realize that there was a tremendous financial impact, both as a result of the disaster and to help recover from it—and it cost quite a bit to get our units out to wherever they were desperately needed.

And right now, loaded in a private jet with two other members of the team, less than four hours to arrive in California, I knew that the fact we were flying after midnight as part of a private charter meant that whatever we were responding to was huge, that they were desperate, and that many lives as well as infrastructure were at stake.

That it was a fire, I already knew and, honestly, given the season, expected. California fell victim yearly to massive conflagrations, some created by nature, and others by the nature of stupidity. I'd not only done my first official on-duty jump out of a perfectly good airplane during a huge hell storm, but I'd also experienced firsthand the various roles, from jumping in and cutting fire line to walking the perimeter to warn evacuees.

Actually, that was how Trish Spence and I had had our first visit with each other after she'd moved out West in the first place. Instead of a normal "hey, come on out and let's hang for a few days" sort of visit, we'd instead both been assigned to walk an evacuation zone—and got caught in a fierce flashover. We'd had to jump into some rich lady's pool and hope for the best—fun times!

I sighed. *Nothing like almost getting the baked potato death sentence to make a friendship solid,* I thought and smiled wryly even as I physically examined every bit of my rig that I could, once again during the flight.

Checked and double-checked and even triple-checked, from the seams to the loads in various pockets, I pulled out my phone and texted Jean.

Bennie: Hey! I got called to a

California fire; won't be able to meet
and catch up tomorrow. But no
worries, I've got stuff with me and I'll
at least get some thumbnails sketched
in. Send me next anyway so I can read
when I get some free time.

I hit "send," then stared at the screen a moment.

I was tempted—seriously tempted—to text Trish, but . . .

I pocketed my phone.

If she was home and sleeping, she'd need the rest; if she was already at the fire—and I was ready to lay very high odds that she was—then it wouldn't matter. And the fact was, given that they were calling my group in, hers was most likely either already there or on its way.

I let out a controlled breath as I tucked my phone back into a safe pocket. With my gear all checked and accounted for, there was nothing left but to cram in as much sleep as I could before we landed. From there, we'd be jolted along in whatever truck they'd supply us with until we arrived at whichever established camp where we'd get as much news as possible, a rundown of the expected procedure—and then we'd get into a perfectly good plane and jump out of it.

I do really wish I'd had that coffee, I thought to myself with faint regret. I could still smell it, and the one good taste I'd had of it clung warm and brown and rich, with its milky smoothness, to my teeth, and the sweet of it right at the edge of my tongue . . . *Well, at least I can sketch it*, I reminded myself as I pulled the pad out from my inside jacket pocket, then reached for the pencils in my bag.

Every call, every event is different. Every call, every event is the same. It doesn't matter how you got there—sooner or later it is always a racing, hopping jolt across terrain that slams you in every direction. Then there's a quick introduction to folks you don't know but whose lives will be in your hands and yours in theirs, with even quicker hellos accompanying grim and hearty hugs and handshakes to the folks you've already met, people you've already depended on to get the job done, who've depended on you, who made it out alive with you. You look at each other with the same look in everyone's eyes, the shine of those who have proven to each other and to the elemental gods that even though it rains fire—and it does—you will be there for each other until the end.

After, you get instructions and the weather readings, headings on wind and fire direction, and you get assigned to your stick: the pairs or even trios that will jump together and in which order.

Next thing you know, you're in a small plane that only luck and God keep up in the air, like a bumblebee falling up against gravity and fighting the laws of physics, while engines run so loud they drown out every last damn thing except for the pulse in your head that tells you—with every second that you fly, with every glimpse out the window at the sun you hope doesn't set too soon—you're the last group to go out for the night (because cover after dark just isn't going to happen), and with every last thing you can think of checked, then checked again, and you know, you know, you *know* . . .

There's a monster roaring just outside the plane, the little airborne island of semi-safety, a monster you, and George the dragon-killer, and all the other saints your grandmother has called upon are gonna have to slay because, if you don't, if you and your crew and all the saints fall from the sky and fail, fail to save, fail to stop, fail to survive . . .

People will die.

And that's all on you.

I was frosty, as in myself and my head personally clear and cold, while we circled to the jump spot. Notes had already been passed back and forth to all of us, alerting us to conditions on the ground and when to expect the next round of air support.

There were things I knew without having to be told. The fact that we'd been called in—and the time we were dropping—meant they were having a bitch of a time getting this dragon contained, never mind getting it to lay its head down, and that several thousand acres of land had already burned, with more being devoured by the second.

I also knew, based on the urgency of our deployment, that whatever lay below us contained something like a research facility, a government installation, or bordered some human encroachment, if it wasn't some combination of all of those.

As we flew to our jump zone, we got more notes, as more specific information was fed to the flight crew: we learned how many personnel were already on the ground, what and where lines to try to contain the beast had been cut and where new ones were being dug. And we learned, very precisely, that ten thousand acres had already been eaten.

This dragon—she was angry.

She was *hungry*.

And . . . there were people down there.

People who had homes. Lives. Families.

Oh God—I shook my head at the news. I really hoped to not repeat the last experience I'd had with homesteaders who refused to leave, not believing how truly dangerous a fire was . . .

"Oh fucking Christ—look at that fucking house!" Romes, a guy I'd jumped with before, yelled over the roar of the engines as he stared out as best he could from the window ahead of us.

"Look at that fucking head!" I redirected instead, even as I did glance where he'd directed, and a charred black spot that had once been a human dwelling flew out of our sight.

Romes turned his head to gaze where I pointed. It felt like I could feel him swallow his heart as we stared, then stared more, because the column was visible even this far out. All eight of us jumpers watched it rage in the tree canopy, over a hundred feet in the air. Deeper reds burst from the heart of it as we swung around to the designated jump coordinates. Smoke rose another ten thousand feet or so.

We had arrived.

A crew member opened the door. Instantly, the volume of everything increased by a thousand. I slammed on my helmet and slid my visor down. I was first man, first stick, first to jump. I tapped Romes on the shoulder, our signal to double-check each other's setups yet again. Everything was present and functional, so we gave each other a thumbs-up.

I grabbed the first set of streamers—a vividly colored roll of crepe paper, attached to a thin gauge of wire—and passed them to the spotter. We flew over the fire, and she tossed the first, then the next, out the door, towards what we hoped might be our landing area. Everyone crowded around as best they could, and we watched the red streaks of flexible paper unwind, each of us aware that we needed to know how they unwound, how they blew and fell, because whatever happened to them would soon happen to us in our chutes.

I observed the way the streamers drifted along the canopy and towards the fire.

The flutter showed there was a little draft—in this case, it was a small current of air with an upward vertical motion, but it was avoidable, so otherwise, so far, so good.

"Are you ready?" the jump supervisor yelled.

"Yeah!" I nodded and gave him a thumbs-up.

"Get in the door!"

I did one last four-point check before I got into position by the door. I stared out into the fire, visually marking the point I wanted to hit, about a thousand feet away from it.

"Watch for the draft!" the supervisor yelled as we banked into position.

Once again, I nodded.

"Get ready!"

I inhaled.

He slapped my shoulder.

I exhaled as I stepped out into air.

Jump thousand.

I flew under the belly of the plane I'd just drawn a breath in.

Inhale.

Look thousand.

I breathed steady out.

Reach thousand.

I inhaled again.

Wait thousand.

Inhale done.

Check my jump partner.

These were all the things that had to be remembered and performed one thousand percent correctly. Every. Single. Time.

I watched Romes jump, coming out good and clear. The others dropped out behind him at their announced times.

Exhale.

Pull thousand.

For a few already rapid heartbeats it felt as if I'd accelerated.

I inhaled into the sharp jerk of my canopy opening.

Check my canopy.

As soon as I had full canopy, I performed the post-open check.

Check my jump spot.

I grabbed my steering toggles, staring all the while at what must have been at least a half-mile-wide fire, its hungry flames whipping every which way they could while the smoke cast a shadow far out over everything, extending into the approaching night.

Only two thousand feet away.

And the roar of it . . .

A dirt road crossed the jump spot, and along it were the remaining houses Romes and I had spotted from the plane.

Two had approaching flames, two were seemingly safe, at least for the moment, and another two had burned to ash.

I was careful as I landed, as careful as I could be, fighting to be certain my speed and my angle were right. It was a known fact that every little thing could go right on a jump, but a landing could always go wrong—and the majority of injuries tended to come from bad landings.

I focused, kept my face into the wind, legs together and knees bent, elbows tucked in close, and then rotated my body to spread impact along the legs, thighs, butt—even the side of my back.

Impacts never get softer.

As I caught my breath during the seconds after I hit the ground and stopped moving, I found myself wishing my hands still held that cup of coffee Linda had made for me, the rich aroma a gorgeous tickle in my brain, but that quickly dissolved into the scent of the smoke and the burning trees as I gathered myself, then began checking for the other jumpers.

As lead jump, I had to ensure everyone had hit the ground in safe and functional condition before the plane flew away, taking its medical kit and communication with the outside world with it.

Once I'd seen everyone had safely landed, the huge cube containers—cubitainers—with our supplies were dropped nearby. Once we were all safely gathered, and our supplies were easily accessible, I knew it was okay to wave the plane off, so I did, then pulled the radio from my suit.

I hit the key to connect to the team already on the ground.

As I'd suspected it would be, it was led by none other than my friend, Trish—short for Patricia—Spence.

"Spence—go!"

"Heya, Spence—we're live!" I greeted.

"Hey hey, Grego—grab all the grub you can and hump it on over! We gotta get this mother to lie down before heat of day hits tomorrow, or we'll never get ahead of it!"

"Yeah, Spence, we can do that," I said, and couldn't help smiling as I did because not only had I been right—Trish was the fire boss—but hey, if we couldn't hang out together in our free time, at least here out in a fire, we knew we could depend on each other. Saving lives had to count for quality time, right?

"We got at least one, maybe two tankers coming in—our best chance at trying to hold this down overnight."

"Uh-huh."

A tanker, maybe two. I absorbed that. It gave me a grim sort of hope, to know that we were set to have at least one small fixed-wing plane fly over to drop a load of fire-retardant cover before full night set—it would help. A lot.

"What are we looking for?"

"Head southwest," she directed. "You'll see the red flag marker. Come over the ridge."

"Yeah, got that."

"Don't be late for dinner!"

I laughed grimly in the heat and smoke. "Wouldn't dream of it!"

Hours become days become one long slog after another. Being an EMT as well as a smoke jumper meant I had gotten very used to spending life in swinging from one to the other of two modes: painfully endless hours of unrelenting boredom punctuated by eternal moments of unrelenting terror.

And sometimes, there were moments like this.

"Jesus H. Christ on a crutch—are you fucking *kidding* me?"

After humping it for just over a mile over the ridge and joining our manpower to Spence's crew, we'd spent a muscle-crunching eternity revving chainsaws, slinging the ever-famous Pulaskis (yes, the combination axe and adze created by the assistant ranger who saved forty-five firefighters during a disastrous wildfire in Idaho), and at times even using our gloved hands and booted feet to cut and clear a control line. We were busting ourselves to create a burnout: a fire set to burn between two control lines to deprive the main flame of fuel—we wanted to starve this burning motherfucker to death. This was a usual and generally successful tactic. But damn, this one, this fire—this one was burning *hot*, just way too fuckin' hot for that to be effective, and there was strong concern that soon it might begin to outrace us instead.

What we were doing had gone from a tactic to a desperate Hail Mary stopgap measure.

We absolutely were going to need that tanker flyover with a full load of flame retardant to keep this fire even barely on a semi-directed path.

So of course, as happens on occasions, the old tanker that had been scheduled to shoot out by us had been redirected instead. The facts as they were fed to us over the radio were grim: there were several areas burning even hotter, and higher, than we were. Any edge that could be used to get this beast to at least back down, if not under complete control, was going to be used.

"What now, boss?" asked Behringer, a just-shy-of-six-foot rookie who had been flown out from Alaska along with a few others happy to "sightsee in the lower forty-eight."

Spence shook her head in a slow side-to-side as the rest of the crew slowly gathered around. Some of them had already been there for two days and going on a third; me with Romes, Behringer, and three others, well, we *were* the relief crew.

While Spence radioed one of the other teams out there to triangulate what we'd do next, I rooted through my pants pockets for one of the energy bars I knew I'd stored there before I'd even left New York for the pre-jump.

"Well," I said as I snagged the edges of the wrapper in my pocket, then pulled it out. I tore the corner open. "We're gonna eat something," I said, breaking my bar in half, then half again. I handed the pieces out while Romes dug through his own pockets to see what he had.

Even though normally—if something could be normal about any of this—we jumpers would land with a three-day food supply, the fact was that some of the crew had already been there for two and were just about to hit their third.

Of course, there was us with our own fresh supplies, but our jump spot, the spot where the crew we were relieving was supposed to also get picked up from, now had a wall of flame sweeping around it—which completely wiped out access to the helispot (the pickup point) the earlier crew had created. No one was stupid enough to go running back into a wall of hell for cans of beans, either.

Besides, if things had gotten so complex that aircraft with necessary flame retardant was being redirected, then I was pretty damn certain the pickup that had been promised for the first crew—which was supposed to arrive in three hours—would be delayed, too.

No matter what, though, we had to either find or create a new helispot.

"Let's make us some coffee!" Romes said brightly, turning around with some freeze-dried packs in one hand and his canteen in the other.

I groaned inwardly, remembering how I had missed out on some of the best stuff when I'd left home God knew how many hours ago.

"Bears, man, bears!" Crespin, a wiry five-foot-three jumper

who'd also come in with my crew, reminded us all as he hopped agitatedly from foot to foot.

Romes stopped in his tracks, then scowled at Crespin from under thick black eyebrows. The rest of us stared, too.

"Bears?" Romes sputtered, incredulous. "Fuck, man—do you see where we *are*?" He spread his arms wide, craning his body around to take it all in. "We're on the edge of a fucking *fire*, man—they've already run the fuck outta here!"

"This is fuckin' San Bernardino—they got *bears* here!" Crespin insisted, head bobbing up and down while he waved an arm wide to indicate—everywhere. "Who the fuck's got a gun for the fucking *bears*?"

"Taylor's group is about three miles that-a-way," Spence said, and pointed south and west. "They've got a good jump spot cleared there and some cubitainers with water—Crayson says they've left us some food." She snorted.

"Apple cores?" I guessed cynically with a grim laugh.

I knew Crayson, having met him on other occasions, and knew we'd be lucky if he'd left us even a spot to scrape out and lick from a can of pork and beans.

"Come on, lardos—let's go!" Romes encouraged.

"Hey—is my butt too big for my pack?" Behringer asked with a falsetto and a flutter of his hand, batting his eyelashes at Romes from a face covered with sweat and dirt.

Romes growled as he adjusted his pack over his shoulder.

"Who the hell gets fat doing this?" Crespin asked everyone.

No one answered as we double-checked ourselves and each other, ensuring we had our equipment, our packs, and our crew.

After a semi-silent agreement that all was present and accounted for, we set off on a small dirt trail, following behind Spence.

"Lard—there's no fucking lard *anything* around here!" Crespin continued as we hiked. "Not unless it's burning in the fucking fire!"

I rolled my eyes and kept walking. Too much was going on, and too much was needed to do for me to engage him, to burn my energy out like that. Crespin did have a point, though: absolutely no one gained weight doing this job.

No one really got old doing it, either. *Aged rapidly though, maybe*, I reflected . . . I sunk myself into the rhythm of the hike.

Every now and again we'd come across spot fires that we put out as we found them, and we'd make note of any smoking areas, too.

We were about another half an hour into our hike when we heard it: the unmistakable heavy bass-drum beat pounding the very air into our ears, the siren song of a loaded bomber flying overhead, the very welcome and even more needed tanker with the retardant.

We stopped where we were, craning our heads up and around to see if we could catch a glimpse of where it was and where it was going.

Crespin eyed the sky nervously. "Great. We either get that shit on our heads, or we're gonna get eaten by fucking *bears!*"

From the sound of the flight path, Crespin was probably wrong about the bears—but right about where that load was going to land, and that was not going to be pretty. Or safe. Or comfortable. But Spence was already on the radio, trying to get the tanker shifted away from us as well as closer to where it was even more needed.

"Direct them north—fuckin' *north!*" she yelled into the communication piece. "That's gonna come right down on us!"

"Hey, Goldilocks—catch!" Behringer called out as he tossed a packet to Crespin. We all laughed at the nickname—and Crespin was from this moment forward Goldilocks forevermore.

He caught the package in reflex, and the strength of his grip burst the packaging, splashing goo all over his fire shirt.

"Oh my God, you're a dick, you're such a fucking *dick!*" Goldilocks howled while Romes, the rest of the crew, and I looked on and laughed—Behringer had tossed him a honey pack that he'd carried in a pocket, and now Goldilocks was covered.

"If those bears eat you first, maybe you'll shut up!" Behringer said laconically.

The rumble of the flying bombers above us came back.

"Grab cover!" Trish ordered over the laughter and the rising roar of the bomber as it approached.

We were lucky enough that there was still plenty of old growth pine for us to cower behind, and I peeked as best I could from behind sheltering needles to look towards the clearing from where we'd come. We'd gotten to cover just in time—a cloud of red dust dropped from the belly of the bomber, right over where we'd just been moments before.

We'd gotten lucky: we were far enough away to see it, but not physically experience it. Everyone took a long moment to watch as the plane flew away.

"Missed us—by *that* much!" Romes said, breaking the silence and holding his hand up with an inch between his thumb and index finger.

We couldn't help it—we all cracked up.

"What do you think normal people are doing right now?" one of the guys asked as we sat around a fire (ironic, I know), resting for the first time in hours.

I glanced up from my little pad of paper to look again directly at what I'd been sketching—a couple of tents that had been set up, a few of my fellow jumpers sitting on the ground—everyone just letting it all drain off a bit, the stress, and the strain, and yes, even the fear.

I looked up into the purpling sky, filled my lungs with the scent of the smoke and the can filled with insta-coffee, the dirt and the trees, all of it blending as we each took a moment to breathe it in and to refuel with both food and sleep for the next morning.

"Betcha they're in normal beds, sleeping next to other people they actually like, and not worried about freakin' bears!" Goldilocks said, his scowl visible in the twilight as he fetched the heated water with its caffeine load, then passed it around.

I put my pencil and my pad down; this had the potential to become entertaining.

"What—you don't like me?" Romes batted his eyelashes at Goldilocks. "I thought we had a moment back there when we were cutting line!"

"That's right, Goldilocks!" Behringer hooted. "Who saved your ass from that big bad chainsaw?"

Goldilocks scowled deeper and passed the heated coffee can to me. "Hey, I acknowledge that it could've gone really bad!"

"Really bad?" Trish mimicked, fingers held up in quotes as she came to sit on a rock next to me. "You're lucky you didn't lose a leg."

"Or worse—your junk!" I added.

That set everyone off into another round of laughter.

Fatigue from firefighting had been robbing us all of both strength and clarity. For a fateful and nearly deadly millisecond Goldilocks had tired all the way to muscle failure, as they say in weightlifting. That failure meant he lost control of the chainsaw he'd been using to cut through and away all of the snags, dead trees, stumps, and huge downed tree limbs—all of which would provide even more fuel for the fire that was headed our way, unless we could clear them. For a space quicker than a heartbeat, the chainsaw kicked back at him, falling towards his upper thigh.

He got super lucky, though—Romes had literally been right behind him, and his quick thinking and acting meant he was able to catch then brace Goldilocks' arm before the ripping and roaring machine had dipped too far.

But even with that miraculous save, there was still one

casualty: right inside Goldilocks' thigh, and uncomfortably close to all sorts of things he wouldn't want to lose or cut, from the femoral artery which would have cost him his life—especially out here with no way of getting immediate help, never mind the leg itself—to his ability to urinate without aid, three inches of cloth from his bunker pants had gotten well-chewed.

Goldilocks immediately leaned over in an exaggerated fashion to both widen and examine the hole in his pant leg.

"Well, oh gosh goh-lee!" he sing-songed. "Ain't you jus' right, Ms. Grego, with your New York City smarts! But at least"—he paused as he straightened—"I got me a window!" And he spread the torn-up part even more, sharing with us all not only the view of the gash but the hair on his leg as well as the knowledge that he wore—

"Tighty-whities, Goldilocks? I didn't know you cared that much!" Romes said. "I'll bet Grego doesn't want to draw *that*!" he added with a laugh, and we all laughed with him, glad to be alive, glad to be sitting still and making jokes about Goldilocks' underpants, gladder that Crayson had left us pork and beans— he and his crew were getting picked up—and that we were about to eat.

He'd left us a note along with the cans, which read:

> You're saving our asses—this here is some padding for yours! Bon appetit (and we left y'all some canned peaches, too). Tell Crespin we'll send him a bear.

"Thank you, Lord," Behringer intoned with his head bowed over his plate.

Everyone joined him for the sacred second. "We lived. The fire's dying. May that continue tomorrow. Amen."

Yes. Exactly that.

"Amen," we all agreed, and dug in.

There are some nights on a fire you sleep out wherever you can, under the open sky, and temporarily safe, and there are some nights you actually have a tent, and this night there was a tent. There wasn't a lot of space, so people shared, and space being what it was, I shared it with Spence—now Trish, just like I was at this moment Bennie, since this was a break.

We all needed it. As it was, I practically dropped into my sleeping bag face first.

"You all right?" Trish asked when she made her way in.

My eyes still closed, I flipped onto my back while I answered. "I'm sore in places I keep forgetting exist until I'm out doing this again, and so tired I'm not sure I'm actually saying words out loud because I'm already dreaming about the coffee I left at home." I sighed. "You?"

Trish gave a tired chuckle as I heard her remove her boots.

"Same thing on the sore—butt-ass tired, too. And"—she let out a heavy breath as I heard her settle back into her sleep sack—"I'm thinking I don't know when you and I will actually be able to get coffee without a fire first. Pickup is arranged for tomorrow for everyone—you headed back to base or to New York after?"

"I don't know," I answered her honestly. "I'll get details on the way back, same as everyone else. And hey," I said as I thought about it. I flopped an exhausted hand in her direction and patted her forearm. "Maybe we'll get lucky, this thing is about to stay down, and we'll work something in before my return flight, or"— I yawned—"why don't you come on out to New York and hang a few days when you're free?"

Trish's equally tired yawn was audible to me in the close space of the tent. "I haven't been back to New York since . . . you know."

I nodded, even though she couldn't see me, because I did know. The shitstorm that had set up camp in her life back then had come down hard, heavy, and horrible, and even though it had been a few years, Trish wasn't really free of the scars of it. Not yet anyway. And maybe not ever.

"New York lost a really great EMT when you moved out here, Trish," I said instead, because it was true: Trish and I had trained together from the beginning in a class at a local college, gone on to come out of the same academy class, then been assigned to the same station. "Not that jumping out of a plane and into fires isn't a great time and everything—" I gave a small chuckle and Trish laughed with me. "It's just, well, trust me, your patient expertise and care is definitely missed."

And I miss you, too, I thought.

I could hear Trish sigh, barely inches away from me in the dark.

"I just . . ." I could hear her shift, and I did, too, leaning up on an elbow so I could look over at her as she spoke. I could just make out her outline and a small shine off her eyes.

"I just really, *really* miss my mother sometimes, y'know?"

The sad and longing tone in her voice made my chest, made my heart ache, ache with her and for her, ache with the need to comfort my friend.

"Yeah, I do," I said, and I reached out to lay a hand on her shoulder, wishing I could do so much more, ease the ache of all of that for her, just make it go away because I really did know, because even though the "how" of it was different, we missed people who were critical to our lives. "I really, really do."

She leaned her cheek against my hand for a long moment, and before it was even a thought, I'd put my arms around her.

I gently pulled her even closer to me, then stroked the back of her head with my hand. Despite the smoke and everything else, her hair was soft through my fingertips. "This fire—evacuating the houses and all of that—it's bringing it all back for you, huh?"

31

"I guess," she sniffed, then sighed against me. "Back then, it—that was . . . bad. It was—"

"It was the worst, the worst it could possibly be," I finished for her, and held her even more closely, my heart aching even more than before with her, for her, over what I knew. "You lost your mother."

I held her so she could safely cry it out—as much of it as she could, and there were parts of it I cried through for her and with her.

And then we talked—really talked—about all of it: the struggle with and witnessing of her mom's growing dementia and her failing body systems, the then-growing estrangement of her father from what was a horribly sad and difficult situation, the parallel one with her then-girlfriend Deb.

"But that doesn't even faze, me, seriously," Trish said quietly.

Even though a fire might have been raging not too far from us, night in the California woods brought cooler temperatures, which would hopefully help bank the fire but could leave us humans sleeping in it chilled.

With Trish stretched against me and tucked up against my shoulder, I'd pulled my sleeping bag over us to ward against that.

"Really? How come?" I asked in just as soft a voice. I brushed my fingertips over the solid curve of her shoulder in a soothing pattern.

She let the very heel of her palm touch under my collarbone. "I'd stopped caring, really—everything with my mom was just all-consuming, and honestly, Deb made no room for me, I made no room for her." She took a deep breath. "It was over, if it had ever been anything in the first place, and when everything was said and done, I was simply, purely, honestly relieved that it was something I didn't have to deal with anymore."

I nodded as I absorbed it. "I can understand that."

"Yeah?" she asked. "That doesn't make me a terrible person?"

I breathed in. "Not at all," I said, and let my breath out slowly. "People who love each other, they show up, you know? You showed up for your mother—and your dad, too, when they needed you—and Deb didn't back you up. And that . . . that's not even a friend, not really."

Trish chuckled softly. "It's funny that you say that—because it was my friends who did show up in those worst days—it was you. You were amazing."

We'd been talking and snuggled all warm together for a while, and that, combined with the pure physical exhaustion of the day, was beginning to get me all drifty. I closed my eyes with the soft and heavy warmth of it all. "At best, it showed that your priorities differed greatly, and you know how it is—life and death—there's nothing bigger than that. It cuts the nonsense very cleanly out, you know what I mean?"

Trish shifted against me, an almost melt along and into my side, the softness of her cheek a rub just against my collarbone. "You think that's just an emergency medical people thing?" she asked quietly. Her breath brushed across my neck, increasing the warmth and the melt and the drift. "Because of everything we see and deal with?"

I continued to trace small circles on her arm as the solid weight of her continued to warm me. "I'm not sure," I said, really thinking about it. "I think . . . I think . . ." I breathed slowly, deeply, floating now in the warmth and the soft of her voice and the oh-so-satisfying way we fit together. "I think maybe it's just something that happens when you lose people you love or watch people you know go through that. It makes you want to—"

"—not waste time," Trish finished for me, nodding against my neck once again. "Yeah . . . that makes sense."

"Doesn't it, though?" I agreed.

"Yeah," she murmured, her breath another brush against the

column of my neck, "I guess it does."

The silence stretched warm and comfortable between us as Trish snugged securely in my arms, and the drift began to turn into a float.

"I do miss it sometimes," Trish said into the new quiet.

"Which? Being an EMT or New York, or Deb or . . . ?"

"Not Deb!" she laughed, pushing at me lightly.

"Are you sure?" I teased. "I mean, you know, didn't she, like, make a good lasagna or something?"

"Reservations," Trish said. "She made good reservations."

"Yeah, well, she sure gave me some, that's for sure."

Trish nudged me and laughed again. "Jerk. You didn't say anything then."

"Sure I did."

"Oh really? What was it?"

I got serious for a moment as I remembered.

"Uh, I said that I could help you drive your mom to appointments, or take your dad out food shopping or whatever."

Trish leaned up for a moment. "You did say that."

"Uh huh."

"Did I ever thank you?" She shifted, no longer in my arms but instead slightly over me, eyes shining in the dark on mine. I could just see the gentle curve of her lips as she waited for me to answer.

"Trish—are you kidding?"

"No." She was quietly serious. "Because I don't have enough words to tell you how much I appreciate everything you did— for me, for my mom and dad and—"

It was a lot, it was making my heart hurt, and my friend was thanking me for something she didn't have to thank me for, not now, not ever.

"Trish, stop," I pleaded. "Just stop."

"But no, really, that was all so—"

"You would've done that and more for me," I told her,

knowing it as I said it so completely that it felt like it was pouring out of my skin.

And in that knowledge and that warmth and the intensity of her eyes on mine, I knew something else, too.

I knew something was there, between us, had always been, and here it was, ready to break through and open, about to—

"So tell me what you miss," I asked her, my voice catching and rough. I couldn't tell if it was from the smoke of the day or anything else—but right now, I wasn't ready for any other answer.

She stared at me a moment, then grinned, like she knew something I didn't. I was okay with that.

"Who, me?"

"Yeah, you said you miss it sometimes, and I can't imagine that it's 4 a.m. fires."

Her hair fell loose as she shook her head and laughed at me. It glinted here and there in the same light that caught the shine of her eyes.

"Uh-huh. I miss bagels and dirty water dogs, Thai at 3 a.m.—and then there's the diners. Oh man!" she said with sudden enthusiasm. "Who doesn't want breakfast 24-7?".

I smiled back at her. "Hey—it's the bacon-egg-and-cheese on a roll that does it! With coffee, of course."

"Oh my God—yeah!" Trish agreed. "*That's* the stuff—you can't really get that here. I mean, you *can*, but it's not the same."

I nodded in agreement, even though I yawned, because my body's need for sleep was overwhelming, and even with knowing there *should* be a relief crew and a flight out for me, Trish, and the rest of this gang, that didn't guarantee a damn thing, should the dragon we had so desperately fought choose to wake again.

"All right, then," I said mid-yawn. "You come out on your next break, and all the bacon-egg-and-cheese on a roll you want—on me, okay? And we'll get coffee, too—no fire," I promised, yawning yet again.

35

"Sounds good," Trish said through exhaustion I could hear as she tucked back onto my shoulder. "All right, then."

"Yeah?"

"You know what? Yeah." There was something firm in her voice as she said it, and her hand reached out to rest across my chest. "Let's do this."

"All right, then," I agreed. "Let's do this."

For a quick moment, my pulse raced as a part of me wondered what it was exactly that we were agreeing to do, but we fit so well, and I was so tired . . . whatever it was, I knew it was going to be okay.

And breathing this thing between us, whatever it was, in and out, the weight of her on me and the weight of her heart released, the warmth beneath the sleeping bag and the trust showed and shared between us, the easy drift took over, taking us with it.

The bellowing howl woke us both.

"Bear! It's a fucking *bear*!"

That shout wasn't from Goldilocks—it was Behringer.

"Oh, for fuck's sake!" I grumbled, and "Fuckin' what?" Trish muttered as she and I rolled apart, then I shoved the sleeping bag off of me, myself into my boots, and crawling carefully over Trish, went out through the flap.

It was oh-fucking-dark thirty, and while the sky glowed sullenly in the distance to the north where we'd left the dragon slumbering, the only real light was the flashlight that Trish had brought out with her to shine on the sight of Behringer— wearing only boots and boxers—holding desperately onto a supply crate while, yes, an actual fucking huge-ass *bear* tugged at the other side.

"Bears! *Bears*! I knew it, I fucking *knew* it!" Goldilocks shouted as he stumbled out of his tent in his tighty-whities and boots, Romes wearing only a T-shirt and boots moments behind him, and the entire camp now up, as ready as could be in varying stages of undress, and yelling.

Someone had had the foresight to grab a pine bough and start waving it.

"Behringer!" Trish barked. "Put the goddamn crate *down*—that's a fucking *bear*!"

Both the bear and Behringer glanced over at Trish. Then, as if coming to, or more likely realizing that the tug of war he was in might remove his arms, Behringer dropped his end, then slowly backed away, his focus on the bear the whole while.

"Heeyah! Hah!" Romes shouted, waving a branch, his tee riding up his back. "Come on, bunch up—we gotta be bigger than it!" he ordered, both arms waving in the air.

He was right, and we gathered a good distance from the bear itself, waving our arms, mostly naked and half-naked people hooting and making ridiculous noises, all while the bear nonchalantly smashed a paw through the crate and rooted around.

"Oh, this is fucking insane!" Romes said as we all kept waving, and the bear blithely ignored us.

"I told you, I fucking *told* you!" Goldilocks howled with both satisfaction and terror. "That's a motherfuckin' *bear*!"

Suddenly, the bear stepped away from the crate, put its nose up in the air, and sniffed.

And just in that second, we saw it—the arc across the sky.

Heat lightning.

The bear took one last swipe at the crate, and then ambled back into the darkness.

"Fuck," I said softly, staring at the flashes overhead.

Everyone looked up with me while Trish pulled out the already crackling radio—operations had seen it, too.

She listened, then nodded. "Yeah, we're gonna beat feet to

the western flank now," she said to whoever was at the other end. She clicked off. "All right, mighty bear scarers, put pants on, then pack it up and let's go. And you!" she said, whirling on Behringer. "Next time you do something so stupid as to try to wrestle a bear, you do that on your own time, ya hear?"

Behringer nodded and swallowed. "At least . . . at least I lived?" he said, his voice shaking.

"Yeah, ya dumb nut, ya did. That's a talk with your mom I wouldn't want to have!"

"Me, either," he agreed fervently. "Me, either."

"Hey, Behringer!" I called as he hurried past me, and I got an unintended good look at the pattern on his shorts. "Nice sailboats!"

"I'm sailing away!" he agreed with a laugh as he trotted past.

With everyone finally wearing *all* of their clothes, we rapidly broke down, packed up, and hiked our way west to the next group in the creeping dawn, hoping all the while that the light show over our heads didn't mean a new fire was about to break out.

"So okay, then," Trish began while we stood in the airport drop-off zone.

We'd done our job—the fire had been contained, and it was time to finally go home.

Although flights to emergencies both global and domestic could and mostly would be by chartered flight in situations like this, going back home was generally some normal airline, which made sense, if you thought about it.

Trish had offered to drive me to the airport instead of grabbing a ride in the truck with everyone else—which was nice because it gave us a little more time together—and the freedom to have the conversation we were having now.

We stood outside the car, my personal gear bag as well as my smaller duffel of personal effects on the sidewalk beside me.

I was simply enjoying this moment and taking it all in, standing in the heat with Trish before me, her hair now loose after days of confinement under a helmet, swinging slightly below her shoulders, free of smoke and mud and ash and shining copper over brown in the sun.

"In about two weeks' time," she continued, summarizing our discussion, "I'll come on out to good old New York City and say hello to bodegas and hot dogs, then we'll—"

"Make sure you get to visit with Tori and Jean, and we will *definitely* grab a coffee without a fire going down," I promised, smiling as I gazed at Trish.

"All right, you've got me convinced." Trish gave a small laugh. "Safe flight home, right? You've got everything you need?"

It was good to see her smile, better yet to hear that laugh.

It was hard to believe that this moment was really happening, was really here. It had actually taken two weeks—yes, an entire fourteen days—to get that fire to put its head down and stay down, and for all that we were grateful that it hadn't been even longer, yet here we now were, seeing each other not only out of grimy and smoke-laden uniform but also safe and clean, surrounded by the sights and sounds of civilization, even dressed in real clean and nice-smelling normal people civilian clothes.

"Oh yeah." I patted my bag and the pocket that held my sketch pad. "I'm all good, and thanks," I confirmed. "All right— gotta go." We gave each other a quick and fierce hug. "I'll text you when I get home," I promised as we released each other.

"Cool. See ya in two weeks."

"Yep," I agreed as I hefted my bags. I saw an airport minder in my peripheral vision coming over to shoo away Trish's car under the guise of offering to help; we'd lingered too long for their liking, and not nearly long enough for mine. Still, it was time to go. "Ciao for now!"

"Ciao for now!" she repeated.

I didn't look back as I walked into the terminal, reminding myself that Trish and I would get to spend some actual free time together in about two weeks, which was pretty awesome.

I can sketch during the flight, I reminded myself. *Maybe I can do a panel or two of Behringer's ursine wrestling match, with the rest of the crew standing around either naked or close to it trying to scare the bear off.*

I smiled to myself as I boarded the plane and took my seat. I'd already checked my emails and read up on the new work Jean had sent me, and I had some good basic sketches to work with. Our project was still on target, which made me happy.

And now, eager to see my cousin and my grandmother—who had both told me they'd meet me at the airport—I was already looking forward to what two weeks would bring. But most importantly, I was firm in the knowledge that whatever work threw at me until I had my next set of promised days off and Trish came to visit, at the very least, there'd be no goddamn bears.

I hoped.

Chapter 2

Bacon-Egg-and-Cheese on a Roll

Trish: One more sleep, and hello NYC,
I'm back! I'm really excited about this!

Bennie: Me, too! So—everything's the
same, right? Flight, times, all of it?

Trish: Yep! We're all good to go—and
I can't wait to see you!

Bennie: Me too! My fam, Tori &
Jean—we're all seriously looking
forward to this!

I WAS ADMITTEDLY impatient while I tapped my fingers on the steering wheel, waiting for the light to change so I could make my turn.

Today was the day we'd been counting down to, texting and talking every day, and Trish and I had confirmed everything about this several times.

Now, with her officially up in the air and not about to jump into a fire, there was hopefully no way she'd get called out or that

41

this visit would get canceled.

"Motherfucker!" I cursed out loud. The jerk driving the car in the center lane and waiting with me at the light now cut ahead of me to make the left, too.

"Fuckin' idiot with a death wish," I muttered, then thought about it a moment—I had to laugh at myself. I'd quite literally made a career out of running around New York City with a piece of foam on wheels and a portable—and highly combustible—oxygen tank when I wasn't jumping out of planes and into actual honest-to-goodness wildfires or landing who knows where to aid and rescue.

"Yeah," I continued, talking to myself, "who actually has the death wish?"

I shook my head at myself. I didn't—have a death wish, that is—but I did have a thing for helping folks out, even if some of the situations were extreme.

I finally got into my turn and headed towards my favorite bodega—I was picking up a bacon-egg-and-cheese on a roll as promised before I swung onto the Belt Parkway, which would take me right to the airport.

"Two? A'right," the guy behind the counter commented, and I waited, the scent of bacon filling the tiny store.

It was probably easier, I supposed, to think about getting some sort of a sandwich with some Gatorade to wash it down with, rather than to think about either the knowing look my grandmother had cast over me when I'd hugged her good-bye or Linda's casual teasing before I'd left—God, sure, technically she was my first cousin, but she definitely was more of a younger sister to me, especially in the way she'd teased me this morning during coffee . . .

"Aren't you concerned your . . . *friend* . . . will take one look at me, fall in love, then whisk me away to California with her?" she'd teased as we sat together over the daily morning coffee, finalizing the details of who was sleeping where.

We lived in a two-bedroom apartment, and those rooms were decently sized. The original plan, when we'd first moved from the small apartment on Staten Island several years ago to here, was that Nana would have one room and I the other, with space enough in the living room for my grandmother to have her sewing machine, cutting table, our shared drafting table, and organizational cubbies with all of the bolts and bits and bobs she needed for her work, both the custom fits and the custom designs.

Ah, that sewing machine . . . I'd fallen asleep to the music of it running, nothing on but the little light that shone on what Nana was working on late at night, after homework and dinner, after her how-was-your-day chat.

And it had been perfect then, what with my being stationed in Brooklyn and the bridal shop that Nana had worked for—still worked for—so nearby.

But over time, more and more of Nana's work seemed to crowd her room, and while the bed was still there, by the time Linda had moved in with us, closer to work for her as an emergency room tech as well as close to the nursing school where she'd been just about to start, it had already become a full-fledged studio.

Sure, it had its religious icons that Nana diligently took care of, but it also now contained Nana's worktable, the shared drafting table, and a pair of closets, each big enough for my gear as well as the constantly rotating bolts of cloth and custom couture that Nana helped work on or even outright created.

And now, too, it held Linda's desk and books as well as the family computer.

Normally it was no big deal that Linda and I bunked together—we were cousins; we'd grown up doing that—but it had been decided for the duration of Trish's visit that, in the interim, Nana would actually use her room (I suppose that even for Nana on normal occasions it probably weirded her out to sleep under the ever-watchful eyes of all those saints), while Linda and I would use the living room.

Besides, it *was* a nice sofa—I'd made certain it was plenty comfortable, since I knew Nana would want to spend time on it—even though she never used the pull-out part, though Linda and I actually would.

And it was only for a few days, anyway.

"Well, *querida*," I drawled as I put my coffee down, then dug into a pocket for a ponytail holder, "last we both knew, you're pretty straight, so that might be a big hurdle to overcome," I said as I drew my hair together, then twisted it into place.

"All I hear you say is that I'm pretty," Linda said, giving me a wide, bright smile as she put our mugs on the table, then sat with me, her hair as long as mine but darker, also pulled back and away from her face.

I lightly shook my head and rolled my eyes with a smile as I looked at her. The scrub shirt she wore today was black with a red-and-pink-ribbon pattern over it. And of course, because it was Linda, the stethoscope she had draped around her neck was the exact same shade of pink, which made me smile; I knew how hard she searched to find good scopes in colors that matched her scrubs. "And you're right, I am—it's a family trait!" She grinned, then poured some sugar into her cup. "But really," she continued as she stirred, "I met her, remember? And what if, between her aura and your discussion about her, I'm ready to do something different?"

"When did you meet her?" I asked, trying to think of when that might have been as I pulled the last twist of the band over. "And aura? Seriously? Since when are you into the whole 'aura' thing?" I air-quoted her.

I knew my family, and I knew them well.

We were like a wolf pack: for those in the circle, there was complete trust, complete affection, complete love.

Those not in the circle . . . Well, everyone would be warm

and polite, and that warmth would either increase or decrease, based on how the person behaved themselves—to everyone in the pack, as it were—but most especially to the person introducing them.

Meaning Nana and Linda would completely judge whether or not they liked Trish by how they perceived her treatment of me.

Which meant I was a bit nervous because not everyone understood the complexities of politeness that my family operated under. And Linda herself could be a bit of a wildcard. Sure, she was considerate and kind, and she was super funny— and that super funny was frequently super sharp. But there were moments that sharp became cutting, especially if she didn't like something or someone, and if Linda had already met her, and she didn't—

"Your hair—*querida*, you're not going to a fire or a shootout, you're going to pick up your—just let me do that," she said with a little sigh and a shake of her head as she stood. She came behind me and took out the ponytail I had just put in.

"I just did that!" I groused, reaching behind my head.

"Shh—let me!" She playfully tapped my hand. "Sit still!" she ordered, holding the length of my hair in her hands.

"Fine, fine—I'm trusting you to not pull or anything like that," I said, rolling my eyes.

"It's like you don't even know me," she said in an exaggerated tone. "Pull, no, but perm . . . that's another story."

"Yeah . . . no," I said, just in case.

"Stop wriggling and trust me," she ordered as she took my hair into her hands. "You know I'm only going to make you look amazing—and in that simple style," she gave a small sigh, "that you love so much."

"Thank you," I said quietly as her fingers ran through my scalp.

"You gotta look good—all that honey mixed in with the

brown of your hair—gotta show it off!" she told me as I felt the tight twist she gave it.

I made a face at the discomfort.

"And by the way, yeah," she said, exaggerating the single syllable into three, "I met her." She continued whatever it was she was doing, pulling strands of hair and organizing them God only knew how. "Twice, at least. Once at your day of assignment, and"—her hands gave a firm twist—"then at the party you had when you first moved here with Nana. Okay, you're good," she said, then let go, only to lean over and put her arms around my shoulders.

"Awesome—did you have to pull quite that hard?" I asked, resisting the urge to rub my scalp, potentially ruining what she did and having her decide to do it all over again.

"You know I only tease you because I love you, right?" she said more than asked quietly into my ear.

"I know, *hermanita*. I know," I said back just as quietly, calling her little sister, which was what she was to me in my heart. I leaned my cheek against hers and let the warmth of her love warm my back. "But be careful of that sometimes—you know that saying about hurting the ones we love, too, right?"

"*Hermana*," she said, and shifted to my front, crouching so she could look into my eyes as she again placed her hands on my shoulders. "Did I hurt your feelings?" She gazed at me with real concern.

"No, *hermanita*," I answered honestly, and covered one of her hands with my own. "It's just something to remember is all, so you never take the teasing, or your sharpness too far—I don't want you to get into bad habits that hurt your life—your relationships—you know?"

"Oh, we're good, then!" Linda said with an easy smile. "And you know, the thing is, even if I did like girls, one, I wouldn't compete with you because *somos familia*, and two, with that gorgeous hair of yours and that incredible complexion—no, don't interrupt me," she said as I began to protest. "You know you've amazing color and such perfect skin!" she enthused, pinching my cheeks.

I rolled my eyes. "I have perma-tan from my shoulders down from being outside for so many years, permanent freckles across the bridge of my nose and my cheeks for the same reason, and then there's the—"

"Oh, hush, you!" Linda said, interrupting me with both a kiss and a tight squeeze. "You know you're gorgeous!"

I rolled my eyes, but I did appreciate her words. I normally never really gave any thought to how I appeared outside of neat, clean, and functional, but still, it was nice to know that at least someone thought I might be nicer than average looking. "Thank you," I said quietly, feeling my cheeks burn.

"It's true," she said quietly. She kissed the top of my head and let me go. She sat back down across from me.

"You know," I began as I reached once more for my coffee, "this is not about that—Trish is my friend. It's been a while since she's been back to spend any time in New York, and this is the first time we're going to be able to actually hang out without an emergency situation happening, or after one."

"Friends are important," Linda agreed, and I could see the smirk she barely hid behind her mug as she sipped. "Important enough for you to even give up drawing time, sometimes."

I was about to ask what she was smirking about, but my watch beeped the hour at me. "Gotta go!" I exclaimed as I pushed away from the table, then grabbed my jacket from a hook sitting by the door.

"*Vaya con Dios!*" Nana said as she hugged me when I stopped in the living room to give her a hug and a kiss.

"Uh-huh," I agreed rapidly as I returned the affection, noted the owl-wide eyes Nana made at me, then made haste to put my jacket on as I went out the door.

I admit, though, that my family's behavior made me feel a

little less nervous—that Linda had fussed over me the way she had, that Nana had given me that particular expression—I knew it meant that Trish, as my friend, already had some preliminary approval.

And now, here I was, smelling bacon, hands carefully clutching two paper bags, one with two bottles of Gatorade and the other with the coveted traditionally foil-wrapped sandwiches.

The sun was shining as I got back in my car, settled my packages into the console between the seats, then safely returned to the Belt Parkway. I opened the windows as I drove, enjoying the smell of the water to my right and the occasional peripheral glances of fishers and bicyclists, joggers and children playing all along the walkway that bounded the water's edge. A pleasant feeling filled my stomach as it all flashed by, and I couldn't help smiling.

One thing I knew for sure: this was already a really good day, and it was only going to get better.

As I pulled into the entrance and followed the signs to the right terminal, I wondered what Trish would think of being back in New York, of being able to spend a few days without having to run out into some sort of emergency. I wondered what it would be like to spend such concentrated time hanging out together—not that we didn't already have a few things planned, including hanging out with some other friends, and there were a bunch of places I was sure she'd want to revisit—but I didn't know if I remembered what it was like to actually spend time with another person who wasn't a patient, a rescue team member, or a family member.

And then, there was that feeling, that warm thrum that I felt whenever we spoke, or texted, an almost cushion over the skin sense of something, the last time we had a moment, like in the tent after the fire . . .

I shook my head and pushed those thoughts away for the

moment—traffic was convoluted around the airport!

I couldn't have timed it better, *and* parking magic was on my side: I pulled up to the curb by the gate, knowing I only had a few minutes before the sharp-eyed guards rushed over and asked—but really ordered—me to drive off and around the circuit again. My eyes focused on the great steel-and-glass walls that had seen masses of humanity coming home, going home, headed back and forth from adventures . . .

And . . . there she was, already coming out through the sliding doors, eyes hidden behind shooter's sunglasses, her smile big, white and bright, hair past her shoulders, and the strap of her bag drawn tightly over her shoulder and across her chest.

A warm tickle of joy spread through my chest then slipped up my neck. I couldn't help the smile I felt myself wearing grow to match hers as I set the car in park, then quickly released my seat belt. "Hey, you!" I called and waved as I got out of the car, that bright feeling still growing and growing in my chest.

"Hey!" she answered back with a laugh as we walked towards each other. She removed her sunglasses.

We stared at each other for another second, grinning like mad, her warm brown eyes beaming right into mine.

God. That shine . . . I had no idea how to capture that on paper, how to make her light shine through pencil and ink. I didn't know if it was possible to just get close enough to—

Hronk! "Heya, Precious! People gotta walk here, ya know!"

The normal sounds of New York City in the day and people trying to do their necessary business shook me from my head and back to where we actually were in the moment, and I laughed at myself and at the moment.

"Give me your bag," I told Trish as I clapped my hand on her arm in greeting. The muscle was firm under my palm.

"I'm good," she said, rubbing my shoulder in return. Still, she did unsling it.

"Yeah, just give it here," I said, reaching for the bag anyway with one hand while I reached behind her to open the passenger door with the other.

"All right," she said with an easy laugh as she handed it over. "I'm not gonna try to out-butch you here."

I laughed. "I'm just being true to my upbringing—and my grandmother would say I was just being polite."

"Your grandmother would say you are lovely."

I blushed as I swung the door open. "Well, I guess she's kind of supposed to," I deflected. Once I ensured Trish was safely seated, I closed the door, then came around to the driver's side, putting her bag into the backseat.

"So," she began as we each snapped in our seat belts, "where to next?"

"Well," I said as I sighted for an opening in traffic. I found it, then pulled away from the curb. The heat in my cheeks had finally started to recede. "If you reach into the console"—I indicated with my hand—"that's what's next. How was your flight and all that?"

"Not bad. A little weird not to be getting ready to jump," she said with a smile I could hear while she lifted the lid of the console. "But still it—oh hey! Is that bacon-egg-and-cheese on a roll?"

"Yeah," I said, and laughed. "I figured there wasn't much more than peanuts on your flight out, and I did promise, so—"

"You are the best!" Trish exclaimed as she pulled her haul out onto her lap. "Mind if I eat this now?"

"That's the point," I said, and glanced over to give her a smile. "Can't have you running around New York City fueled only by peanuts and bad coffee, right?"

The sandwich may have cooled, but still the awesome smell of bacon filled the car as she unwrapped it. "You," she said around the first bite she took, "are truly a great friend."

"Yeah, I am," I agreed, and chuckled. "There's Gatorade in there, too. Dehydration, you know," I added as we finally entered the Belt Parkway for the return trip to Brooklyn.

"Thanks. So . . . this is your place in Gravesend?"

"Technically, yes, but there are those who'll insist that it's actually Bath Beach."

"Uh-huh," she said around another bite. "Yeah, that's the part of Brooklyn that's always been a bit confusing for me."

I laughed. "It's Brooklyn, and it's near the beach, so it's all good! But," I said while I signaled for a lane switch, "I figured you might need both some rest and a shower before New York actually welcomes you back, so whether it's called Bath Beach or Gravesend, that's where we're off to now."

"New York doesn't welcome *anyone*," Trish reminded me. "It grudgingly lets you buy a hot dog, grumbles 'have a nice day' at you if *and* when you get a taxi—then takes your wallet and asks for change."

"Oh, so you *do* remember what it's like to live here!" I teased while we eased to a stop. "Pass me the other sandwich?" I asked, suddenly ravenous. "The scent is driving me insane!"

"Sure," she said, and there was rustling before she handed me the awesome bacon-egg-and-cheese. She'd even taken the silver foil off in such a way that I could still eat the sandwich and not get anything on my hands.

"You're awesome—and thank you!" I took a bite. Yeah, that definitely hit the spot in all the right ways! "Well, you can't say you've not been welcomed back properly!"

Trish reached over and lightly pushed on my shoulder. I could feel the gentle connect from her fingers through my shirt. "Hey—it would've been great, even without that."

I glanced over and saw her warm grin and the brightness of her eyes shining on me. "Ah—sometimes it's just that one little thing that makes it all work, ya know?"

"Yeah," she nodded, and rubbed her thumb against the muscle in my arm, making everywhere she touched feel like liquid sunshine. "Yeah, it is—and it does. Thanks."

I peeked over at her again and answered her smile with one of my own—I just couldn't help myself. "Hey—it really is my pleasure. And besides, what are friends for, right?"

We drove in contented silence the rest of the way to Brooklyn.

"Oh . . . wow!" Trish said admiringly as we approached the gated property the building was on. The building stood on its own bit of landscaped lot complete with garden, while the beach and the water were less than three hundred yards out. "I'd forgotten how nice this place is," she said as she looked around. "It's this little oasis of peace in such a busy city."

"It really is," I agreed. "And it's safe, too—so when Nana's up for it, I like that she can go out and about, sit in the sun, watch the kids in the park, walk over and look at the water. Hell," I admitted as I hit the button on my key ring to open the bay door to the parking garage, "I do that, too, more often than even I thought I would."

"Second floor," I reminded her as we walked to the elevator.

"High enough for a good view, low enough to jump if you've got to," she said knowingly as we walked through the hallway.

"Yup—exactly," I answered as I hit the elevator call button.

What she said and what I agreed to was true, was and is an absolutely very real thing among many emergency personnel, whether we worked with fire, crime, medical emergencies, or some combination thereof: to not have a living space higher than the second floor, third in the worst-case scenario, because everything forbid there was a fire with no easy exits—well, most folks would survive a second-story jump and even a third-story (especially if you had a second-floor window ladder to bring you just that much lower to the ground), even though they might have some serious fractures to contend with after.

Broken bones could heal.

Roasted bodies could not.

As the doors opened and we exited onto my floor, I knew Trish was taking note of where the exits were, how clearly they were marked, and even more important, how easy they would or wouldn't be to reach in total darkness.

It didn't bother me at all that she was doing that or that I knew she was, even though she wasn't obvious about it in any way because, frankly, it was something I did, too—every place I went, every single time, whether it was a family, friend, or work visit.

Hmm ... Is that like an OCD—obsessive compulsive disorder—thing? I asked myself as we walked. *I mean, yeah, sure, it's normal to me and Trish as well as other emergency personnel, but would civilians ...* I observed Trish taking in the layout as we walked and found it reassuring I wasn't the only one who could find the way out if something terrible happened. *You know what? It doesn't matter*, I decided. After all, what we did, observing and learning these little things, these bits of knowledge all helped give us an edge in saving lives.

"If you remember the layout of the place, you'll have the room in the back corner while you're here," I told her as we approached the door. But oh, I could smell something delicious, and I was certain that—

"Welcome back—food's ready!" Linda announced brightly through the door she pulled open before I could even put my key in the lock. She literally reached out past me to take Trish into an enthusiastic hug.

"Uh, okay—thanks!" Trish said with a laugh behind me as I brought her bags inside. "It smells incredible in here!" she said as Linda continued to crush her.

"*Pero*, Linda, *da le un momento para respirar!*" Nana said behind her.

"Yeah, let her breathe!" I agreed as Trish was finally free to fully walk in. She immediately greeted my grandmother.

"*Es un placer estar aquí con ustedes,*" Trish said to my grandmother in perfectly pronounced, if very American-accented, formal Spanish.

I could see the smile on my Nana's face grow from happy to delighted as she opened her arms up to hug Trish as well, and I admit, it made my heart swell to see that Trish knew—without any coaching on my part—what the right thing to do and say was.

Hell, had she said the same thing in English, it would've been enough. But that she learned to be able to say it in Spanish—

Wow.

"And you are always *bienvenida—es tu casa, también,*" Nana told her with real warmth.

"*Gracias, señora,*" Trish answered as she bent to give her a return embrace.

"So come on—food's ready and it's going to get cold!" Linda announced. "Seriously, Bennadette—why are you taking so long to show Trish where her room is?"

I rolled my eyes good-naturedly. "This way," I announced to Trish, who followed me down the hall.

"You've really got this place set up beautifully," she commented as she followed me through the apartment.

"Thank you," I answered. "And . . . here we are." I opened the door, walked in, and placed her bag on the foot of the bed.

I turned to look at her and watched her take it all in. "This is really nice," she said finally. "And thank you—thank you for inviting me, for having me stay here, and"—she shifted her weight from one leg to the other—"thank you for lending me your room."

Her sunglasses were hung from the neck of her shirt, and the expression on her face—she was so serious, but the lines of her mouth were so soft, and her eyes—there was something in them that I didn't recognize but wanted to understand . . . and

I again found myself wondering how there was any way I could possibly catch that remarkable light in a sketched portrait.

"It's totally my pleasure," I said around a growing dryness in my throat that made no sense, and I hadn't realized I'd stepped closer, but I had, and—

"Bennie—come on—food!" Linda called. "What is taking you so long?"

The moment broke as Trish and I both laughed. "This way to the dining room," I said as I led her to the promised meal, the incredible scent of it drawing us on. "I'm pretty sure it's *arroz con pollo*—and no one makes it better than Linda or my Nana—not even me."

It was cool—as in seriously really cool—to hang out with Trish, and at the same time, it was a bit weird because, after the very delicious lunch cooked by my Nana and Linda (and yes, we both ate, despite having already had sandwiches, because the food smelled and tasted so good, making it irresistible *and* it would have seriously insulted both Nana and Linda not to), I made certain the very-tired-but-hiding-it-well Trish knew where the shower was.

With the dishes washed and put away and the next meal already planned, I was taking a moment for myself, simply sitting on the sofa, enjoying a cup of coffee, and thinking I might just stretch out for a few minutes myself while Trish showered, then rested for a bit.

Of course, we'd already made all sorts of plans during our texts and calls, and the biggest one was to meet mutual friends Tori and Jean for dinner at their house on Staten Island—which was our very next thing to do.

I knew we would definitely have fun, it was more than probably going to be more than a bit noisy, and that Trish would be seriously tired sooner or later, given the time difference between the East and West Coast.

"So hey, querida—we're off for a few days, then. Have fun!" Linda announced, breaking the quiet as she came out of Nana's room with two packed bags.

What the heck . . . ? I stood up. "Wait—what? Where are you—where are both of you going?" I asked, surprised and confused.

Nana came out just behind her, wearing a very nice suit, her hair all made up, and—I peered closely—*was that . . .* yes. That was definitely makeup she had on.

"Got a bonus at work, found a great deal online, and *voila!* Reservations for a few days in Atlantic City!" Linda informed my very stunned self cheerily, giving me a very bright smile as she bustled by me with the bags towards the door. "Plus, Nana has a client who's doing some sort of gown show thing there," she added with a grin.

"*Si, es para un cliente,*" Nana agreed, her eyes owl-wide.

Yeah . . . I knew that look. Something was up.

"Uh . . . how are you getting there?" I asked stupidly. "Linda has been borrowing my car because hers is in the shop this week."

"*Es un Uber,*" Nana answered. "*Es muy easy.*"

"Oh. Okay," I said, just as dumbly as I followed behind them to the door. For whatever reason, none of this was making sense. At all.

"Any numbers you want us to play for you?" Linda asked with her hand on the knob. She glanced at me over her shoulder and grinned. "You know, like . . ." she put a finger against her chin and pretended to think on it. "Hmmm . . . How about two? Does two work for you?"

"Linda!" Nana exclaimed as she lightly slapped her arm. "You tease your *prima* too much! But"—Nana turned back to me, then reached up to hug and kiss me good-bye—"*nos vamos* so we don't cramp your *estilo.*"

"Oh my God!" I said, alarmed, and dropped my voice to a harsh whisper because this was embarrassing me *and* I didn't want Trish to overhear; we could all hear the water for her shower had just shut off moments before, and this place wasn't *that* soundproof room to room. "You—she—seriously, there's absolutely *no* style to cramp—we're just friends!" I spluttered indignantly—and to seemingly no avail.

"*Sí,*" my Nana agreed from within the hug and pulled me in a bit closer. For such a small person, she was incredibly strong. "*Y es así que se hace mejor.*" She released me from the embrace with a kiss to my cheek.

"*Estoy de acuerdo,*" Linda said, offering Nana her arm as she agreed with her. "Friendship is the best foundation for everything."

"Hey, I'm clean and refreshed!" I heard Trish call from deeper within the apartment. "Let's go see Tori and Jean and go explore—sleeping is for way later!"

"Jesus Christ—you guys, just—whatever!" I hissed to Nana and Linda by the door.

If they were going, better they leave before Trish came out and could hear the two of them and their suppositions, embarrassing me eternally. "Go—win big money or something!" I encouraged and hurried them.

Nana's eyes narrowed at me briefly at the mention of Christ. "*Pero esa boca . . .* that mouth!"

Oh no . . . I'd really stepped in it with her. "I'm sorry, Nana," I began contritely, but Nana's eyes narrowed on me even further. Right. The apology wasn't just for her. "Oh—and Jesus, okay? I'm sorry, Jesus," I added hurriedly.

Nana squinted at me as she grudgingly nodded her forgiveness, and I assume transmitted the deity's, too.

"Where's everyone going?" Trish asked from just behind my shoulder.

"Atlantic City!" Nana announced loudly. "We go see a show,

maybe get massage *y un* mani-pedi, *y* then—"

"Maybe we'll win a new car!" Linda said with a huge smile. "It's a weekend for gambling, after all! Any special numbers either of you want us to play?" she asked, and her smile turned decidedly sharp. "How about six and ni—"

My eyes widened in alarm at what was about to come out of her mouth. I think I levitated the few feet between us to help push her out the door before she could finish that statement. "So okay, by now your car's downstairs. Go, so you don't miss it!" I said over her instead.

Linda turned a very obviously wicked grin on me.

I rolled my eyes at the pair of them, with their self-congratulatory smiles and too-wide eyes, hugged and kissed and shooed them out the door.

"Have fun, good luck, win big money!" I wished them hurriedly as I closed the door behind them.

I could hear them laughing and joking as they made their way to the elevator. I leaned against the door a moment, simultaneously embarrassed by the teasing, relieved they were gone, and glad, because the teasing meant they liked Trish.

"Was that weird," Trish asked, waving to the door, "or am I goofy from being tired?"

"It was weird," I admitted as I set the last lock and waved her to follow me into the living room. "I mean, yeah, you might be goofy tired and all that, too, but there's nothing wrong with your powers of perception."

She stood in the center of the room, her hands on her hips. She'd dressed in a fresh pair of jeans, engineer boots, and a collared shirt opened at the neck, a small medallion of some sort centered in the hollow of her throat. She glanced about, not knowing what to do next.

I honestly didn't blame her; I was definitely feeling a little weirded out by that abrupt and unexpected change in plans myself.

"Coffee?" I offered. *That's always a good place to start*, I thought. Not only would it help ease some of the tired, but it would definitely give me the moments I needed to collect myself and settle from the confusion the last few minutes had created for me. "I could for sure use some."

"You know . . ." she said, then pursed her lips thoughtfully. "Yeah. That'll probably do the trick."

"Give me a few minutes," I said and smiled before I made my way to the kitchen.

The simple acts of measuring and grinding beans, pouring water, setting everything up on the stove were mindful, calming, and allowed me to recover from the not-so-hidden—I didn't know if they were observations or accusations—from my family.

And given how very certain *they* were of what they saw and said, I wasn't so sure which of those things they might be, myself.

I'm missing something, I told myself. *I bet it's as simple as—*

"Milk and sugar?" Trish asked hopefully, her voice closer than before since, instead of being in the living room, she was in the doorway, and somehow, knowing that she'd followed me to the kitchen—well, it somehow made me feel better.

"Yes, and yes," I promised as I poured. I handed her a generously sized mug, the side emblazoned with "I Heart an EMT."

"So . . ." she began as she set her mug on the table and took a seat, "seems like your cousin and Nana want us to hook up, huh?"

I shook my head and chuckled as I pulled out a seat of my own. That . . . was the Trish I knew. Trust her to succinctly name whatever a situation might be. And that sort of honesty—that was the sort of thing that went down very well in the wolf pack that was my family.

"Uh . . . yeah," I confirmed as I sat. It might have made me a little uncomfortable, but why deny what was so obviously true, right? I took a sip from my mug and smacked my lips. *Uh-huh, yes, I do make a good cuppa*, I noted, *even if I do say so myself.*

"Is it because . . . we're really good friends, because we're both gay, because we do the same thing, because—what?" she asked, waving a hand to emphasize her question.

I almost choked on my next sip because that wasn't something I had expected.

"Don't die on me, Grego," Trish warned. "I'm supposed to be off duty this weekend!"

"I'm fine, Spence, I'm fine," I said hastily as my throat and vision cleared. "And how about we figure that out later? I'm not caffeinated enough to think that deeply."

"Okay, okay," Trish said with a light laugh. She took another sip from her mug. "But damn, you always do know what to do with coffee!" she said admiringly. "And okay, again, what've you got planned for next—after Tori and Jean's, I mean?"

I studied her as I thought about it and sipped again—carefully, this time. Yes, I'd planned for some things, but the reality was that Trish wasn't a tourist: she was a native who'd been gone for a little while, was all. I was completely certain there had to be things she'd want to see and do, too, in addition to the bacon-egg-and-cheese sandwich.

And because she was my guest and because she was my friend, whatever happened next was completely up to her—and I'd be more than happy to help make it happen.

"Your move, your choice, Spence," I told her. "Your move, your choice."

We were sitting for a moment, enjoying the Starbucks we had picked up on the corner and resting at a random table and chair we'd found under one of the many trees in Bryant Park.

Light filtered through on and off as the trees rustled in the light breeze, dappling the table and creating an occasional blink off the sunglasses Trish again wore.

She's just so perfect, I thought. *If I memorize the light and the angles perfectly, maybe I can finally find the right way to draw them sometime.* I breathed while I watched. *I think about that a lot,* I realized.

"Thank you for the coffee," I said as I leaned back in my chair with a contented sigh, enjoying the air, the trees, the view before me, and the general bustle of the city around this small island of green.

"Hey, no coffee, no life!" Trish answered with a smile, then held her cup up. "*Salud!*"

"*Salud!*" I answered back, and touched my cup to hers, then sipped. God, that was good—and necessary . . . "So," I began, feeling expansive. It had been a really great afternoon, starting with the hearty lunch we'd had earlier, through the trip into Manhattan, and the walk around that had led us from Union Square all the way up here, just on the other side of the library with the famous lions on its front steps. "We've enjoyed the thrills that are walking up Broadway—where to next, Captain?"

"Uh . . ." Trish paused to take a long sip from her cup, and she glanced down at the table, her fingers fiddling with the sleeve. "There's a store not far from here I'm kinda hoping is still around and open."

"Yeah?" I asked with sincere interest. We only had a few days, so wherever she wanted to go and whatever she wanted to do, well, we were going and doing.

She cocked her head and furrowed her brow. "It's, uh . . . it's . . . it's a comic book store. I used to go there when—well, you know."

I put my cup down and leaned a bit forward. This was surprising—this was something I hadn't known about Trish before at all.

"Uh . . . by any chance, is it on Thirty-Second Street?"

The crease on Trish's brow eased, and she gave me a small grin. "Jim Hanley's Universe?"

"The name's changed slightly since you were here last," I told her as I stood. "It's JHU Comic Books now, and yeah, it's still there." I pushed my chair in. "Let's go!" I was smiling broadly now as I stood.

Because seriously, comic books? They were totally my thing, so much so that my friend Jean and I were working on an ongoing project, one that took up all my free time, the one thing that, whenever we got enough material to complete a story arc together, we paid to get physical copies made.

Like, for people.

To read.

In fact, we even sold them on occasion at JHU. *Oh hey*, I realized, *I* should *probably stop there and ask—*

"Really?" Trish, smiling and obviously surprised, stared up at me.

"Yeah—come on!" I grabbed her hand and pulled her up with me. "Stories told through sequential art sequences await!"

She laughed. "Yes, they surely do."

"I can't believe you never told me about this before!" I told her as together we practically ran the few blocks to the store.

"Wasn't a chance before," she said with a shrug.

A few steps more, and we were there.

"All right!" I announced as we stood before the store. "It's all still here!" I waved an arm to take in the entire display window, which included a statue of the Silver Surfer hanging a cosmic eternal ten while he stared intensely into the middle distance, just across the street from the Empire State Building. "Thirty-two on East Thirty-Second!"

It was at that moment I realized we'd still been holding hands, and momentarily self-conscious, I quickly dropped the light grip between us so I could open the door. "After you," I said, and glanced up to see Trish wearing a delighted grin.

"Thank you," she said quietly as she walked past me. She patted my arm as she walked in. "You've really surprised me."

"What?" I asked as I walked behind her. "That I'm also into—"

"Hey, Bennie!" a male voice I knew called from behind the counter. "I've got some money for you and Jean, and some new issues on your pull list ready for you!"

Trish turned back to look at me over her shoulder and over her sunglasses. "They know you here? I'm impressed!"

"Uh-huh," I confirmed, once again a bit self-conscious. I stood a bit behind her, even as I tried to wave the equivalent of "don't say anything" to Robbie; Trish didn't know that I moonlighted as anything other than a smoke jumper, and I wasn't sure if I was ready to have that conversation just yet.

Luckily for me, Trish seemed to have not heard the first part of his statement. "Yes, complete with a pull list," I told her with a grin, keeping us firmly in the I'm-just-a-customer-here territory. "Hey, Robbie," I greeted him as I walked to the counter. "How ya doin'?"

"I'm good, good," he said, and lifted his eyebrows at me to show he understood my weird gestures. Or maybe he didn't but was going along with me anyway.

Robbie was the same Robbie I'd always known, and from what I understood from friends, the way he'd always been: dark and wavy hair that sometimes came past his chin, sometimes down to his shoulders, although here and there, silver streaked through the waves.

"Got those after I bought this shop," Robbie would tell anyone who asked—and even anyone who didn't. "I think because of it, even."

"How *you* doin'? Watcha up to today?" he asked, still wriggling his eyebrows at me.

"I'm good," I told him. "Just bringing my friend Trish here around for a visit."

"Nice to meet you," Trish said, extending her hand over the counter.

"Hey, yeah," Robbie said as he took her hand. "*X-Men*, right?"

"Yeah," Trish laughed, surprise on her face as she took her hand back. "How can you tell?"

Robbie chuckled. "Eh—it's not a guess. I remember you! You used to run in, your partner waiting in the ambulance just out front, grab the latest, then run back out. I think at least twice you got a call, left your books, and had to come back later!"

Trish laughed. "Yeah, I guess a moment like that might be memorable!"

"Hey, these are not just gray hairs; these are memory files!" he told her, and winked as he grabbed one of his curls and shook it at her.

"Well, it's nice to officially meet you. Oh wow!" she exclaimed, looking at the wall behind and over his head. "Is that actually an *X-Men #1*?"

I glanced up with her, and yes, mounted on the wall among the many collectible issues of various titles, there it was: a giant-size *X-Men #1*. It even said exactly that on the cover, complete with the original lineup.

"Oh man—that would be some score!" I enthused.

"Damn, yes!" Trish agreed energetically.

"How much is it?" I asked. I nodded as Robbie answered, thinking all the while, because *yeah—that would be amazing to add to my collection, and—*

"So hey, sorry to interrupt, but do any of those memory files know if the bathroom is available?" she asked Robbie.

"What—you don't know where it is?" I asked her with a grin.

"Nope," she answered succinctly. "Never here long enough for that. And"—she grinned at me "—you know how it is—caffeine is just like alcohol—they're substances you rent, never own. So—," she clapped her hands together—"where to?"

Robbie directed her, and we both watched her walk away

before she disappeared into a side aisle.

"So," he began, "I owe you and Jean some money. Maybe we should do an event here, like a signing and drawing thing sometime with you two, schedule it when—"

"That's a great idea," I agreed, "but can we discuss it some other time? Not too many people know what I do, and I kinda want to keep it like that for a bit, or at least for right now."

Robbie gave me an odd look. "Yeah, that's fine," he said slowly, "but let's not leave it for too long. I want to get the calendar all set up sooner rather than later."

I felt so awkward, I didn't know where to look first, and as my eyes searched about, they came to rest on the *X-Men #1*, the one that Trish had admired.

And an idea occurred to me.

"Hey, Robbie—I want to buy that X-Men—but—" I thought about how I wanted to do this. "Don't take it down until after we leave, then mail it to"—I scribbled Trish's address on a piece of paper—"here, okay?" I said. "I promise, we'll talk later this week about scheduling something, and"— I slid the paper to him—"whatever the shipping is, just add it."

"Okay, we'll talk, and sure, I can do that—no problem," he assured me as he read what I'd written. He turned from me to ring everything up. "Shipping's on me, though. Figure it'll get there in a few days or so."

"Really? Thanks," I said, surprised.

"Eh, it's no big thing," Robbie said, then gave me a bright grin. "Besides, your girlfriend's always impressed me as being a good person. She'll really like this," Robbie commented as he began to gather some things behind the counter—probably my pull list. "And I'm thinking she'll really like that her girlfriend is working on a cool indie title."

"She *is* a good person, and I do think she'll like it," I agreed. "But"—I shook my head—"she's not my 'girlfriend,'" I said, using air quotes around the word. "At least not in any sense other than we both happen to be female and that we're friends with each other."

"Uh-huh," Robbie said noncommittally as he put a bag on the counter. "But . . . you like each other."

Seriously. What's with this vibe everyone's getting? I wondered.

I faced him. "Uh, Robbie? Why are we having this conversation?" I asked as I reached for the bag with one hand and into my jacket for my wallet with the other.

I mean, of course we like each other, I thought loudly to myself. *We're friends, after all. And yes,* I conceded to myself, *okay, I did kinda have the idea that maybe we might like each other a bit more than that—well . . . maybe—well . . . kinda. But . . .* I reassured myself as I found my card, *I surely wasn't* that *oblivious—or obvious—about it. Right?*

Robbie cocked his head to the side and stared at me a moment, eyes still smiling. "Don'tcha think I might have seen this movie before?"

I gave him a sidewise look of my own. "Have you, now?" I asked dryly and passed him the card.

"Yep," he chuckled as he rang me up. "And—I won't give you any spoilers, but I'll bet you anything you want that I know how this one ends!"

"Spoilers? What movie are we discussing?" Trish asked from just behind my shoulder, making me jump slightly.

"Uh . . ." I started, flustered. "We were talking about—"

"X-Men!" Robbie answered, handing me back my card and the receipt to sign. "I know some stuff about the next one. You know, they"—he held both hands up, making quote signs with his fingers—"tell us . . . you know . . . *things,*" he said as I gave him a look that was probably a combination of *thank you for not embarrassing me more than my family did* and *oh my God—please stop talking!*

Which was exactly how I was feeling.

"Okay . . ." Trish said slowly, glancing from me to Robbie

and back again as Robbie handed me my bag.

"Let's take a look around—see what we find?" I suggested hastily, not wanting to get into any of this further—at all.

"Sure," Trish agreed easily. "That's sorta the point, right?" She gave me a quick grin. "So," she started with a long, low drag-out of the sound as we headed down the first aisle, "have you seen them all?"

"All them what?" I asked, more than slightly distracted, because this was a lot of pressure, from the teasing and then the rapid disappearance of my family, Robbie pointing out the obvious—which I really wasn't ready to deal with yet, and even me and Trish planning before this visit on having a cup of coffee—which was a really super noncommittal way of feeling each other out about maybe going on a date, yet still keeping our friendship intact if it didn't work that way.

It was . . . a *lot*.

"X-Men. The movies," she answered, gazing at me over her shoulder. I'd never seen her grin like that before. "Have you seen them all so far?"

That pulled me out of my head. "Hey, I'll have you know"—I stopped in my tracks—"I *have* them all—all the released ones so far, that is—on every format you can watch them on—from DVD to streaming media, just in case there are differences—and so I can watch them wherever I am," I added hastily. "You know, when I get to travel to all those exotic locations . . ." I said and grinned back.

"Yeah, because there's so much time to watch a movie during a fire or an earthquake or a flood," Trish joked.

"Well, I download them before I get on the plane—usually for the flight back," I amended. "It's not a bad way to decompress."

She nodded as we continued down the aisles. "How about you?" I asked finally, honestly curious about the answer, even as I eyed, then picked up a thick hardcover *Love and Rockets* collection.

"How about me what? Oh—that's the *Love and Rockets* collection!" she exclaimed as she saw what I was flipping through. "I didn't know you read that!"

"Yep," I nodded. "Hence the pull list." I let her take the book from me to flip through. "And how about you and the X-Men?" I glanced up to watch her scan through the pages.

Trish closed the book and looked back at me. "All I have to say," she said, her expression growing very serious, "is make mine Marvel!" She gave me a huge smile as she handed me back the tome. "And since you have them all, whattaya say we marathon?"

"What?" Was she saying what I thought she was? I could feel the unspoken question on my face

"X-Men. Marathon. You— "she pointed to me, "—and me." She tapped her chest with her thumb. "Deep in the heart of Brooklyn." She watched me with an expectant smile.

Oh. *Wow* . . . that was so cool! I couldn't help the grin I felt grow across my face as I shook my head. "You're something else, y'know?"

"I just might even be mutant!" she agreed brightly. "So— yeah?" And her grin became a huge smile that made me feel like I was standing in the warmest sunshine.

I couldn't help it. I laughed. "All right," I agreed, still laughing. "You got it." Impulsively, I held my arm out for her.

"Yeah?" she asked, glancing at my arm, then back to my eyes.

"Yeah." I nodded.

"Mutants, unite!" she said as she took my arm.

And still grinning like mad, off we went.

"But that's the saddest thing," I said to Trish. "I mean, if you think about it."

She shifted to face me instead of the screen.

"What, you mean, to see yet be so far?" she asked as I faced her in return.

"It's as bad, maybe even worse than death, really, to know that never again can there be talk or touch or . . . to never, ever know the truth of what should have been."

I couldn't help the wave of sadness that filled me, and I gazed down at my hands in an effort to control it, tamp it down, back, *away*, place it somewhere other than here at this moment.

"Hey," Trish said softly with a genuine concern I could hear as she scooted over to gently touch my shoulder. "Want to stop watching? Is this getting you down?"

We'd just been watching a movie about the origin of the character Wolverine: the life he'd led before it was all taken away from him, even his mind, with the memory of the woman he had loved and who loved him in return, and yes, that was a really sad thing. He had, in essence, lost everything that mattered emotionally.

And even though I knew (and knew Trish knew as well) that this was "just a movie," as the saying goes, and therefore only fiction, it did just so happen to be that, once upon a time, and maybe not all that long ago in the way human lives are counted, I'd lost everything that had seemed to matter to me, too.

Not that I hadn't moved on, not that I'd not kept going . . .

"Yeah . . . no, not really," I answered slowly. I continued to stare at my hands as Trish keyed the remote to shut off the movie. "I just . . . I just get these moments sometimes when I really, *really* remember . . . stuff . . . things I used to want and be, y'know?" I gave her a small grin and hoped the fullness I felt in my eyes wouldn't overflow.

"Yeah, I do," she said softly, and she shifted even farther to give me a side hug. "I really, really do."

Without even thinking about it, I turned her head into my shoulder, and before it was even a thought, she'd put her other arm around me.

She gently stroked the back of my head with her hand, her fingertips soft and soothing against my scalp. "Something about this is bringing stuff all back for you, huh?"

I breathed in to relieve the fullness in my head, breathed out to relieve the weight in my chest, and found that some of it escaped from my eyes anyway.

"I guess," I murmured against her, breathing in a measured way to keep myself here and now, and not back in such a painful then. "It . . . that time . . . it was . . . really bad. It was—"

I sighed with the effort of trying not to remember.

"Anything that has you this upset, then whatever it was, I know it was the worst—the worst it could possibly be," she finished for me, and she held me even more closely, a closeness through which I could feel her heartbeat against my aching one, a closeness where I could feel the ache she held, too.

"And when you're ready—to talk, I mean, if you ever want to, and even if you never do—I'm here for you, Bennie. I'm right here for you," she whispered over my head. "Whatever, and whenever you need."

Trish let me cry it out against her as much as I was able, and there were parts where she cried with me, too. And so, finally I guess, I talked about some of it, if not all of it, of a time when I was so small and the hope of my father returning was a real thing, of the Dennis the Menace, Little Lulu, and Richie Rich comic books my mother bought and shared with me for the little time I'd had her with me and something that my grandmother had continued after she was gone, of the treasure trove of Batman that I'd discovered in my father's personal effects when my grandmother and I had finally moved from that first apartment I remembered only as the place where I'd last seen my mother, to the one we'd live in for years before we came here.

The sun had set just a short while ago, and with its light disappearing from the sky and hence the living room, it had gotten not only darker but also cooler.

I'd turned on a light on the table next to the sofa to combat the first, and now that I was stretched all along Trish and tucked up against her shoulder, I'd pulled a blanket over us from the back of the sofa to ward against the other.

"So I guess that's kinda where it all started for me," I said quietly. "And boy, after I discovered the X-Men when I was in high school . . . that changed the whole world!"

I chuckled at the memory, and Trish gave a light laugh with me.

"Oh man, that was probably one of the best things I'd ever read, too!" Trish said with real enthusiasm. "I have to honestly say I seriously wished I could meet them!"

"I got to the point where I wanted to *make* them!" I admitted to her. "I mean, yeah, I was doing premed in college and all that, but that was really what moved me, and when it hit me that I could change my major, well, I figured that even if I couldn't get *that* job—"

"What, actually drawing the X-Men?" Trish asked with a smile I could hear.

"Honestly—yeah," I confessed. "But I figured until then, I could work maybe as a graphic designer in publishing or something."

"Really? So why didn't you do that?" she asked me, her voice serious and soft. Her fingertips brushed over my shoulder in a soft and soothing pattern, making me feel safe and warm and incredibly comfortable in the circle of warmth we created. "You still draw, right? I mean, you did that funny one with the guys in their underpants and boots with the bear, then you did that really pretty piece from that stream we stayed near—and there's all of those other ones of the crew and other sites I've seen you do, too."

I sighed heavily.

I didn't know if I was truly ready to talk about this . . . this *thing* . . . that had been a part of who I was, of who I'd become, for so long.

Especially when no one else—no one that mattered, really—knew about all of it either.

"That . . . that part—it's really hard to think about, never mind talk about," I said honestly, letting my breath out slowly. I rubbed my fingertips against her collarbone, finding the hardness of the ridge and the contrast with the silky soft skin that covered it fascinating.

"I'm sure it is," she said quietly. "You don't have to, if you don't want to—it's totally okay, Bennie. It really is."

"You sure?" I asked her because I wanted to be certain, because if it wasn't, then okay, but for Trish, for everything she'd shared with me, I'd try.

I wanted to.

"Of course," she said, and pulled me as close to her as she could. She kissed the top of my head. "When you're ready, you're ready, and not a second before."

"Okay." I nodded against her chest. "One of these days, really," I promised quietly, and I closed my eyes. Once again, us talking all snuggled warm together was making me light and drifty.

It was an incredible feeling, this float with Trish, with its sureness and its comfort and its . . . safety, the sense that here, in this time and space where we were, everything was okay. It didn't matter if we were in the middle of a northern California forest, facing fires and bears, running emergency calls, or checking out comic books in Manhattan, it always felt like we fit, lock and key, and no matter what, everything was already all right—and would continue to be.

And with that same surety, I knew that even if I couldn't tell her about the hard part of it, the "what" had happened that was behind the "why" I stopped going down the path I'd started, I *could* tell her about the new one I'd found, the one I was pursuing now.

My heart began to beat hard. Other than my family—which in many ways included Tori, Jean, and their kids, too—no one else really knew this, not even my cousin Linda—about me.

And still to this day, I was the only one who knew all the details.

I breathed in for a count of four softly, held it for another count of four, then exhaled easily, because I didn't want to think about it—or remember any more of it—right now.

I focused on the positive, on the here and now, on the present moment that held us close and safe and warm, the air filled with the possibility of . . . something, something I couldn't yet name, but I already knew was something good.

The heartbeat under my ear proved it.

"Hey," I began softly, "you're right, you know—I do still draw."

"Yeah, I know you do—all those awesome little pieces you do on the job and everything," she said lightly and easily, squeezing me to her even more closely for a moment.

"Uh . . . actually," I began, leaning into the hold. "Jean and I do this small comic thing—she writes it, I draw it, and um"—I shifted just a bit so I could see Trish's face, gauge her reaction—"we fund and print a run about every month or so, and JHU sells them on consignment for us."

Trish's eyes opened wide, and she sat up straighter. Her face filled with what I could only describe as delighted surprise as she smiled at me.

"You're kidding! Really? You do? What's it called? What's it about? Do you have pen names? Would I have read it somewhere? Where else can I find it? When do you—"

"Okay! I can answer all of those individually!" I said and laughed, because her enthusiasm and excitement surprised

73

and delighted me.

"Yes, I do, well, me and Jean do," I hastily corrected. "It's called *Hex*, it's normal people fighting super, extra, and paranormal baddies, we use our actual names, maybe you've picked it up if you like indie comics, and . . ." I ticked the answers off on my fingers, "we create in every free moment we can find. Did I get them all?"

"Uh, maybe? But I still have questions—more than two!" she warned with that smile that made me feel so damned good.

"Well all right, go for it," I told her, feeling my own smile grow so large it almost hurt.

"Okay," she began and there was no mistaking the excitement in her voice, "how did you and Jean get started? Does this make you like a superhero by day and a mild-mannered—well, maybe not so mild—creative by night?"

"Truthfully? We got started because we started talking about this whole story world in between calls," I told her. "Huh." I chuckled a bit under my breath. "Something like that—though yeah, maybe not so mild," I agreed. "So . . ." we settled back into each other, "now you know. Whatcha think?" I asked, sincerely wanting to know—this was something so different than anything we'd ever discussed before and it wasn't something, well, usual among our peers, I knew that for a fact.

"What do I think?" Trish asked me softly as we curled further into each other. "What do I think?" she repeated. "What I think . . ." she murmured as she traced small circles on my arm and back, "is that you're perfect. This . . ." she held me tight to her. "This is perfect."

"Yes," I sighed in very contented agreement, tucking my forehead against her neck. "It really is."

I took a deep satisfied breath, and it hit me—*I love this*, I realized, *I love every bit of this*—the sharing and the laughing, the enthusiasm . . . every. Single. Thing. And more than anything else, I realized that I loved this . . . *us* . . . we had created.

"I love this, Trish," I told her, whispering across the silky-smooth skin of her neck, feeling completely suffused by this whatever it was we had created together, this space that was so small and all us, yet felt like it was flowing and growing, would soon fill the room with all the feeling between us.

"Bennie, my Bennie," Trish whispered softly against my hair as I felt us both continue to float in the comfort of the warm drift. "I think . . . I think we have something very special between us," she said, and kissed my head. "I want to explore this with you."

"Yes," I agreed, breathing out the headiness of it, my breath now again a warm brush against the column of her neck. "Me, too."

"As slow as you want or need to go, Bennie, okay?" Trish told me as we settled in somehow even closer, tighter. "However and whatever you want."

"All right," I nodded, now full of warm and sleep and the gorgeous feel that was us snuggled up together under this blanket, within her arms and she in mine, and it was perfect and beautiful, us curled together, closer, closer, so close . . .

Which is how Linda and Nana found us when they walked in the next morning: Trish and I curled up together and fast asleep on the sofa.

Chapter 3

There's Always Something Happening and It's Usually Quite Loud

"IT'S YOUR bat phone!" This time the voice that called outside the bathroom door while I showered was Nana's.

"It's—" I sputtered, trying not to swallow water and soap. "It's all right!" I called back as loudly as I could. "I'll call them back!"

"*Es una emergencia!*" Nana yelled back through the door.

"I know!" I yelled back, now spitting suds and trying to get the rest out of my hair and eyes. Because honestly, on that phone, there was nothing else it could possibly be. "I'll call right back!" I ran rapid fingers through my soaped and soaked hair to quickly rinse it.

"Is for you!" she said emphatically, her voice so much clearer, closer, and very much louder now.

And there, below my dripping chin, just behind the spray from the nozzle and barely in through the curtain, was my levitating phone, the screen bright, letting me know the call had, in fact, been answered.

Well, the phone wasn't really levitating, obviously; Nana had decided to come into the bathroom.

"Nana—that's going to get ruined in here," I said, even as I was already shutting the taps.

I made an executive decision while I mentally rolled my eyes because I understood why Nana had both swiped to accept the call and come into the bathroom: it really *was* an emergency if that phone rang.

It was too bad Nana didn't understand that it was okay for me to let it go to voicemail and call back, I thought as I wiped my finger on the curtain. Hoping at least that part of me was dry enough, I gave a quick prayer that I'd neither insult the handler calling me, nor—more importantly—damage my phone as I blew my breath out in a huff and hit the screen to end the call.

"*Gracias*, Nana—I'll call them back as soon as I get out of here," I said from behind the curtain.

"*No te entiendo*," Nana said, taking the phone with her, "I don't understand you. *Dices que siempre*—you always must, with that phone, and now—you wait? *No te entiendo*," she repeated as I heard her walk back to the door.

"Thank you, Nana—just put it back on the counter in the kitchen, please?" I asked while I squeezed the last of the water from my hair.

"Hmph," she said, which I took as "yes." She closed the door behind her.

I sighed as I rapidly reached for, then wrapped myself within a towel. It didn't matter how often or apparently how well I explained to her that it was okay if I didn't answer right that very second if I was doing something, like already on a call at my regular job, very deeply asleep, or—as in this case—occupied in the bathroom. Besides, there'd probably be a text about the situation, too . . .

I wondered what it was as I towel dried my hair and went back to my room to dress. Of course, it would be on my three-day swing, I thought while I smelled the coffee Nana was brewing and pulled my pants on.

Five days on, two off, five days on, three off. That's the way the emergency medical service worked, and generally, that schedule meant I was in a good position to plan things—like working on

Jean's and my book or, most important right now, the next time Trish and I would see each other—except for those times when something urgent happened.

Which it seemed right now was the case . . .

And then there was the next issue of *Hex* that Jean and I were working on—we weren't late, but still, I didn't want to get behind, either.

I grabbed my regular phone to text Trish—it was too early to call California, and we'd just spent hours on the phone the night before, which meant that she was (hopefully) sleeping. I sighed as I remembered. It had been a great talk, too, the best one yet . . .

"I can't believe you did that!" Trish had said when I answered the phone. The happy surprise was obvious in her voice.

God—just hearing her voice had warmed me all through and made me wish we were in the same place at the same time, so much so that I felt the ache of it in my arms. But if this was all we could do for now, then I'd take it.

"What did I did?" I asked because I honestly didn't know, but I smiled anyway because I loved hearing her voice and, even more, hearing her so happy.

"You had JHU send me *X-Men #1*! Really and truly and seriously? I can't believe you *did* that!" she repeated. "You— you're amazing, you know that?"

I laughed because, in the interim with how busy the job could be, I'd forgotten that I'd arranged the whole thing with Ron just a little over a week ago. "You like it?"

"Like it?" she asked incredulously. "I *love* it—I love *you!*"

I caught my breath and my heart stopped for a painful second. My head heated and filled and buzzed. Did she just tell me—

"Uh, I mean . . ." she began, her voice now quiet. "Ah, fuck it," she said with strength, and I could hear her blow her breath out in a low huff before she inhaled again. "Bennie, I . . . I love you," she said quietly, firmly, the low tone of her voice, the richness and depth of it telling me just how serious she was. "I really do—and I know, I know, I probably should've told you that when I was in New York, maybe sooner. And thank you, because this is so fucking awesome—*you* are just so fucking awesome, and well, it's true—I just do, I mean. I love you."

I had never expected to hear that from her, and certainly not that day. My heart was beating so hard I didn't just feel it, I heard it in my head, and it wasn't mere warmth, it was pure heat that spread through me, a brightness starting in my chest that flew up my neck until I felt my cheeks burn with it, and the fullness of my heart followed, until it felt like my skin overflowed. I knew I had a moment, just this one, to say whatever it was I was feeling, or let it go and forever hold my peace . . .

"Oh Christ, Trish," I said softly, "I . . . I love you, too . . . I can't even begin to tell you how much . . . and"—I caught my breath—"I'm really glad you like it."

"What—that you love me, too, or that I like your gift?" she asked, and there was laughter in her voice again, light and airy, and I realized I was hearing her smile.

"Either, both—Christ, Trish—I really wish I was telling you this in person," I told her, really feeling the ache of distance between us grow from just the chafing in my arms to a weight of longing that filled me as much as the love did. "I wish . . . well, there it is," I said, my head buzzing with the reality of what I was saying and what I was feeling. "And now you know—I love you, so incredibly much."

It just seemed weird and even wrong somehow to have this moment and be so far away from each other.

"Me, too, sweetheart," Trish said, and sighed softly. "Me, too."

The missing and the longing threatened to take me over, until it hit me—*oh hey! not this weekend because it was already too close to plan, but two weeks from now*—

I said it as I thought it, before nerves or my overthinking brain, or anything else could stop me. "Uh . . . assuming you've got some free time, I've got another three-day swing in two weeks—maybe we could spend some time together?"

"Oh—oh yeah!" Trish began enthusiastically, "that would be—oh damn, I've got to be on call, though," she finished, her voice sounding crestfallen.

"I could come out to you, actually, is what I was thinking," I offered.

"Yes! Awesome! Please!" she said with such vigor it made me laugh again. "When can we make this happen?"

So right then and there we had planned it. The good and happy feeling of knowing we'd see each other in two weeks had sung me to sleep and stayed with me through the wake-up and the morning ablutions.

But the call I'd just received . . . sigh. If it was an emergency situation, then maybe plans were perhaps about to change whether I wanted them to or not . . .

I texted her, just in case.

> Bennie: Missing you. Just got a call.
> Don't know what it is yet, but either
> we'll have to reschedule my visit OR
> we're gonna see each other that much
> sooner!

The answering ping came through as I was pulling a shirt over my head, and I admit I couldn't help smiling, knowing that it *was* Trish answering.

> Trish: Missing YOU! We're just about
> to deploy here. I'm on the next round.
> Find out and let me know. If I don't
> get back to you, you know where

I am! So much for the end of the
season, right?

Trish: And Bennie? Let me know
where you're going. Please be safe!

The happy smile I'd been wearing on the outside and feeling on the inside almost instantly vaporized into concern.

The facts were the facts: *everyone* always hoped the end of season was just that—the damned end. For all the adrenaline rushes and challenges and triumphs, it was always a relief when fire season was done, at least for a few months. And for those few months, no one was jumping out of planes, or ducking away from flame-retardant shower dumps or flying debris from chainsaws. For a few months, there was no worry about being caught between closing walls of flame and hoping that the fire shelters, also known as flashover bags—bodysized sacks made of a flame-resistant material—would hold long and cool enough and not just turn you into a baked potato. For a few months, you didn't worry about you or your friends getting hurt, or worse.

For a few months, everyone was safe from the wildest of dragon fires—at least insofar as the natural ones went.

I frowned at my phone and tried to ignore the hammering in my chest as I texted back.

Bennie: Yes and yes. And YOU be
careful too, ok? I'd like to see you all
in one HEALTHY piece! Text me as
soon as you're clear, ok?

I stared at what I'd sent and kept thinking . . . I was missing something. There was more to be said. I hesitated, still scowling at the screen. *Oh, fuck it*, I thought. *God forbid something happens, right?*

I typed and practically squashed the glass to hit "send" before I could change my mind.

Bennie: Sending you a lot of love.

I blew out my breath. It was silly that this had me at all stressed. I mean, it wasn't as if we hadn't said we love each other before, right?

But still . . .

I was still frowning to myself as I followed the scent of coffee out of my room, past the sounds of Nana running her own morning ablutions, and into the kitchen. The silence in the rest of the apartment reminded me that Linda had had an even earlier morning with appointments today. I grabbed the bat phone off the counter, then reached for a mug for coffee. *What the hell am I getting all hung up about?* I wondered as I poured.

I let myself simply breathe it all out while I added milk and sugar. There was no way I was going to make a phone call to *any*one, let alone to my handler, without caffeine first, especially after the way the last job had gone down.

I took my first sip and closed my eyes.

Oh . . . yes. At least now I could pretend to start thinking.

I hit the button on the side of the bat phone to wake it, and sure enough, there was a text along with a voice message.

I swiped to read it.

Ryan: Stand by for Alaska. Pickup in
6 hours if confirmed/you're available.
Please advise ASAP.

Oh *fuck* . . . the season wasn't done after all—anywhere—it seemed.

Dammit. I keyed the number, ready to call back, but my regular phone buzzed twice in my back pocket, making me jump.

The first buzz was from a text, the second was a continued ring. I checked the screen and recognized the number; it was from my station. That had *never* happened before, so I answered immediately, my brain already snapped into emergency awareness mode.

"This is Grego."

"Ms. Grego, this is Captain Hookweis. Sorry to break into your three-day swing, but there's been a—a situation just outside of Kennedy Airport. A plane has crashed, and we need all able-bodied personnel available. A unit is already en route to you, and further information will be supplied as you approach—conditions are shifting on the ground. We do know there are 149 passengers, plus the crew."

I felt the blood drain out of my face, even as my brain further cooled from prepared to ready mode. Without thought, I'd already put my cup down, toed my civilian shoes off, and was pulling my shirt out from my jeans in preparation to change into my uniform. "I'm there," I answered as I raced down the hallway to my room, undoing the button on my jeans one-handed, then opening my closet to pull my uniform out.

"Great. I've others to call and deploy. Check in via radio; we'll handle the clock in and out paperwork when you get back to base." He clicked off without any further formality.

I tucked my shirt into my pants and checked my belt while I raced in stocking feet back to the gear room where my work boots, gear bags, and all the watching saints were.

I jammed my feet in and laced up as fast as my fingers would allow, then swung my bag over my shoulder.

I nearly ran Nana over on the way out as I checked the next text that had come in.

> Scanlon-Scott: Get your boots on, baby! Got a unit already en route to get you!

I smiled reading that because it meant at least I'd be working with people I knew, respected, and liked, and it also meant I didn't have to tell Jean anything since that text had come from her wife and one of my closest friends, Tori.

I stopped my headlong rush just before crashing into my grandmother.

"*Pero, hija, donde vas?*" Nana asked me, gazing up at me with deep dark eyes, dark hair wrapped in a white towel, and her small frame seemingly engulfed by the fluffy cotton-candy pink robe she wore.

Oh God . . . where *was* I going, in every single way? I stared for a long moment at my grandmother, and in that space of time, I took in everything about her—the way her robe enveloped her, how small she really was, yet how big her eyes were as they gazed at me, even the fluffy white slippers she wore on her feet, how everything seemed to wrap her up in outsized softness—while underneath I knew how fragile she'd been while recovering from the horrific flu she'd had, how fragile she still was . . . we *all* were, really.

I wanted to protect that—protect her, protect *everyone*—from everything I knew was right outside the door waiting for each and every single one of us, waiting for that right moment to pounce. Hell, it was literally, *actually* on its way to me in a heavily loaded vehicle, just to take me to the scene directly.

I leaned down and gave my Nana a gentle but secure hug as I answered her question honestly. There was no use in not telling her what she'd see on the news soon, anyway. "There's been a huge accident, Nana—a plane has gone down near Kennedy. They're calling everyone in, and I have to go."

Though I could feel how thin Nana was under her robes, there was still no mistaking the very real strength in the hug she gave me.

"*Te doy mi bendición,*" she said, loosening her hold with one arm for a moment to pull a tiny bottle out from one of her robe pockets.

"You carry one everywhere?" I asked incredulously, realizing it was a travel-size holy water bottle she held. *Oh, of course she does*, I thought and sighed, mentally shaking my head.

"*Tranquila, hijita*," she quieted me, then began to whisper the same prayer she always said "*Dulcísimo San José . . .*" as she put holy water on my head in the ritual cross. It was a mark of how concerned she really was that she said it in Spanish, not taking the time to translate it like she usually did, " . . . *mantennos siempre unidos, siempre fervientes en la imitación de la virtud, y siempre fieles en la devoción a ti. Amén.*"

"Amen," I repeated. "*Gracias—te adoro.*" I told her as I kissed her cheek.

"You'll be careful . . . you'll be *safe*"—she pulled me in to kiss the crown of my head—"and you'll come home soon," she said, speaking it as a foreordained certainty as she always did. This was as much a part of the ritual as everything else, and we never neglected it.

"Yes, Nana," I agreed. "I will—all of that. *Yo te amo.*"

Nana held me even tighter for a moment. "*Yo te amo más.*"

With my boots and coat on, loaded gear bag over my shoulder, and Nana's blessing on me, as well as my promise to return in her heart, out I went into the unknown gray of whatever awaited.

By the time I arrived with my unit to the scene, it had already become—to put it politely—a clusterfuck. Not one but two triage stations had to be set up on some civilian's front lawn (and we were all grateful that the homeowners were decent human beings who wanted to help as much as possible) while response from other units—city, voluntary, and otherwise—was so huge that there were moments when radio signals to and from commanders and the hospitals couldn't get through.

Insofar as we could ascertain, the aircraft—a four-engine jet airliner—had somehow lost power and thereby its ability to stay airborne, clipping several trees and posts as it came down before it crashed onto a hill.

The fuselage had ripped into three separate pieces.

And God . . . the noise that surrounded triage itself . . . the sound that seemed to drown everything else out as you got closer to the planes—it was people. You could still hear the people trapped within.

Calling out in pain.

Calling out for help.

Terrified.

And not more than five hundred feet away from them was, already, the makeshift morgue. The fog and the chilly mist-rain made the terrain treacherous; we on-scene needed more hands to help, but they couldn't get here, due to the once-limited and now-blocked access. Worse yet, the very same weather that hindered every movement on the ground also meant helicopters could neither arrive nor leave to take the critically injured to the surgery suites they so desperately needed.

"Oh Christ—what the fuck are they *doing*?" Tori—a great friend of mine, as well as work partner since the very beginning of this crazy career—exclaimed next to me as we headed with a stretcher back to the fuselage.

This was not our first run to the wreckage itself; we'd been in another section seemingly a million times, though in reality, it had been only a handful or so.

The only way to and from the wrecked interiors was with ladders that the fire department had erected into the safer openings that were either part of the plane's structure or had been created by earlier rescue teams. This had been done after each of the three sections the plane had broken into was braced to some form of stability—or as much as could be found on the slick ground—with a combination of sawhorses and two-by-fours.

Organized madness sung around us, and exactly as Tori had noticed, a new song had just joined the chorus.

Oh, but I knew that particular voice so very well, that unique sound: the sound of chainsaws rarin' and roarin' to go.

I glanced over to where the sound came from—it was the copse of trees between another access road and the overall crash site—then back to Tori.

"Betcha anything you want, firemen are gonna cut a path from the road to the wreck," I said, and sure enough, that's exactly what they were yelling at each other to do.

Tori shook her head as we both tried to maintain our footing over the terrain. "Hope they take the stumps out!"

I shook my head, too, and shot her a rueful grin as we continued to struggle forward over the slick and mucky terrain. "Yeah . . . we can hope!"

It wasn't as if that hadn't happened before: a path cut through but not down. In the urgency and adrenaline of the situation, sometimes people needed reminding that vehicles—or at least most rescue vehicles—could neither plow through trees nor roll over tree stumps.

"Okay—there you are! We've got something here!" The call came out from the hole in the fuselage we'd been directed to. An EMT I didn't know appeared right at the end of it. "I'm too big to get in there—you, you two!" He pointed to Tori and me. "You two can make it."

His partner appeared behind him.

"Whoever it is, they're under a tangle of smashed seats and shit against the front. It's too tight," he explained as we helped Tori up the ladder; then I handed her the bright orange gear bag that was ubiquitous to the service. She adjusted that over her shoulder and pulled a flashlight from her pocket as I climbed up just as carefully behind her.

Well, at least I know why that supervisor pulled us off from triage and sent us here, I thought as I reset my own gear bag over my shoulder, pulled a flashlight (two lights as well as two heads were better than one), and carefully picked my way forward, as it were, to the more compressed end.

It made sense: everyone I worked with knew about my training and work as a rescue specialist. Hell, there were times when those emergency situations could and would take precedence over anything local—meaning directly here in my own city—while Tori herself was a ranking officer in a volunteer brigade with accompanying really high levels of disaster and operations training. There couldn't be two better people to send into this dangerous rescue scenario. And we were both already on-site.

I took a breath as I stepped in, already looking all around, spotting for whatever, hyperalert, even while not really noticing that all my skin buzzed, despite the wet and the cold, or that my heartbeat was a constant companion in my neck, in my head, underscoring the sound of everything that surrounded this moment.

Initial observation revealed every overhead compartment had burst open and apart, sections slamming off and scattered in bulky obstructions, while the seating itself—rows made of extruded and shaped aluminum, fitted with cushions, then fixed to tracks on the floor decking—had slid, collapsed, then slid again, crashing and twisting and tearing into complex braids and tangles that made it so difficult to not only find folks but also to safely extricate them.

And so many of those we had already found had broken legs, broken by the impact, then the concussive force of their seat being thrown into the seat in front of them, and so on and so on, until it was all a mix of metal and bone, blood and foam.

Again, this wasn't my or Tori's first trip up and into one of the shattered plane sections, so at least the scene, although tragic, no longer had the power to shock us the way it initially had—and I was honestly grateful that I hadn't been deployed to search around the debris field for the poor souls who had once been the pilot and copilot or the others similarly ejected from the plane.

Well, when we saw the size of the tree that speared through the cockpit windows—yes, plural—we knew the chances of those two folks being alive were less than good.

"You hear that?" Tori asked, stopping before me.

It was a weird thing, if you really thought about it, but it was something that happened automatically. Despite the sounds that surrounded the entire scene—from yelling crew, the people calling out for their loved ones through their pain, as well as the roar of the several chainsaws now running just outside, and all of it now under the steady constant hit that was the rain, which had just now begun to come down in earnest—there existed this expectant waiting, not-quite silence—not that there was something to be listening for so much as there was something we needed to realize was missing.

So I listened very hard.

"*Choo.*"

It was the tiniest, faintest sneeze.

"I hear it!" I said, filled with excitement and hope that we'd found someone and filled with dread at what that tiny sound most likely meant.

"Yeah—me, too," Tori said, her voice low and hard. I heard her swallow.

I knew she was thinking what I was: that small noise, the tangle of crushed and mangled seats before us, the most likely spaces to be available for a living creature . . .

"I'll go." I said decisively, then huffed out my breath. "I'm smaller than you." I carefully edged in front of her.

Because it was true and it made much more sense: I was a few inches shorter than Tori, which meant I could wedge myself in farther.

"They're under that front-most pileup," Tori said, indicating with her flashlight the tumbled mess that had slammed against the front of the compartment—beyond which there was a several-foot drop to the ground.

A segment of the overhead compartment had sheared and blocked the entire mass diagonally, which under our flashlights revealed a small, perhaps sixteen-inch high and maybe twenty-inch-wide access. Within that, all either of us could see were wedged foam parts and aluminum tubing.

"We need to either shift or stabilize that overhead, then somehow move those seats, get to the space underneath to reach them."

"Yeah," I nodded. "It's tight up here," I said, shining the light along the presenting face of the mass.

We needed to both get through the wreckage to get to the kitten-delicate sounds we could hear beneath while somehow maintaining the integrity in such a way that the remaining mass wouldn't collapse—either on us or whoever was under it.

Blood and whatever else was already streaked and pooled everywhere. I crouched down and shone the light through the opening.

"Choo!" This time it was louder, and with my head in the hole, it was easier for me to narrow down where it was coming from.

"Got it!" I said excitedly, attempting to both lean and see farther in. "Sounds about another three, maybe four feet in!"

I still couldn't see anything or anyone yet, but Tori was already on the radio and calling for some muscle backup.

"We hear you—we've got you, we're coming," I said as soothingly as I could in the general direction where I'd heard the sound, knowing that sometimes hearing a voice, especially one that said it would help, could be the most calming and effective tool at my disposal.

I could hear the careful clomping sounds of two more

personnel who had entered the fuselage behind us, but I didn't move from where I was, scouting well as I could for the next logical move through this tight little maze, but I recognized the voice of the first rescuer who had hailed us moments ago, even as I heard, then felt the presence of his legs next to me.

"All right—I got this part. *Oof!*"

My peripheral vision caught sight of a firmly planted and booted leg with turnout pants, and from the slight groan and almost shift of the hole before me, I knew he had somehow taken the bulk load of the container over his back, either as full support or pure stabilization.

A slight shudder ran through the entire deck, and we all froze a moment, fearing the worst—but it settled and stayed still.

I could feel each of us relax just the tiniest bit.

"We're good," Samson—that's what I'd decided to call him—breathed out, and I nodded.

"All right," I said as I mentally readied myself to climb in, trying to both physically and mentally visualize what I might encounter. "I'm gonna hand things out as I can."

I won't pretend for a second that I didn't sincerely hope none of the debris I found was human in origin. Because that was never easy to deal with.

"I've got light on you, too," Tori said from just behind me. "Just hand straight back to me." I nodded again, and flashlight first, both to see and reach for obstacles, as well as to minimize my width, I carefully stuck my head and shoulders in.

My first obstruction was a cross-placed and braced aluminum tube. I needed more light to see where it went, what had caught it, if it could be moved safely. Under the glow of my light, I saw that it had caught up within an armrest, fully attached and bent almost parallel to the back cushion.

I tugged lightly and experimentally on the crosspiece—not to remove it, but to see what else it impinged on.

It was stuck from the top. I had some play back and forth, though, with a bit of side movement. If I could just wedge it a bit more to my left, I might be able to create a better opening, crawl closer to where I'd heard that second sound come from.

God, I was careful, the hammering in my chest and head now a normal noise to me. At this point I was terrified I might bring this all crashing down on us, but I could do this, I could do this, I could *do* this . . .

I progressed six inches, found another ripped-up armpiece on the bit of floor before me, and carefully handed it out behind me, announcing what I was doing as I did it.

The rest of the trip through the interior was just as agonizingly slow, just as painstakingly careful, mostly on my belly the entire time.

I was grateful for the thickness of my jacket as I went over the debris before me.

I ignored the smears of blood.

The smell of it—the fuel and smoke and burst perfumes, the blood and the spit and the sour sweat of pure fear, along with the tang of metal and mechanics that always seemed to surround a vehicle incident of any sort, hung heavy and thick in the air of this small space.

Every so often, a shudder would run through the structure, forcing us all to statue stillness until it stopped.

My own fear was a harsh metal taste I bit on, a grim thing I dug my teeth into and pushed past, just a part of each second that I literally clawed and crawled through.

It felt like I'd been crawling and pulling and moving and shoving and passing things behind me forever, for hundreds of feet. But in all reality, it couldn't have really been more than five, maybe six feet at most.

And suddenly, there it was.

Designed by chance or math or God, the perfect protective lean-to, made up of a jumble of seat cushions and backs, was right before me.

My light shone through the seams left between red cushions, shining on something knit in white and pink.

And then—it *moved*.

"I found her—pretty sure it's a baby!" I yelled back behind me as best I could, and now all the pounding and pressure I'd ignored became a huge lump pressed into my chest as I examined how I could best get this little one out of here.

"All right," I announced to my team, "there's a lot of weight on the frames of these cushions—they're bearing up the load. It's like the perfect combination of cross pressures."

I desperately wanted to see more of the little patient, to begin assessing and caring for her, so I carefully pushed against the foam from the closest upright angle, pressing enough to compress the foam, but not enough to shift the frame.

I shone my light into the depression, and there I saw—

"*Choo!*"

I gazed at a tiny face turned towards me, eyes squeezed shut against the light, pink knit hat still on her head. She blinked against the glow, then smiled at me.

For a moment, everything halted—the rain, the noise, the vibration, even the tragedy of the event and the situation as I gazed at the soft round face before me . . . and I smiled down at her.

And then another shudder wriggled through the frame.

The warm moment I had froze and broke. There was nothing more vital than getting this child out—getting us *all* out—alive.

I pushed experimentally on the foam again, attempting to make enough room to remove the tiny patient without shifting the support structure.

Damn. No luck with that.

They were already as compressed as they could be, and there was so much weight on those seat cushions, the frames of them bearing up as they were beneath the wreckage above.

"Hey—if we can get you a hacksaw—" Samson called.

"Are you fucking *crazy*? She doesn't need a fuckin' hacksaw!" Tori interrupted sharply.

"Can't use that in here!" I called back at the same time. "Way too tight!" Seriously—was he out of his mind?

I couldn't move the structure at all without endangering us all. *But* ... my brain worked the puzzle. *If I can somehow cut into the foam, the center parts, make a larger opening without touching the supporting frame* ...

"I'm gonna try to cut into the foam without touching the structure," I told them.

I pulled my EMT shears from my pocket: they were capable of cutting through a penny if need be, were lightweight and had blunted ends, so if somehow they fell or I lost control in some way, the ends wouldn't hurt anyone. *Definitely the right tool for this job*, I decided, while outside the wreck I could hear the increased patter of rain on the metal hull.

"Tori!" I called. "Shine that light maybe about another inch to my right!"

The light shifted, and I slid mine back into my belt. I was going to need two hands to accomplish this.

"Here goes nothing," I muttered to myself as I pinched a bit from a center line closest to me. I prayed from the depth of my very marrow to whatever or whoever might listen that we would all come out of this alive—then made the first cut. *This is probably my most frequent request to the Universe*, a part of me noted.

"It's working!" I called back, and the light jogged a second.

"All right!"

"Good!"

I cut again, then kept cutting, slowly, methodically, testing in between as best I could and hoping for continued structural integrity. The little one made soft sounds, and I did my best to prevent anything from falling on her.

Finally, I had about ten inches—a little jagged, yes, but *that should be enough to reach through and pull her out*, I figured.

I knew better than to trust the integrity of the supports outside or within. The light Tori held behind me wasn't enough. Quickly and carefully, I pocketed my shears, again pulled my own flashlight, then carefully shone it in the opening I'd made, making certain I didn't aim straight for the little one's face.

I reached my free hand in and felt around the child's body for encumbrances; I'd check later, once I got her out and my work gloves off, for any damage.

But she was quiet in a not-ominous way, just normal baby gurgling, despite the environment, and that gave me hope that she wasn't injured.

"I've got a space—she looks okay!" I called to the crew behind me.

All my hands found was baby and, just beyond her foot, more foam wall.

I swallowed, then took a deep breath. Once again, an envelope of silence seemed to surround me as I let it out slowly, then reached both hands through the hole, the rest of me balanced on the front of my thighs and my belly, like an odd sort of cobra pose, while I trusted my spatial sense and memory to accurately find and secure my tiny patient.

"I'm in!"

I slipped one hand under her head, the other just a bit farther down her spine, and carefully, so damn, damn carefully, my elbows almost locked together as I lifted . . . I pulled her out.

From the shape and size of her, my rapidly developing working patient profile said she wasn't more than several weeks old, perhaps two months at most.

"Got her!" I called behind me in a tone I hoped wouldn't disturb her more, while I carefully tucked her against my chest. She didn't kick, she didn't cry, but she did squirm and make soft sounds of protest. I leaned on my other elbow, took a second to collect myself.

All we have to do now is get out of here, I thought, *crawling backward . . .*

Easy-peasy, right?

"All right, kiddo—here we go," I whispered to the knit hat under my chin. I lifted my head. "We're coming out!"

"I'm spotting you!" Tori called back.

Once again, it felt much slower and much farther than it actually was. I trusted my memory, I trusted my sense of space, I trusted myself—and I absolutely trusted my partner to keep me on track, her voice guiding me through the spots I was unsure of.

"Almost out!" she assured me, then I felt her gloved hand warm on the back of my calf.

Another shudder ran through the structure, and I felt it through my legs, through my belly, through the arm that supported me.

And I knew, I *knew*, as I arched my back to get as much distance from the deck below, my jacket just shy of pressed against whatever it was above me, that—

"Holy fuck—get her out!" Samson yelled.

In that very second, the world shifted, a hard right tilt that dropped a very solid *something* from the tiny distance of the makeshift ceiling above me.

It slammed hard and heavy across my shoulders. Somehow I managed to control the breath it shoved out of me, so I didn't further scare the baby I held, while my brain numbed knowing I might be the only barrier between her and crushing death.

Everything went very still.

It seemed even my heart stopped for a moment, and all I could think was that I had to protect the baby I held in my arm; I had to keep her safe.

"Are you okay?" and "You all right?" Tori and Samson called while Tori's guiding touch on my leg became a grip, a slight tug.

I didn't even know if anything hurt. All I knew was that

the little one had gone from wriggling to making sounds that indicated incipient crying.

Crying was good.

Crying meant she was conscious, which meant the likelihood of her having a critical internal injury was lower.

Crying meant her lungs worked.

Crying meant she was alive.

"We're okay!" I answered.

"We need to get out of here," Tori said, her voice low and steady.

I could hear the terseness beneath it.

I evaluated my own condition. Arching my back earlier seemed to have given me an inch or so to play with. I carefully, carefully lowered myself a bit, hoping to hell the ceiling didn't further collapse on me.

"I've got less room," I told her. "It's down tighter over my upper back."

"I've got you," Tori assured me.

She didn't say what we both knew: the structure was too unstable to allow any other rescue personnel within it. Any addition could jeopardize our already precarious position.

"It's okay, little Choo, it's okay," I said softly and soothingly over the knit-covered head before I made my next move.

I carefully stretched my body back, leaving my hands stretched out before me, the baby's head in them, her body over my forearms.

As long as her head stayed below the level of my own, nothing would touch her, but I agonized with each and every inch of movement that I'd miscalculated, that there'd be another shift, that despite the crying that had now quieted down to exhausted squeaks, somehow in the dark and the small space I'd missed something vital and—

"Gotcha!" Tori had my shoulders, and finally able to almost kneel, I pulled the baby out the rest of the way with me.

"She's out!" Samson yelled.

Relief was short-lived because vibration now went in waves through the structure. "Get out—get out *now!*" Samson ordered, and little Choo had finally had enough and began to wail.

I handed the now healthily screaming baby to Tori, because she was closest to the exit. I straightened further, then painfully stood to see Samson, flashlight strapped to his helmet.

In a moment, I realized he was literally supporting the bulk of the compartment on his shoulders.

"But you—"

"I got this—fucking *go!*" he growled out. "Get clear, and I'm right behind you!"

He was right, and I knew it.

I cautiously hurried as I made my way behind Tori, and I could hear the shouts that went up as first she handed the baby down the ladder, then stepped out.

I was next, rain beating on my back amid the shouting and the planted klieg-style lights that who knows who had brought, while everything under my hands slipped and shook in the cold.

I glanced up at the light coming from the hole to see Samson, light still attached to his head, framed in the entry, hands braced on either side waiting for me to clear enough steps for him to come out after me.

I could feel the movement through the gloves, through the rails of the ladder, feel it grow from rumble to shake to—

"Jump! Fucking *jump!*"

The shouts came from seemingly everywhere and everyone. I glanced down to see Tori clear the last step, glanced up to see Samson staring down, and the rumble grew, kept growing.

"JUMP!" I yelled up at him, then checked to my left. It was clear enough to try.

I let go and pushed off, and as I did, I glanced back up to see Samson's eyes close, his head drop. "Fuck me," he muttered as he shook his head from side to side.

Time suspended, and the rumble became a roar. The very air seemed to tremble as I watched Samson's grip on the edge tighten, then loosen as the front of the wreck pitched towards the ground, and Samson slid down, away, and into the dark, the fuselage taking him to its crushed and crowded deeper interior, deep into the belly of the beast.

The ground slapped up at me, a crush of mud and grass and a pound of feet that surrounded me, hands already lifting me up even as I struggled to stand, to race back to the plane, but those hands were holding me back. Voices insisted on checking me out, and as I watched and swatted the hands away, the ladder I'd just jumped from slid then crashed down as the last of the wooden horse and beams gave way, and the end of the wreck I'd just been in slammed to the ground with a force that shook the world.

People scrambled out of the way, and it was a combination of my own feet and people tugging on me as the once-flying cave gave a slight roll towards us, then shuddered to a rest in the mud and glass and wreckage.

It would take a crew of approximately sixteen rescuers, a combination of EMTs, emergency services personnel, and firefighters, to get Samson—whose name I later learned was Ben Sharone—out of the remains of the wreckage.

Probably one of the things that made everything harder than it already was, was knowing that this was not only a massive multi-casualty incident but also an active investigation scene. This meant every last thing had to be observed, documented, and left as intact as possible to allow for a full forensic analysis. This was something each and every single one of us was achingly and painfully aware of as we moved and shifted and cut our way through and over and under to get to the injured folks within.

Samson—Ben—had a severe bruise to both the lower bones of his left leg, which meant it would hurt and take as long to heal as a break, but he'd definitely recover.

Thankfully.

Hours or days, or maybe it was only a forever later, covered in sweat and mud and blood with all of it crowned under a layer of diesel, I was back at the station.

"Oh *fuck* . . . I don't have my car," I groaned as I finally punched out.

"You do know I'm gonna give you a ride home, right?" Tori said behind me, clapping a hand to my shoulder as she waited to punch out next.

"Thanks, buddy," I said with sincere gratitude as I turned. I gave her a smile. "You're seriously the best."

Tori smiled tiredly back at me. "Eh—takes one to know one."

"I'm gonna go take a shower first, if you don't mind," I told her while she punched her card. "I can't go home like this," I said, and indicated all of me.

"Me, too," Tori agreed. The smile she gave me was as tired as I felt. Her eyes were large and dark, and where her face wasn't smudged with dirt, she was pale. "Can't take this home."

No.

Neither of us could, although I knew, in a real way, we both would, anyway.

Once in the shower, I was mercifully blank for a few long seconds, standing underneath the shining steel showerhead, water pulsing over my head.

I lifted my hands to my head—and I could feel it: the sharp hurt across my back where something had landed. I felt carefully as best I could, but given that I'd been on the scene for quite some time afterward, had no trouble breathing, and could still move everything, even though it might hurt a bit . . . *Just the usual bumps and bruises*, I decided. Still, though, maybe there'd be an Epsom salt bath in my near future . . .

Knowing it was the best way to let things go, let events process, I let my mind drift as I soaped and rinsed.

For whatever reason, I found myself wondering about my father, a man I'd never really known, and my mother, whom I'd only known just a touch more.

Oh, I knew a few things about him, such as he'd been a paramedic in the army, fallen in love with my mother, got deployed to a jungle, came home just long enough to get married and make me, then went off again.

My daddy—he jumped out of planes, I recalled.

My daddy had jumped out of helicopters into gun and rifle fire in his face, and with mortar blasts and bombs waiting to go off because he was a medic and that's what he did: he was a hero, and he saved people's lives.

And my mom had been a nurse working with a non-governmental organization, which was how they'd met in the first place. Technically, she was transported by the same perfectly good planes and choppers my dad jumped out of, to do essentially the same thing.

I scrubbed the blood and the mud from myself, the diesel and death, as I reviewed what I knew and what I remembered.

I had a picture of them: it was a little faded and had turned slightly orange and yellow, but still, it was my parents: my dad holding an itty-bitty me, complete with white christening dress, in one of his arms, with the other wrapped around my mother. As small as the image was, there was no mistaking the expression on his face, how proud, how happy and loving he was, or the way my mother loved us, too.

In the picture, I, of course, was making a little face because what did I know of any of it?

Huh. *Not much yet*, I told myself.

Because one day, after I'd been born, he'd gone back to active duty, and not that much later, my mom's organization went there, too. All I ever really knew was that they were together at the end.

No more Mommy.

No more Daddy.

There were the pictures kept in an old book now in my nightstand, a set of dog tags wrapped in with them, and all of that underneath the wedding picture I had of them, which rested on the stand itself.

Not that I remembered my mother that much either, most of the time. *Maybe . . . maybe I don't want to? Am I afraid to?* I asked myself. I had barely been three, when we lost her—*not lost, she was with Daddy*, I reminded myself with a rueful shake of my head, then sighed as I reached for the tap. *At least they were together*—

The pain was sharp and sudden, enough to make me wince as I felt the muscles in my back pull.

"You all right?" Tori's voice asked, just on the other side of the shower door.

"Yeah—caught a nasty bruise when the debris shifted, is all," I answered. I winced at both the pain and with embarrassment. I must have made a sound . . . I hadn't meant to do that.

"I remember that," Tori said with audible concern. "Lemme check you out. You should probably file an incident report, just in case."

I sighed again as I grabbed my towel off the wall. *She's right, just in case this becomes an issue*, I reminded myself as I wrapped up. "I'm all right," I said, stepping out of the stall to see Tori, hair still wet, standing in her underwear. "It's just a bruise."

"Uh-huh. They all are," she said with a roll of her eyes. "Turn around."

"It's nothing a little ice—and a little time off—won't cure," I said, even as I did as she asked. Tori's fingers were competent and careful across my back as she examined and tested.

"Ow!" I breathed out sharply as she found a particularly sensitive spot.

"Yeah, you're right—it's nasty looking," she agreed, "but nothing broken. Still—incident report, ya know? Cover your ass is always the name of the game."

For whatever reason, the irony of the statement hit me hard, and I laughed. "You realize that I'm in a towel, right? And I would like to go cover my ass and go home!"

"Oh my God—you're right!" Tori laughed with me. "Yeah, go cover your ass—then cover your ass, and let's get out of here."

Finally, everyone's asses covered figuratively and literally, we were in her car and on the way back.

"You all right?" I asked Tori as she drove off the lot.

It wouldn't be the first—or the last time we had a conversation about the events of the day, especially when they were rough like this day had been: multiple injuries, multiple deaths—at least ten on scene, and . . . a baby.

That baby . . . Tori had little ones at home. I knew how easily children on a scene affected us all, and I was certain that the toll had to be higher for those who loved children.

"That . . . that was pretty intense," Tori said as she sighted for a turn. "That might well be on the top of worst things we've ever seen."

"Seriously, yeah," I agreed. "An almost fifty percent casualty rate on-scene." Which was—sadly—true. There had been over 150 people on the plane; at least seventy-three bodies had been found, including the ones ejected from the wreckage. Tori and I had both had our share earlier of extrication and what was politely referred to as recovery: the discovery and removal of the dead.

And that number, that almost fifty percent, didn't take into account the people who'd died in triage, too injured for us to do anything for them, or the dwindling golden hour of rescue inexorably winding down to minutes while we waited for grounded helicopters to be able to fly, or those who would die later in the hospital, no matter what—

"We saved a baby—*you*—saved that baby," Tori said, interrupting the thoughts that were beginning to spiral in my head and take me down with them.

Which was why we had these conversations in the first place—and for which I was also very grateful

I gave a grim chuckle. "I was fuckin' terrified, every inch of that. She didn't have a scratch, though," I added thoughtfully, thinking about it. "And at least Samson—Sharone," I quickly amended, "wasn't too seriously hurt."

"Samson?" Tori threw me a quick grin with her glance. "I was calling him that, too!" She laughed, and I laughed with her.

It felt good to laugh, to be out of the rain, to be clean and dry and on the way home. To be away from the mud, the blood, the dead and the dying, and the hoping to be saved.

"They found her mother—alive," Tori said quietly. She glanced back over at me, eyes glinting in the predawn dark.

"I was glad of that," I said quietly. "Man, Tori—I am so fucking *tired*," I said, feeling it all wash over me, the tired and the chill, the soreness everywhere, and the middle of my back starting to ache.

"Yeah, me, too," she said with a soft sigh. "Me, too." She reached into a jacket pocket and took something out. "You gotta be getting sore—take this," she said, and handed me a small envelope with Tylenol in it.

"Oh—thanks!" I gratefully took it from her. "I didn't think of that," I admitted as I tore the pack open and dry-swallowed.

"I'm wondering if there are other things you're not thinking of," Tori said lightly.

"Really? We're going to have this conversation now?" I asked, looking at her pointedly. I knew exactly what this was going to be about.

"Sure, why not?" Tori said in the same light tone. "We just watched a whole bunch of people die for the usual reason— absofuckinglutely *nothing*." She said it with vehemence. "And let me be very frank with you—"

"Oh sure," I said with feigned grumpiness. "Because you've never been *that* before, and it's not like I could stop you!"

Oh, but I could swear that this was payback still for that bet I'd made with a mutual friend of ours years ago, about whether or not she'd date—

"People were killed, *we* almost got killed—now we're going home, and I'm dropping you off with your grandmother and your cousin while I'm going home to my wife and my babies. You should have that, too, Bennie—you deserve that. The way you were with that—"

"What—you want to share Jean and your kids with me? I didn't know you guys did that!" I said in a loud joking tone.

"Ah, c'mon Bennie, don't be a jerk," she said. "You know what I mean." The smile she gave me told me she wasn't mad.

"All right. My simple answer is, since you're married to Jean and she to you, the two best and hottest women I know are completely unavailable, so I'll just have to wait until you guys have at least one clone made."

Tori rolled her eyes and shook her head. "You wanna do this now? Or are you avoiding a topic by bringing up another avoided topic?"

"Hey—I'm smart like that!" I said with a smile. "You get to choose which rabbit hole you're gonna go down—assuming I follow, that is."

She shook her head at me. "Yeah, you're a smartass." She sighed. Rain started to pour down again. "What happened with you and Trish?" she asked as she put the wipers on.

I sighed.

Tori was my friend. We'd known each other since even before our Emergency Medical Service Academy days, from back when we'd first taken the emergency medical training class at a local community college.

And we were tight, *really* tight. I'd even been part of her wedding party, back when she and Jean got married, and her wife and little ones were dear to me—family—there wasn't a thing I wouldn't do for any of them.

And my best friend would do the same for me. Which meant she was asking because she cared. And because she *was* such a good friend, and I didn't really want to be a jerk, not even to myself, she deserved an honest answer.

So did I.

I took a breath. "Nothing," I said finally, letting it out slowly, watching the wipers sweep back and forth. "Nothing's going on."

"Why's that? It's not like the two of you aren't into each other—that was unmistakable when you guys came over for dinner. The way she looks at you, Bennie! And you—oh man, the way you guys interact. Seriously, though, I thought—"

"You thought wrong, Tori," I said firmly. "Look, you know the deal—she had all that shit with her mother to deal with, and I *do* live with my grandmother and my cousin—that's not ever changing. It's a lot for some folks, you know?"

Tori blew her breath out. "Stop, Bennie—don't use the excuse of family. What's stopping you? You're not really holding on—out—for . . . something else, are you?" Her tone was uncertain and the words weren't sharp, but still . . .

It stung, and I squared my jaw and my shoulders as I angled my head at her.

"Ego, much?"

I could literally feel the heat that was the stirring of Tori's anger as she shifted in her seat. "Christ, Bennie—you know what I mean!" She blew her breath out. "Outside of Jean, you're my fuckin' best friend—and I'm supposed to be yours. Which means I'm not doing you any favors if you're holding out or holding on to something."

She shook her head as we came to a stop for a red light. Rain pounded down. "C'mon, buddy, tell me." Tori glanced over at me and held my eyes with hers. "You care so much about others—what happened to *you?* I know it's . . ." She hesitated for a long moment, then gave a small breath. "I know what happened with your parents was horrible, and maybe that's all—maybe that's enough—but I *know* you, Bennie, I *know* you—and I know *something* happened and . . ." she gave me a small smile, "everything in my gut tells me it's an unfortunate thing we have in common." She returned her attention to the road, and in the half-second before her eyes went back to the window, I got to really see them—and I realized that part of the shine in her eyes was unshed tears.

That . . . that broke through to me, dissolved more of the internal walls I kept so firmly in place, had been doing for years, since just before I'd taken that class with her . . .

I found my own eyes filling as we moved through the rain again. *How does she know?* I wondered as I stared into the rain. *Or does she? How do I even begin to say . . . anything? It's . . . it's too much to put on anyone,*

"It's . . . I'm not ready to talk about it. It was a long time ago—right before we met, actually—and I just . . . I just can't right now, okay?" I said finally.

Tori sniffed as she nodded. "Yeah . . . I get that, I really do. But, Bennie," she said as she pulled into the entrance for the parking garage of my building, "I'm here—when you're ready, okay? I mean it."

I quickly dashed at my eyes, which were starting to overfill. I really appreciated the concern and the love from my friend.

"Sure," I said as we pulled in. "Done deal."

A heavy and warm, almost expectant silence filled the car as she pulled to a stop by the door that led to the building interior.

"Thanks for the ride," I said as I put my hand on the latch. "Go enjoy your family—and give them love from me, too."

"Here." She hefted my bag out of the backseat. "And of course. It's your family, too, you know." She grinned warmly over at me.

I couldn't help but smile back because I knew it was true. "Thanks. Go relax or something," I said as I got out of the car.

She chuckled, and as I began to swing the car door shut, I made a decision. Tori had been right earlier, that I was avoiding one discussion for another. And even with my diversions, she still cared, was still a great friend. *Maybe . . . maybe at least on one thing, I could say something . . .*

"Hey," I said softly through the still-open door. "There was a time back in the day when I thought we might date." I said it with a smile because it was a nice memory, Tori and I getting to know each other in class, becoming friends.

Tori smiled back at me. "Yeah? Me, too, but—" Her smile grew wider, and I knew she couldn't help it because I knew why she was smiling.

"Jean," I answered for her, feeling warm in a good way. "Yeah—the moment I saw you guys together—and it wasn't anything, just hanging out for coffee during a break when we were all at the academy," I said as I readjusted my bag over my shoulder. "I knew—knew you two belonged to no one else but each other."

She laughed, and Tori, who was already so pretty it was almost unreal, grew even more incredibly beautiful under the flush that rose in her face as she thought of her Jean. "Yeah, I guess—but I was a little stupid because I didn't know it then!"

It was true, so true—the very second I'd seen them together, not doing anything more than chatting outside, drinking coffee with the usual groups that gathered during break, I knew they belonged together. There was something that was so much more than just a spark; it was a light that flowed and meshed and made them glow together, brighter and brighter the nearer to each other they got. Tori and I would have never had that—and there was no way I would've stopped or stepped between them and something that obvious, that beautiful.

"I know!" I said, still smiling. "I had to help you!"

"Christ—that stupid bet!" She shook her head and laughed outright.

"Well, it was more of a nudge," I conceded with a grin. It was true: in order to spark Tori into asking Jean out—*finally*—I'd told her that if she didn't, I would, and I'd made a bet with a friend of ours who was also there that night that Tori *would* do it—and I won.

"Hey—you know I thank you for that. Why do you think you stood where you did at our wedding?"

"Because of my charm and style, of course," I said, faking a glamour pose. I batted my eyelashes and pulled out the side pockets of my jacket in imitation of a skirt curtsey.

Tori rolled her eyes at me while she laughed even louder. "Oh my God—of course! Go home, Bennie! Kiss your grandmother, hug your cousin, give them my love!"

I laughed, too. "I'm going! And good night—or good morning or . . . whatever!"

"Hey, Bennie?" Tori asked, leaning across the passenger side so I could hear her better, just before I closed the door. "You know I want that for you, too, right? I want to be there at your wedding, chill with your family, worry with you about baby fevers, celebrate holidays and anniversaries. Because you deserve all of it, you should be just as happy." Despite her serious expression, her face still wore the glow that thinking of Jean brought her.

And that—I was always happy to see. It was beautiful to have such love and joy in this world.

"I know you do," I said quietly. "Me, too. Just . . . not in a rush or anything, is all."

Tori nodded. "Yeah, and you shouldn't be. I just don't want you to miss it when it comes your way, y'know?"

"Hey, I'm sure you'll play Captain Obvious for me if ever I need you to," I said, and gave her another grin. "Or Cupid or whatever."

"True enough," she agreed with a nod and a smile. "True enough. G'night, Bennie."

"G'night, Tori."

I shut the door, then made my way inside.

Chapter 4

Everything Else Is Just That

I FINALLY got upstairs into the apartment, stripped my gear, then made my achy way into bed. I slept long and hard.

"Oh . . . ow . . . ." I couldn't help but groan out long and loud as I rolled onto my back, the pain in my shoulder singing through me. Linda had already gone for the—well, if the light streaming around the edges of the curtain shading my window was any indication, we were well past morning and into afternoon—the day.

That spot on my back was so damned sore . . .

I took a deep breath, and then another, just staring at the ceiling over my head, orienting myself to daylight, to warmth, to the mattress beneath me, the sheet above me.

With every inhale, I took it all in: *the day looks lovely and sunny and bright . . . I hear sparrows and starlings twittering in the shrubs outside . . .* with every exhale, I let out every memory of every moment from last night: the cold and the wet, the fear and the sorrow.

Daylight. Warm. Dry. Sun . . . I breathed it in, feeling each and every one of those things as I filled my lungs.

Dark. Cold. Wet. Blood . . .

I breathed it out with the memory playing over my skin.

Soap-smell hair. Clean sheets. Nice pillow . . . very *nice pillow!* I inhaled deeply, literally enjoying the scents, feeling the textures

111

under my hands, shifting my head along the comfortable pillow.

Burning engine parts. Mud. Dangerous sharp edges . . .

I exhaled with steady strength. *I am grateful to not be choking on fumes, that my feet aren't slipping or sticking, that I'm no longer ducking jagged edges.*

But today, right now, I had:

Good friends. Beloved family. A life I loved . . . I breathed it all in, smiling at each image of each person that I loved as it came into my head.

The so-recent memory came rushing in.

People crying in fear. People crying for their loved ones.

And with that pain, the door opened, and the past, the past, the past . . . Oh . . . God . . . it was so many years ago, but I could still see that face, and there was that bruising grip on my arm, and I'd been sleeping but—

Whoa—okay, hold on there—that's more than enough of that! I told myself, and tossed my blankets off, using the movement and the texture to anchor myself fully.

I am here. I am now. And I will not *be defined by that!* I told my memory defiantly.

I jumped out of bed and glanced over to my dresser where both my phones lay. They each blinked at me, letting me know I'd received texts and voice messages.

First things first, though. I grabbed my personal phone to text Trish, only to see her text already waiting for me.

> Trish: Christ, Bennie! We heard about the crash out here. I'm so sorry. Let me know that you're ok. And Bennie? Love. You.

> Trish: Oh hey. I'm taking a break. I'll come out your next 3 day swing? What do you think?

I couldn't help but smile—I was okay, and the thought of having Trish come out for another few days—yeah.

We could do that. And maybe Tori was right. Maybe I *was* using family as an excuse. Maybe . . . there was already no doubt that we—Trish and I—cared for each other, loved one another even. We had now taken to actually saying so—well, okay, texting so, but close enough for now, until we did talk again.

We did say it—every time we spoke.

And . . . I didn't just think about it, I let myself fully feel it as I stood there, finger poised to text her back.

Yeah, I thought to myself, *I miss her so intensely my chest hurts with it and . . . God . . .*

I sighed.

I shook my head, not knowing what else to do with myself, with this truth I held. Because I could no longer even try to pretend to myself.

Yes, I was crazy attracted to her. And the deeper truth was, no matter how much we skirted around it, there *was* something here, something between us.

My shoulder and back again twinged sharply as I reached for a dresser drawer, the pain forcefully reminding me of how it had happened.

The dark, the tight space, the slip and the fall, and the smells of the mud and the rain and the burning electrical parts, the people who had lost loved ones and didn't know it—yet—the people who themselves had been lost . . .

None of those people had expected their lives to be so drastically and dramatically ended—and the very stark fact of it was that, even if someone from that incident survived it, whoever and whatever they were before—it was gone.

And that really was the nature of things, wasn't it?

My daddy had jumped from planes; he did it all the time. My mother had been an aid worker and had been deployed with him—and one day their jobs took them both.

And me—it had been a project, that's all it was, a class project with a partner, but he didn't like—

Enough.

Life was short. Sometimes it was brutal.

But I'd been in so many ways very lucky. Things could have been just as equally, brutally different.

But I was healthy. I was alive. I still had a life to continue living.

So maybe, just maybe, a part of me cautiously said, *there could be something beautiful within it.* Because Trish was very much a beautiful person.

Suddenly, I ached—*everywhere.* There was a tearing through my arms, filled with longing to see her, to hear her voice, maybe to even hold her again while we talked until we fell asleep—my entire chest felt like it could burst with warm joy at the memory of it.

I could do that forever, I realized as I laid my palm over my chest to rub that spot of warm and tingle and buzz.

No, I realized as I rubbed and the feeling grew and grew, *I want to do that—forever.*

There was only one thing to do, now that I knew that with such certainity.

> Bennie: You know what? Yeah, I love that! In fact, I'll take some comp days. Let me know when you want to do this and we'll get it set! The honest truth is I love the idea, I'd love to see you, and yeah, I love YOU. So yes, please?

I didn't know how she was going to manage the time, but if she could find it, I would totally be certain I could be there for it. And . . . *maybe this time, take a step farther into seeing what we could be*, I thought, still rubbing the spot in my chest that felt as if it contained a small sun of its own.

Well.

Okay.

That message was sent and maybe some new potential put out there, right? Right, I told myself as I scrolled through my phone for the unread text it indicated I still had from the night before.

> Linda: I'm home. What a fucking day!
> Left you dinner on the stove when you
> get in, my querida cuz.

Oh wow, that's right—Linda had already been out on a shift when I'd gotten called in, which meant she had definitely been in a nearby emergency room, working her tail off with the same multi-casualty incident.

That she'd come home after and still taken the time to make food for all of us ... I shook my head and smiled to myself, even as I felt the warm glow fill my chest.

Linda was amazing—and I was lucky that I got to call her not only family but friend. I guessed that, despite the chaos of last night, she still had to work today, otherwise I would have expected her next to me in the morning. Wait—*had she been there when I'd finally crawled in last night?* I shook my head because I couldn't remember, but then again, I'd been so tired ...

My bat phone—which I was going to look at next anyway— flashed at me as I picked it up. I unlocked the screen and saw that I had several texts, not all of them the same.

> Ryan: All personnel advise on standby
> for Alaska.

> Cadell: All personnel be advised that
> all able-bodied active 911 members

of service for NYC departments have
been deployed to an active crash site.

Ryan: All personnel not part of NYC
911 please advise standby for Alaska.

Ryan: Standby for Alaska.

Ryan: Standby for Alaska.

Ryan: Alaska confirmation.

That last one had come in about the time I'd first gotten
home, I noted. I put the phone down on my dresser. *Well*, I
thought, filled with mixed feelings about jumping a fire in
Alaska versus taking care of a plane crash in New York, *at least I
didn't have to call or text and let someone know that something other
than Alaska was going on—and that no way was I able to go out
there, not with an emergency right at my doorstep.*

I knew there wasn't a single handler who wouldn't understand
that, but still . . . something niggled at me as I pulled a T-shirt
over my head.

It's probably just that it was a bad call, a really bad call, I told
myself as I found a button-down shirt to go over it. And it would
make sense, right? I mean, trauma would bring up trauma, it
would make me a little hyperaware—

I jumped when my phone buzzed but smiled when I saw the
message flash across, telling me who the text that had just come
in was from.

Trish: I can get a flight tonight, or is
that too soon for you?

My heart quite literally jumped in my chest and fluttered

in my neck as I read that because, yes, I wanted her to do that, I wanted her *here*, and it could *never* be too soon—not for me. And if she wanted to *be* here as soon as she could, then maybe, just maybe . . .

> Bennie: Sweetheart, you can't get
> here soon enough!

Heart still beating in my throat, I sent it. Her answer came back almost immediately.

> Trish: Good, because I can't wait to
> see you either. But if we can both
> hold on about 10 hours, here's the
> flight info. And I'll rent a car.

I read it and memorized it—and it was fine if she wanted to rent a car, sure, but I honestly didn't want to wait longer than we already had to.

> Bennie: I'll pick you up. Let's get a
> rental nearby. I just want to see you.

> Trish: Yes, love. I want to see you, too.
> ♥

My heart hammered even harder in my chest, and heat—heat I'd only felt when running a fever or coming in out of a freezing day—flooded through me.

I touched my cheek, marveling at the warmth in my skin, stroked down my neck to my throat, surprised at the flame I felt.

When was the last time, I wondered, that I really wanted to get that close to someone, to anyone? I loved my family, gave hugs and kisses to friends, had spent some really wonderful hours curled up with Trish next to me, on me . . . I breathed out.

The last time we'd been together, it had been so hard to *not* let anything more than that happen.

"I really . . . I really want to kiss you," Trish had whispered up into that sensitive join between my jaw and neck, her fingers brushing softly along my jaw. And she did, pressed her lips into that tender spot.

"Oh . . ." I had breathed it out softly, the feeling of her in my arms and wrapped over me, her mouth against that spot, so filled with love, with warmth, feelings that poured out from her and over me, through me, back to her.

"God—me, too," I said through gritted teeth, loving the feelings she was filling me with, the touch on my face and against my neck, the gorgeous solidity of her on me and in my arms. I shifted my face so I could kiss her forehead with all the emotion I had.

"I . . . I don't . . . I don't want us to take this too far," I said, holding her tightly, my mouth pressed against her head. "It's just . . . there're things that—"

"Hey, hey," Trish said gently, and shifted within our embrace until she was almost over me, looking at me, her eyes large and wide and glowing and warm, so warm, so full of everything, so full of love as they gazed into mine. "It's okay—it's really okay. We're not gonna go anywhere you don't want to, okay?"

I gazed up at her, up into the shine of her eyes, saw the absolute care, the concern—I was scared to call what I was seeing, what I was feeling—love . . . And the pained pounding in my chest settled, became something different, still hard, still solid, but without the edge of—was it fear? Panic? I didn't know, but it was gone.

Her eyes were so bright on me, I couldn't help but touch the soft high plane of her cheek. "I want to—I do, it's just— Trish, we won't stop—if we kiss, I mean—you know that would become—"

"Making love?" she asked softly, her fingers warm on my face. "Yes," she said softly, then kissed my forehead. "You're right, we would—and we already are," she whispered against my hair, shifting ever so slightly, and I noticed finally how entangled we already were, how naturally, perfectly her legs entwined with mine. "This—" her hand was warm as it crossed my chest, just under my neck, "—this is love, Bennie, the way you're holding and touching me," she whispered as I rubbed lightly against her back. "This right now, this between us this very second—it's an act of, a speaking and showing—of love."

She wrapped her arms around my chest, her hands firm on my back, and laid her head on my shoulder, her lips once again near my throat. "And this, all of this—with you—it is all absolutely perfect," she told me as she nestled in. "*You* are perfect."

"Thank you," I said softly into her hair. I kissed the crown of her head. "You . . . you are amazing," I said as I closed my arms around her even tighter. "I'm just . . . I'm not . . ." I sighed.

Trish partially released me, only to put her hand over my heart. She nuzzled against me again. "You're not ready, and that's okay. It's okay if you never are—this is fine, we're fine—perfect, even."

We lay like that, breathing and drifting in the warmth and the silence. Her fingers rubbed lightly on my chest.

"I love you," she said softly. "Exactly as you are, I love you."

"God!" I exhaled softly, then pulled her even closer so I could kiss her head again. "I'm so glad you do because I love *you*, I really, truly love *you*, too. I swear I do."

Trish nodded against me, another lovely rub just below my shoulder. "That's all that matters—everything else is just that: everything else."

And that's where we'd left it then, her last visit here, our last time spent together that wasn't in the midst of an emergency. So yes, we talked more, we texted more, we told each other we loved each other, and that was lovely and wonderful, it felt so damn good, but I was missing her, her presence, the solidity of her in my arms, and the ache of it had begun to override everything else.

And yes, with the plane disaster in my head, with everything I'd ever seen, done, what I did for a living, what my life was before any of that—all of it—I didn't want—I didn't—

Dammit.

No one was home as I paced around the already clean apartment, and considering the studio closet was half empty, I figured Nana had gone out with some finished work for clients or maybe even to meet new ones.

Oh, but I didn't know what to do with myself as thoughts and memories of different times and places went rushing through my head.

Can I do this? I asked myself. Could I really be that close—to *anyone?* Would I feel anything? Would Trish care? Would I? Did it even matter?

I hadn't, I mean—I didn't—

Oh . . . fuck.

I blew my breath out in frustration as I found myself wandering in the kitchen. There on the stove was the dinner Linda had made me. Maybe eating would make me feel better or at least give me a good basis to begin to figure this all out.

I opened the lid on the pot closest to me and inhaled deeply.

Oh wow—it was *arroz con gandules!*

We might not be Puerto Rican, but we were New Yorkers, so what did that matter? Good food is good food, and Linda made *amazing* rice with pigeon peas. Curious, I peeked into the next pot and was overjoyed to see and smell stewed chicken.

"Linda, you are the absolute *best!*" I said to the empty room as I pulled out a dish for myself.

Prepping gave me something to do, kept my hands busy, and somehow that made the scurrying, clashing, and clawing thoughts all swirling through my head slow down just a bit.

All right, I told myself after I'd taken a few bites that I gratefully savored, *this isn't the biggest deal to anyone else but me, but that's okay, right? I mean, Trish did say more than once that how we were, it was perfectly fine, that she was happy with us—with me.*

I chewed thoughtfully as I tried to tease it out, settle my thoughts as well as the restless, riding buzz that rode through me, the skitter pouring out over my skin that was the anticipation of seeing Trish again, of being so close to her.

It wasn't that I didn't want to be even closer—I did, I really did—nor was it that I was unfamiliar or unknowing about how that closer could work. It was just . . .

I swallowed, then sighed.

I stared at the food before me. I hadn't—hadn't been that close to anyone or, rather, let them get *that* level of close to me, since . . . since . . .

I took a deep breath. *I can do this*, I told myself. *Take the memory out as a package, handle it carefully, put it back, not let the edges cut me.*

And I could see it in my mind's eye: the college campus, the sun as it cut through the panoramic windows in the hallway that led to the arts department classrooms, how much warmth it brought to that space, even though it was already an unusually chilly September, and the heat hadn't really been put on yet.

I walked down that hallway from my first class in my new major, the one I'd just changed that year, that week.

I'd not really told my grandmother yet, but I figured that sooner or later she'd notice that my biology and chemistry texts, my lab books, and my math notes were now all sitting on a shelf in the living room that doubled as a study area and dining room.

Right now, though, with a brand-new copy of *Gardener's Art Through the Ages* under my arm, and a bag slung over my shoulder filled with what a syllabus said would be the first shopping list—a multimedia-grade pad, some charcoal sticks, and of all things, a standard No. 2 pencil with three different types of erasers—I walked into my first ever art class.

Everything about that place in that moment stayed in my head, from the way all the seating was arranged, the small stages of varying heights waiting for whatever would be presented to us as models . . . The building was new, an addition to the college. We would be the first class in this building, in this room.

It smelled of fresh wax; the tiles gleamed.

Even the dust motes riding the beams that slanted in from the windows seemed fresh and new, shining as they did in their suspension.

I remembered that day, and I let the joy of it, the memory of the excitement and anticipation, the feeling of "yes, I belong here" fill me.

All right, I told myself. *I remembered that, and it wasn't painful. I can get through the rest of this*, I encouraged my brain.

Because I needed to.

I needed to remember where I was, what I had been. I needed to really and fully understand what had led to the leap that made me what I now was.

And that understanding, I wanted to use that to move forward, to see what new—what *next*—I could become.

Because I wanted to.

I wanted to at least see if I could be, do something different from what I had been, done before. Because I wanted to grow.

Because I wanted Trish in every way with a primalness of need, with a cell-deep desire to close the distance between us, and not just physically but in a way that meant the physical was in itself speech, the most profound communication, the direct translation of her to me and me to her of just how much we meant to each other.

Of just how much she meant to *me*.

How did I get that across? How did I explain myself, the things I was, the things I'd done and become? How in the world—no—*why* in the name of everything did I expect her to understand when I barely understood it myself?

But she does understand—she knows, I reminded myself. She did know because she'd said so when we were wrapped up so closely, so tightly, beautiful touch and embrace between us. I heard her words all over again. "This right now, this between us this very second," she'd said, "it's an act of, a speaking and showing—of love."

Knowing that she thought that, that she felt that way, it made my heart warm and filled with love and gratitude and just missing her so much.

It made me want to reach farther, see what more I could be.

I finished eating, and while I let my hands mechanically wash the dishes in the sink, I tentatively probed through my mind and memories, testing as though I were searching for the "ouch" spot in my teeth, for the place that still, even now, *hurt.*

When was it? I asked myself, although I knew the answer, didn't know how I could forget it, ever, that day or that night in October—October 8, to be exact.

Oh, but that day . . .

"Hey, pretty lady!" Russell, all shaggy red hair, two days of beard, and the faint smell of barbecue potato chips, came up, swung his bag of books on the table before us as he put his arm around my shoulder, then planted a quick kiss on my cheek. "You wanna take some time, go over that plan?" He settled down on the bench next to me in the small campus cafeteria.

"Yeah, sure," I told him, brushing a very quick kiss on his cheek. I put down my pencil, closed the pad I'd been working with, and slid a bit out from under his arm when I put everything in my bag. "We're supposed to meet later anyway, right?"

"Yup," he agreed. He dropped his arm from around me. "You, uh . . ." He fiddled with the button on his bag, a genuine World War I intelligence document bag. "We're wrapping up really late—so you're staying over, yeah?"

"Uh . . . maybe?" I hazarded. "I've got a crazy early class tomorrow, and it's faster to get to campus from my apartment than yours."

"But that's really late to travel," he began, and laid a hand over mine. "It's not safe," he said earnestly. "You know how dangerous some of those late-night drivers are."

I nodded. It was true, I did. Earlier that same morning, it had been in the local paper about a woman assaulted by a cab driver from one of the many local companies.

"We'll see how late it is," I said as I took my hand back. It really did depend on—

Buzz!

The vibration of my phone made me jump, breaking me away from the memory and back to the here and now. I hastily dried my hands on a dish towel, then whipped the buzzing glass and plastic out of my pocket to see who was reaching out in my direction.

Scanlon-Scott: Checking in—you okay?

Ah, Tori—always such a sweetheart! Yeah, I'm okay, I thought as I read it with a smile. And then our last conversation was playing in my head, even as I began texting her back.

"I *know* you, Bennie, I *know* you—and I know *something* happened," Tori had said as we drove home in the rain.

"It's . . . I'm not ready to talk about it. It was a long time ago—right before we met, actually—and I just . . . I just can't right now, okay?" I'd told her.

"Bennie, I'm here—when you're ready, okay? I mean it," she'd assured me.

Maybe . . . maybe now, I was.

Maybe now . . . I should.

And maybe . . . I could check in on Tori, too, make sure she was okay, and maybe between us figure out if this was something real that I was going through or just the trauma crap that a really horrible incident could bring to the fore.

Now or never, right?

I texted, then hit "send."

> Bennie: I'm okay—are you? And if you're off this afternoon, what do you say to meeting me down by the pier in Sheepshead Bay, grabbing some bagels, and chatting?

> Scanlon-Scott: Bodega on the Sheep side, then hang Manhattan Beach side?

> Bennie: Just across from the Ocean Ave pedestrian bridge, yeah.

> Scanlon-Scott: Gotcha. See you in about 40 min!

"So how much time do you have before her flight arrives?" Tori asked me, then took a bite out of her bagel.

We sat on one of the many benches that dotted the walkway skirting the bay itself, and while technically we were on the Manhattan Beach side of things, the water we gazed upon was still Sheepshead Bay itself.

There was something just so soothing about being able to smell the salt of the ocean, hear and see the gulls wheeling overhead while the water below splashed along the retaining wall.

"About another three hours," I answered, pulling my own bagel out of the paper bag. I peeled the wax paper away. "A little less."

I took a bite. Ah yes, an egg bagel, lightly toasted with butter and jelly. Definitely a New York indulgence, and I was really glad of it.

"Stressed?" Tori asked lightly.

I glanced over at her to see her staring out over the water, too, then returned my attention to the waves.

Now or never, I reminded myself. I'd asked for this, right?

"Yeah," I said slowly, "but . . . it's not in the way you'd think."

"Uh-huh," Tori nodded, still looking at the water. "So . . . stressing about . . . getting, uh, closer?" she asked.

"Something like that," I agreed, and nodded, still staring at the water, too. I took another bite and chewed.

"Yeah," Tori said softly. "I get that."

An easy, open silence drifted between us. Far up in the sky, seagulls called to us, to each other, to the boats that made their way in and out of the docks. "It's hard, really hard to open up to someone, and even harder after—" she swallowed, then took a breath "—after someone wrecks, just totally betrays and tries to absolutely destroy you—it takes your trust," she said softly. "I really do know." She sighed.

I glanced over and stared hard at my friend. "Because of the—what happened to you a couple of years ago?"

I let it hang right there because I didn't know—not for absolute certain, anyway. But . . . if it was what I thought, if it had been something as painful as I suspected, then I didn't want to make Tori feel self-conscious and vulnerable, didn't want to lead her mind down paths that were hurtful and damaging to travel, even in the remembering.

And I didn't want her to say or reveal anything she didn't want to.

"You mean when I got 'assaulted'?" Tori asked and hooked

her fingers into air quotes. "Yeah." She nodded and continued to stare out at the water as she spoke. "Although at the time, from a strictly by-the-letter-of-the-law legal point of view, nothing criminal happened because there was no law specific for that back then, so no one could do anything."

She gave me a small, tight smile. "That, and since some guy had used the 'she's a lesbian, and that made me temporarily insane' line as a successful defense, it meant there was no way anyone in the local courts could—or maybe rather *would*—do anything. All of it makes it kinda hard to go forward sometimes."

I felt the blood run out of my face at Tori's words. "Did—" I swallowed, then tried again. "Did you say 'temporarily insane' because she—" I couldn't finish it.

Tori's eyes were now sharp on me. "Her being a lesbian drove him insane? Yeah. It was a legal defense that worked—and it set such a strong precedent that the local law wouldn't look at the legal possibility of a sexual assault by a woman on a woman."

I didn't know what to say. Just hearing that again, that very specific phrase—his defense and how well it had worked for him, that meaning, made my head whirl with images of what had happened, the small trial that went nowhere, the humiliation and full degradation of it all—and the way it had played out for future cases—

Oh. My. God.

My face, my head, my hands went numb. My skin was too tight everywhere while I could feel my heart pounding through my neck, hear the pulse pounding in my ears. I'd honestly had no idea that there had been anything further, that this had legacy, that this—

"Hey—hey!" Tori had closed the distance between us and put a hand on my shoulder. "You're right here. It's okay—I'm with you!" I don't know how long it took, how many times she'd repeated herself before I could actually understand the words I realized I was hearing. Tori's voice was low but strong. "You're okay, Bennie. You're okay. I'm right here with you."

I was shocked to realize I'd been staring at nothing, unable to process the blue of the sky, the sound of the water, or even the gulls that had begun to scream.

It was as if I was coming into my own self from a distance, a heavy snap back into today, into now, into here, as I turned my head to see Tori's eyes on me.

"That . . . that was *me*," I told her, my throat dry, my lips even drier as I said it. Even the sound itself was a faint rasp, like the smallest handful of sand flying against the cement wall.

Tori just patted my shoulder and waited.

I took a deep breath. God, I felt so fucking bad, as if somehow this had been my fault, that maybe I could have done something to— "Tori, I didn't know, I really didn't, and I'm sorry that that came up against you. I'm so, so sorry!"

"That—that had nothing to do with you, what are you apologizing for? It's all right, seriously. It's okay," Tori assured me.

But I was stuck in space in that place, and before I was really clear about what I was even thinking or feeling, it all came spilling out, the story I'd told only one person besides the police and the prosecutor I'd had to speak with at the precinct, the person who'd gone with me to make the report in the first place, who knew what the outcome had been. ".And I didn't tell my grandmother—she still doesn't know—her heart, you know? I just couldn't do that to her, add to everything she'd already been through, while Russell . . ."

I was surprised that I was crying, aching with hurt, shame, and rage at the absolute unfairness of it all. "I mean—he offered to *marry* me, as if that would change it all, make it okay! And absolutely *nothing* happened to him—nothing! There's not even a record. Because he already was on probation for some other offense, and why should a momentary lapse of judgment ruin his potential, right?"

The indignation and revulsion at the thought of ever voluntarily marrying anyone who had forced themselves on anyone in the ways that he had—that he'd offered it—that's what had made everything seemingly okay with the prosecution, even the arresting officers.

I was surprised at the depth of the anger as well as the bitterness I felt in remembering,

Tori nodded at me, eyes wide, mouth set. "Yeah. That's beyond fucked up. And I'm really sorry that you had to go through any of that—at all."

"Me, too," I said with a nod. I caught my breath. "Me, too."

"Bennie . . . I'm really humbly honored that you shared this with me," Tori said, and gently rubbed my arm. "I know that wasn't easy—to go through, to live with, then to decide who to talk with, especially after, well, the travesty of the legal process—as you now know I'm familiar with. I sometimes think that's the part that hurts even more—insult to injury, as it were."

I patted Tori's hand. "I'm so fucking sorry," I said, meaning it with the deepest part of me. That was something I wished on no one, and especially not anyone who was as good a person and friend as Tori was. "I wish I could change that for you."

"Yeah," Tori said with a shake of her head, and looked down at the ground beneath us for a moment. "Wish I could change it for all of us."

I nodded in agreement, and we both stared out at the water for long moments.

"Kinda funny in its own way that there's such a strange connection between those events—something like a year and a half or so apart, huh?" Tori commented.

She picked her coffee up from the bench next to her and sipped, eyes still on the harbor.

I sat back and stared at her. "Christ—you're right! Tori—I really am sorry. Maybe there was something I could have—"

Tori turned and gently took my hands in hers; I hadn't

realized I'd been waving them. "Nothing you did or didn't do made him do that to you; nothing you did or didn't do made Trace do anything to me." She gave me a gentle smile.

I stared at her. It *had* been her ex, Trace. I'd never known for certain.

"Trace. Trace, the lab proctor, Trace who convinced me to go to the precinct, Trace, who, last I knew, worked as a respiratory therapist at SIU, the one that you were ..." I let that go awkwardly because I didn't want to be insulting in any way or bring up something that was either embarrassing, painful, or—given how people were—probably both. "*That* Trace?"

Tori dropped her eyes a moment and withdrew her hands. "Yep. That one."

Oh, but something went cold and hard and numb within me at the confirmation because it was *Trace*—and once upon a time, I had trusted her.

And so had Tori.

I was stunned, and now I was hurting, too, hurting for Tori, hurting for me, hurting that there was always, always some nonhuman crap being hiding behind the face of a person.

"There was nothing anyone could do. And—" she gazed up at me again, "—that has absolutely nothing to do with you, other than maybe she learned how easy things might be to get away with."

"Oh . . . fuckin' A," I muttered as I shook my head, not knowing what to do with all of this new information other than somehow, it fit with everything else. "It just fucking figures," I said, finally, because it really did.

"Staten Island was—*is*—a small place," Tori said.

"You're so not fuckin' kidding," I said with another shake of my head. I sipped at my coffee, which, although now cool, was still milky and sweet. "So . . . but . . ." I didn't know the right words to use, to ask what I wanted to, and I stumbled through it. "But now . . . you're okay now, and Jean's okay, and you—I mean, she knows, yeah? How do you—?" I shrugged, not knowing exactly what I what I wanted to ask and hoping that Tori would know what I meant, anyway.

"Of course Jean knows," Tori said, slight surprise in her voice. She cocked her head as she looked at me. "She's my best friend—that's why she's my wife. And I had to—we couldn't, I mean—it's a really big thing. Hey . . ." She reached out and touched my arm again. "Is this what you're worried about with Trish? Telling her, or . . ." she sighed softly, "is it the whole closeness thing itself? Because I know Trish, too, remember— and I know she'll understand."

I nodded at Tori, hearing her. "All of it," I admitted, and put my hands into my lap. I stared at them. "What if . . . what if I'm wrong? What if there's something wrong—with me, I mean? What if I freak out or something? What if she thinks I'm— "I cast about for the words, "—I'm broken, or something? What if I am? What if—"

"Stop . . . stop, stop, stop," Tori ordered quietly, and took both my hands again. "You're not . . . that's not going to—"

"But what if it does?" I persisted, finally fully setting the fear I had free. "What if I *am* broken? And what if . . . what if . . ." I swallowed, then finally glanced up to see Tori watching me, eyes filled with concern. "What if I don't feel anything at all? What if I just *can't*?"

I let tears I didn't even know I had fall freely as I blinked at her.

"Oh, Bennie . . ." Tori sighed softly. "I'd like to hug you—can I give you a hug?" she asked, then came closer.

I recognized what she was doing, the asking of permission, allowing me to set boundaries. It was something we'd learned to do as a matter of course, it seemed, for some of the patients we'd had, and very specifically for those who'd been abused and physically assaulted in any way, but especially intimately. And odd as it might be to be on the receiving end of it, it was also comforting in its own way. I sniffed and nodded.

"All right," Tori said, her voice still low and even.

And then I was caught up in her hug, and I found myself quite literally crying on her shoulder. "Let it out, Bennie . . . let it out. You're all right, you're okay. You've been holding this in for so long . . . too long, my friend . . . You're okay . . . let it go."

"I'm scared, Tori," I admitted into her shoulder. "That changed everything—every single last little thing—for me."

Tori nodded. I could feel her cheek move against my head. "I know. I'm so sorry. It does that. And you lost a lot. But—"her hands were warm and solid on my back and shoulders "—it didn't take *you*, Bennie. You're still *you*, and that's what you're bringing with you every day, to the job, to your family—to me, and to Trish."

She rubbed the back of my head. "No one can take that from you, Bennie, no matter what, the internal, the real you—because that can't be broken."

"You think?" I asked quietly as I held onto my friend.

"I know," she said emphatically, and rubbed my back. "I swear to you—I *know*." She kissed the top of my head.

I slowly disentangled from the warm hug. I felt . . . I felt empty somehow, and tired, and as if I'd just woken up after a fever or a bad dream.

I wiped my eyes. "So . . . just do this, then?" I asked as brightly as I could, attempting to smile while I wiped my eyes.

Tori wiped at her own eyes and smiled back at me. "You do whatever your heart tells you to do," she said. "Start, stop, start over, backwards, forwards—what's right for you is right for you," she said emphatically. "And if Trish is what I've known her to be, it'll be fine."

"All right."

"Yeah? All right?" Tori asked, catching my eyes with hers and giving me her usual grin.

"Yeah, all right." The smile I gave her this time was real.

"And now you've got, what, about an hour before you have to be there?"

I glanced at the watch on my wrist. "Oh Christ, yeah!" I gathered the little debris I'd created, crumpled it into a single ball, then tossed it into the nearby trash can as I stood. "Tori . . . thank you. Seriously, I don't know what I would have done or—"

Tori stood with me. "You would've been okay. I know that, too," she assured me. "I'm just . . . I'm just really . . ." She shook her head at me with a small smile as she reached for the words. "I'm really humbled and touched that you've shared that with me, I really am."

"You're a great friend, Tori, you really are. And that—that was a really big deal to share with me, too. Seriously, thank you for trusting me with that," I told her, meaning it from the deepest part of me. "I just really so very much appreciate you."

I opened my arms to give her a hug. Because we were friends, and Tori was a great one.

"Well, I really appreciate you, too," Tori told me, and gave me a hearty squeeze that I returned. "'Cause you're pretty fucking awesome—and I'm pretty damn sure that Trish knows that, too. And if she doesn't," she continued as we released each other, "we can always ask Jean to do something funky to her car."

I laughed. "You're kidding, right?"

"Actually?" Tori answered back with a laugh of her own. "I'm not—but I also think it won't be necessary!"

I chuckled as we began to walk back to our cars. "Tell me about it sometime?" I asked.

"Definitely," Tori said with a nod. "And maybe you can tell me more about what it was like to be something *other* than a premed major!"

I smiled as I thought about it, remembered the joy of what that had been. "You got it." Maybe, maybe I could, maybe I *would*—talk about it.

Someday.

Because after what I'd revealed and discussed today, all things were possible.

"Hey, Tori?" I called as I reached my car.

"Yeah?"

"Thanks—for listening, for hearing all of that. I don't know why I thought you could, but . . ." I shrugged my shoulders. "Thank you."

Tori nodded and took a breath. "It's all right, Bennie, and I'm glad it was me. It's one of those . . . takes-one-to-know-one things, you know? And we are both very much survivors." She grinned at me. "Now go on and get out of here—go get your girl."

I got into my car and started it, then watched Tori through my rearview, making certain she was safely off, and we waved to each other as she passed me.

I squared my shoulders, let my breath out in a big huff, and sighted to pull out.

Because if Tori was right, and the feelings I had were right, and everything said between me and Trish was the truth, then Tori was right again about where I was headed: I *was* going to get my girl.

Chapter 5

Coffee and Bacon

"LIKE THIS?" We were close and melting and silky smooth. The words were a breath, hot, low . . . intense. And the answer—

"God—yes—just like that, baby, just . . . like . . . that."

Because even after everything was said, there was still more to say, and that part, the most important part, could only be spoken by showing, by doing. Because in the doing and the showing, this . . . this closeness and this intensity, this sharing and oneness, not merely between us but of us, was easy, so easy . . .

It was as natural as breathing, as composed, directed, and essential as a heartbeat.

Because when I first saw Trish and her bag over her shoulder coming to me through the terminal gate at the airport, she saw me—and ran those last few yards.

She caught me in her arms, and I realized she was crying. "Jean told me—Christ, Bennie, that was so fucking close! And—" she gasped for breath, then crushed me even closer to her, "—I couldn't take it if anything happened to you."

I held her just as closely, just as fiercely, and though I was stunned at the vehemence of her words, at the extent of her feelings, I also found that I was amazed in ways I didn't expect with not just the strength but also the ardor, the pure fervent strength I felt from her as she held me.

"It's okay—I'm okay," I assured her, stroking her head,

135

holding her to me with equal need, rubbing her arms and her back and her shoulders because I was glad, just so goddamn glad to see her, and this feeling of her in my arms . . . I felt so damn good, so damned complete—whole—with her next to me. "I'm okay," I said again, and she buried her face into my neck. I could feel her face was still wet with tears.

I kissed the back of her head. "Let's get out of here, yeah? Do you have any other bags or anything?" I asked softly.

"No," she murmured, "just this. Yeah . . ." She sniffed, then straightened.

I looked up into her brilliant glowing eyes, lashes still shining bright with tears. "Let's just go," she said, and gave me a smile.

"All right, good," I agreed easily, because all I wanted to do was whatever she wanted, and with her hand firmly in mine, we walked back to my car.

With the exception of the occasional need for both my hands on the wheel to make turns, Trish and I held onto each other the entire way back to my apartment.

We didn't say anything, at least not out loud. We just held onto each other as tightly as we could.

The pressure of her fingers through mine was a gorgeous constant as we rode along the highway that edged the water.

I honestly can't say why we were silent for the ride, but the silence was filled, filled with touch and filled with us constantly gazing at each other whenever possible, filled with the sound of the beat of my heart and the joy that grew within me, enough to pour out through and over my skin. The ride was filled with the glow of her eyes, the heat and buzz that her nearness gave, the amazement that, yes, we were here, we were now—we were *together*—in the same space and place . . .

What silence was there, really, when we were constantly talking, constantly telling each other through glance, through touch, that we were so very, very happy to be here?

"How . . . how many days can you stay?" I finally asked as we pulled into the parking garage.

"As many as you want," she told me as I parked. She touched my arm. "I told my squad leader I had a personal emergency."

"I'm so glad you're here," I told her, and I knew everything I felt was showing in my face, could be heard in my voice as we stepped out of the car. "I'm just so damn happy you're here." This time I opened my arms to her, and it was mutual, the wrap and the need and the hold, each of us to the other.

Trish rubbed her head against my cheek. "I just . . . I just couldn't not see you anymore. This friends thing—dammit, Bennie, if that's all you want, fine, and I get it, I do, I'll take it because I *need* you—I *need* you in my life, Bennie, and I can't—"

Her hands were strong, so strong on me. I returned the hold, the touch, wanted to tell her what I realized I was feeling, what this was for me—for us—all along.

"Trish—"

"Bennie, I can't stand the thought of anything happening to you, and you don't know that, that I—"

"Trish—"

"And it's okay, Bennie, it's okay if you don't want this, if you don't feel the same—"

"Trish, it's okay—"

She was holding me so close, so, so damned close, and her lips were warm—hot, really, as they touched my ear. "It's not just that I love you—I'm *in* love with you, Bennie, and—"

And suddenly I knew, I *knew* exactly what to say, and how to say it. Knew exactly what I had to do.

I shifted my head, felt the brush of her lips against my cheek, pulled away just a touch and then—

I kissed her.

For the first second, her lips were oh-so-soft against mine . . . then they answered my message with a language of their own.

I understood it perfectly.

"Trish . . ." I whispered against the gorgeous silk of her

mouth. "It's okay—I'm *in* love with you, too." I cradled her face in my hands, let my forehead rest against hers, filled with the desire to kiss her again, to never stop kissing her, even as we both breathed heavy and hard against each other.

"Oh . . ." she said, her voice still low, but it was filled with a surprise I could hear. "Yeah? Really?" Her eyes met mine, and I couldn't help the smile I felt grow from the inside out, a warmth, a shine that I knew radiated.

"Yeah," I said softly as I nodded, her face just so, so *beautiful*, warm and precious in the careful hold of my hands. I kissed her again, the reality—the *truth*—of it all in the press of my lips, in the very gentle taste and touch of her tongue to mine. "Really."

Her hand once again firmly gripped in mine, we leaned against each other as we went into the building, and as unsaid as it was, we both knew this: where we were headed, whatever we did from here forward, it would be unchangeable, while it would change—everything.

Once inside my apartment, her bag got dropped by the door I locked behind us both as we kissed again, hard, needing, wanting, wanting so much, just oh-so-fucking *much* . . .

Because I did, did want this, wanted *us* with all that it would bring and mean, here and now, and for tomorrow.

We were mute except for the language of our bodies, the exchange of lips and taste and tongues, and another door shut behind us as we made our way through the apartment. Just inside my bedroom, I discovered my hands were already pulling the shirt from her waistband.

My breath caught with the sudden realization that *this . . . this is about to happen—Trish and I are just a breath away from—*

I gasped against her neck, filled with desire, filled with fear, overwhelmed with the knowledge that once this happened, there was no going back, only forward. And what if that forward was a jump into the abyss for me, for her?

But oh, the longing . . . the love and the want, the absolute wrenching and overwhelming purest need to touch the warmth and soft of her skin—it was a flood, a force, a slam against the barriers my mind had defended for so long. I brushed my lips against the column that framed her throat and breathed out. "God, Trish . . . I want this—this *us*—so much . . . and I . . . I just don't want to rush, I don't . . ."

But God, her hands, her fingertips were strong, caring, bursting with love and tenderness as they lifted my face to hers and she kissed me softly, gently, her lips filled with the same sensual promise, the touch of her tongue to mine something I craved, and instantly knew I'd want constantly.

"I know," she whispered against my mouth. "I know—it's okay, we won't—I swear." She kissed me again, and her hands, oh, her hands, they felt so good on my back, along my ribs and my waist. Her body was beautiful and strong, long and hard in the right ways and places, soft and receiving of mine so damned perfectly . . .

My heart was beating so fast, so hard I could hear it in my head, and I could feel it pounding in my chest against hers. "It's just . . ." I had no words left.

Because I loved.

And because I wanted.

And because I was so scared, afraid that this . . . this *thing* I carried with me . . . might leak out somehow, hurt me, hurt *her* in some unknowable, unpredictable way, and that—that I could never forgive.

Trish caught me up even closer, her face a rub against the side of mine, her lips a brush against my ear. "Bennie . . . it's okay. I know there's something—"

"I know, I know—I'm sorry—I just . . . I *want* to tell you, but . . ." I tried to explain, find words through everything happening within me. I found myself pulling my head away, even though I didn't let her go.

"Bennie, Bennie . . . it's all right," she soothed, her hands gentling me. She pressed kisses against my neck, my cheek.

"You tell me what, when—whenever *you* want. Nothing has to happen," she assured me. "This, just this—this is all I need—this"—she held me closer, laid kisses on my temple—"here, now, with you." She shifted, but only so she could see me. Her eyes found and held mine. "Bennie . . . you love me?" she asked so softly, and the expression in her eyes, so full, so bright, brimming with tears, tore at my heart, filled my entire body with everything I felt until it overflowed, and I knew my eyes shone like hers. "You're in love with me?"

Her touch, her tone, her words, and oh God, the way she was looking at me, her love, her heart, all there and open and present for me to see, and I could only answer her with the same openness, the same love.

The words tore out of the aching spot in my chest. "Oh my God, yes—yes, I am." I cradled her face, her beautiful, shining face in my hands. I was awed by the courage she showed, humbled by the love she shone in her—for me. "Yes."

Trish nodded at me. "Then it's all good—it's perfect," she told me, her voice still so soft, so low. A fully formed tear shone in the corner of her eye. She swallowed and ran gentle hands along my arms, my neck, lightly rubbed her fingers through and under the hair along the base of my head. "I just want to be with you. I don't care how it is, so long as it's you and me."

And it was exactly that—just her and me—the sacred *us* already created before we even made it to my bed, a union that had been founded and forged in the many days and nights spent under fire both ballistic and thermal, strengthened and maintained through countless conversations and hours of closeness, reaffirmed with kisses and touches through mutually granted permissions: permission to reach, permission to touch . . . permission to love.

So when, during this deepening of our new connection, of our first speaking to each other in this, this new language we now had between us, she asked me:

"Baby . . ."

It was a low and oh so sexy groan into my ear as we pressed against each other, her lips against mine as she spoke. "Can I . . . can I come inside you? I . . . I really want to come inside you."

The love and the lust so heightened with her words, I felt my heart jump in my chest with this elevated sense of joy, while the arousal she stoked for me was so complete I felt it—everywhere.

And yet, even within this space of heightened sensation and joy, I had a moment of slight distance in which to make a complete decision—because I knew the answer to this question, this beautiful request that was so deep, so revealing of who Trish was at heart in so many ways . . . this answer would affect the future of who we were—of *how* we were—to each other.

This answer would both reveal and determine some very key things about me, for me.

Did I want that? Did I want to welcome another into my very body?

Did I want to be completely self-contained, belonging wholly to myself and none other?

Did I want to take that sort of power over both of us, deny her—and myself—that access? How afraid was I, really? And of what, and of who?

Did I not want to know finally, even if it was just for once, what it would be like to completely give myself to another, to surrender to the love that poured out of and over us both, so rich and heady it felt as if the room were filled with it and we swam within its sea . . .

"I love you," she whispered as touch between us became more urgent, and once again, not only did her touch do every single right thing but I could feel *her*, feel her body, feel the coil and tension and the hardness as that beautiful blinding moment came closer. "And . . . I want to share this with you, Bennie. All of it." And oh, her voice was strained and beautiful and so raw, raw with honesty and openness and a vulnerability I wanted nothing more in the world than to protect and love and cherish. "Because it's *me*, Bennie, coming inside of you, it's *me* . . . and I'm so completely yours."

And I knew, I *knew* it was true—Trish was completely, beautifully mine.

And I knew the answer, I was oh-so-very clear.

I belonged to myself; this was *my* body and my decision. This was my joy to have and my risk to take, and I could feel the joy and the love and the hope for the future—our future—surge through me as the gorgeous slip and gorgeous kiss from Trish's lips and tongue met and answered mine.

My body.

My decision.

Because no one—absolutely *no one*—had the right to decide what I could, would, or wouldn't do: it was up to me.

I realized in that very second, with the decision right then and there: if I let that past control me, if I let someone else's actions dictate my decision in the right here and now, constrain or compel me to actions that ran contrary to my desire, then yes, I was letting something—some*one*—else control me.

That wasn't happening, not now, not anymore.

And not ever again.

Because this was my moment, my opportunity to let Trish know beyond any shadow of doubt that I loved her, wanted her, needed her.

I pushed my fear aside and took a deep breath because I had decided: for this moment, this here and now, I wanted to be equally hers, too, I wanted to for once—for *me*—to know what it was to completely belong to someone other than myself in love, in trust.

If . . . if that was betrayed, I wouldn't blame myself for acting on an honest heart. I wanted to know what it was to be so completely loved, and I wanted Trish to know that I was equally vulnerable.

And if . . .

If, for whatever reason, this was the wrong decision to make, well, at least it had been my decision—and my mistake—to make.

But still, even with that possibility, I wanted to show Trish how deeply I loved and cared, how much I wanted and desired her—her and no other—and I had to know, for myself, what making love truly was, with someone I was so utterly in love with.

I kissed her again, deeper, my fingers sure, pressed and sliding, stroking in silk, reveling in the growing hardness, too, that responded so beautifully to my touch. I shifted so that we held each other even closer. "Yes, baby . . ." I whispered against her neck, then kissed her cheek. I kissed her mouth again even as I raised my leg to wrap over her waist, opening myself further to her love, her touch, her very welcome and wanted exploration. "I want you too—I want you to come inside me."

I had no fear of anything anymore, not the future, not of nor for us, not of myself nor the things I'd known, because all I knew was Trish's body pressed so closely to mine, the hardness of her pushing back urgently against my touch even as her folds heated and held me with ever-growing intensity while her touch on my desire became both ardent satisfaction and growing need, as she played against my entrance.

"Oh baby, I'm so close . . ." she said, and somehow between hearing the words so hot against my cheek and feeling the very certain proof of it in my hands, my own desire and arousal rose to heights I didn't know I'd been capable of, was taking me down the path she was going. "May I?" she asked, throaty and raw.

I answered her the only way I could, the love and the need, the purity of the moment and this new language we now spoke urging me on, ensuring I would tell her with the unmistakable want and response of my body.

"Yes, baby," I told her. "Please."

"Look at me, baby, please," she asked, and I did, I looked up into the glow of her eyes.

"I love you," she whispered, and she began to slide into me, beautiful and shocking and wanted. "I love you," she said again, then closed her eyes to lean her cheek against mine, as I closed mine with her.

"I love you, too," I gasped out, welcoming her within me, and there we were, with the oh-so-satisfying feel of her within me, the grasp of her hand on my shoulder and back, the tight fit of her within my arms, the tiny close circle that was her head buried in my neck and my cheek pressed against her hair, and then that feeling, that growing, swelling wave that was the push and the pull and the stroke and—

"I—I'm gonna come," she gasped out into the skin of my throat.

I could feel her within me, without me, this touch and taste and movement between us, urgent and beautiful and ours, all ours, she was taking me with her and—

"Come, baby," I urged her through my heart beating with love and joy and a fiery desire I never knew I was capable of, through lungs that gasped for air, from a body that felt what she was feeling, a gorgeous tension that was climbing and climbing and—

"Come inside me." I kissed her deeply, fully, feeling her swell even more in that final approach. Her body pushed even closer to mine for a holy second as she moved within me, full and beautiful, the gift of *her* as she came for me, inside me, loved and beloved. And in those eternal moments, the ones where we hung together, joined stars in a sky filled and made of love, I felt the joyous burst of my heart, the overflow of it all, the beauty of her, the beauty of this *us* we'd just created, the gorgeousness of her heart and her feelings pouring through and over me, too—and she took me with her.

—⟶— —⟶— —⟶—

"I smell coffee . . . and bacon," Trish murmured into my neck, then pressed her lips gorgeously and warmly against my skin.

"Mmhmm," I agreed, and my eyes still closed, I tightened my arms around her. I kissed her head, let my cheek rest against her hair, still happily lost in the beautiful drift that was us, warm and close, silky soft and muscle strong, and oh-so-damned beautiful . . .

I nuzzled deeper into her hair, inhaled deeply of it all as I relished the feel of her and me and us all wrapped and pressed together . . .

And then it hit me.

Linda.

My Nana.

My eyes popped open. Oh . . . boy. Wow. I hadn't thought of any of that at all. When did they get home? Where did Linda sleep? What was I going to—

"You okay, baby?" Trish asked me as I stirred a bit beneath her, and she laid more soft kisses along my collarbone.

"Uh, yeah. I, uh . . . my family," I said, still holding her as I sat up a bit more. "I didn't think—I mean, I—"

"Shh . . . it's okay," Trish assured me, stroking gently against my skin. "Linda popped her head in a while ago, and I'm pretty sure both she and your grandmother are fine with, well, everything."

"Really? Not the fine thing. Linda, I mean."

"Mmhmm," she said, and nodded slightly, rubbing her cheek on my shoulder. "The door opened, I raised my head, Linda stared a second," Trish told me softly. "Then she smiled, blew a kiss our way, and now—well, we smell food, so I'm sure it's all okay, baby," she repeated, and rubbed her fingertips along my chest.

I nodded as I absorbed that. I had not meant to bump Linda like that, but I supposed that maybe we might have to rethink the gear room moving forward, since Trish and I—

Wait.

Am I doing that U-Haul thing? I asked myself. I mean, here I was assuming that Trish and I were a definitive together thing, that changes would need to get made because we would be ongoing. But . . . *what if that's not what she wants? What if*—

Oh, forget that line of thinking. It was stupid to guess when she was right here with me and I could simply ask. I or we would work around whatever the answer was.

"Hey, are you okay with all of this?" I asked, stroking her arm.

Trish snuggled even closer to me. "What, us?" She kissed my chin. "I don't think I've ever been more okay than I am right now."

"I mean . . . I mean my family and all of that. Are you all right with this? Because I . . .

Trish shifted and leaned over me, her eyes beautiful and bright as they gazed into mine. "Bennie," she began, her voice low and serious. She touched my cheek, tracing the line of it with her fingertip. "I know who you are—and I know your family is very deeply a part of you. So yes, it's all more than okay." She gave me a very soft smile. "I love you, you know—*all* of you."

Oh, the expression on her face when she said that—it made me want to melt and hold her forever, it made my chest feel like it had expanded, made my heart feel too large for my body.

"I love you," I whispered up at the wonder that was Trish as she gazed down at me, meaning it with every single part of me that existed and even the parts yet to come into being. "I love you," I told her again, reaching up to touch the beautiful lines of her face. I glanced at the perfect curve of her lips, stroked across them with my thumb. "I just so fucking love you." I drew her down to me so I could kiss her.

And I did.

Oh . . . once again we were joined and joining, the beautiful entwine and the language of love bodily expressed, growing and expanding between us as we didn't so much learn as remember ourselves, each other, and—

"The food *will* get cold—if Nana and I don't eat it all first!" Linda sing-songed right outside the door.

I couldn't help it. I started to laugh, and so did Trish. "Oh, I suppose we should say something?" Trish murmured, her lips brushing against my ear.

"Oh, I suppose we should," I agreed. "In a minute." We shifted together, and Trish wrapped her arms even tighter around me, pulling me even closer to her.

"In a minute," she echoed, and she kissed me again, soft and strong with a taste I couldn't get enough of.

"Seriously!" Linda said outside the door. "Don't blame us if you starve to death!"

It was the hardest thing to do, to take my mouth from Trish's, but kissing and laughing proved to be too much of a challenge, and we really were laughing too hard.

"Thank you, Linda. Thank you, Nana. We'll be right there!" I finally called to the door while Trish chuckled into my shoulder.

"Great. Don't forget clothes!" Linda answered. "We're all still eating; you don't want to blind us with all that beauty!"

"Beautiful clothes—you got it!" I called back. I kissed Trish's head while she did her best to smother her laughter against my skin.

"Are you *sure* you're okay with all of this?" I asked her again, waving a hand to take in everything.

"Ah God . . ." Trish said, laughter in her voice as she chuckled warm and wonderful against my skin. "I wouldn't have it any other way, my love, I wouldn't have it any other way."

Chapter 6

Lions, Tigers, Bears—and Occasional Daisies

"IT'S ALL RIGHT. We're gonna work this all out. I really believe that."

That, spoken just before "I love you," were the last words Trish and I had exchanged in person—and while we spoke and texted almost constantly, it certainly wasn't even close to being the same as being together, in the same space, sharing almost the same breath.

> Trish: I am missing you so fucking much, baby!

> Bennie: Seriously, me too, love! Kinda aching without you, honestly.

> Trish: I feel you, sweetheart, I really do. It feels like this season is never going to end! But as soon as it does, it's me and you—I don't care how we do it.

> Bennie: Me either, love. We'll make it happen, I promise.

"Oh my God—I don't think Jean and I text each other that much—and our kids get into messes and stuff!" Tori said with a laugh as I hit "send" on my phone.

I gave a self-conscious chuckle as I slipped my phone back into my pocket, then glanced over at Tori as she drove our rig down Broadway.

"Yeah, well, you guys do have that advantage of living in the same home and all that. You've got that going for you," I said, adjusting myself in the seat.

Tori chuckled as she expertly maneuvered us around a bus. "Hey—believe me, I'm glad of that every day. And"—she glanced at me—"I'm so glad things are going well between you two," she said, and smiled. "Makes my heart happy—and you already know Jean's opinion on it!" She laughed.

"Oh, you mean the balloons and the cake?" I asked, laughing with her.

"So you noticed them, then?" Tori said, then laughed again.

"She put sparklers on the cake—it was hard to ignore!"

Because the last time I'd been to their place, both to catch up on next steps in Jean's and my project as well as to visit with them and their little ones for dinner, they'd planned something special for me.

We'd been sitting in their living room, drinking coffee after dinner, watching an age-appropriate superhero movie, Tori and Jean snuggled up together with the littlest baby—tiny Trick, short for Patrick and only seven months old—on one sofa, and me on the other one with the other little ones—Daisy (short for Marguerita, since Jean's mother was Margaret) and Anna (a traditional family name on Tori's side)—draped over me.

"*Tia?*" little Anna asked into my ear.

"Yes, sweetie?" I leaned in closer to hear her. I loved that Tori and Jean's kids were bilingual and called me "aunt" in Spanish.

"Will you draw that for me?" she asked, pointing to the screen.

I tried to figure out who she meant among the characters flying on-screen. "Which one?"

"*Tia!*" Anna's voice was reproachful as she gazed up at me with a little frown. "The girl!"

"Yes, Annie Banannie, I'll draw that for you," I promised, then kissed the top of her head as she settled back in.

"*Tia?*" she asked again.

"Yes, *amor?*"

"Something, something—and something," she whispered, covering her mouth.

"What was that, honey?" I asked, leaning in even closer.

"*Mami dice que tu novia es Trish,*" she whispered to me in Spanish, meaning she didn't want anyone else to hear her—which was only a little silly, since every single one of us spoke Spanish, including Jean—and I assumed little baby Trick would be taught English and Spanish simultaneously, like the girls had been . . .

"Did she?"

"Uh-huh," Anna nodded. "*Mami* said Trish is your *novia*, and Mama said if you get married, then I can go to the wedding, right?" she said, then twisted in my lap to look up at me, her eyes imploring me with her earnestness. "Because I can hold the flowers—I don't use the sippy anymore!"

I chuckled softly because I didn't want to hurt her feelings, didn't want her to think I was laughing at her. "Yes, you're a big girl now, huh? And yes, Annie Banannie, of course."

"Really?" she asked breathlessly. "I can go?"

"Yes, sweetie!"

She jumped up. "I'm gonna hold the flowers!" she yelled and threw her arms around me.

"What flowers?" Daisy jumped up. "I *am* a flower—*I* want

150

to hold them!"

"Yes, yes. You, too. You can hold flowers," I said, hugging them both and now laughing. "Nothing is planned yet, though!"

"When *Tia* gets married to Trish, I get to hold the flowers!" Anna shouted as she wriggled free and jumped around excitedly.

"Me, too!" Daisy yelled, just as excited. "I get flowers, too!"

I glanced back at their parents, who were now outright laughing behind me, too. "So . . . y'all are planning something, then? Because I've no such thing on my calendar!"

"Hey, doesn't hurt to be prepared!" Jean said through her laughter. "Girls," she said, handing Trick over to Tori, who was smiling broadly, even as she shook her head back and forth, "let's go get the surprise for *Tia*?"

"Oh! Yes!" Anna exclaimed and took off into the kitchen.

"Wait for me!" Daisy yelled as she took off right behind her. "Not without me!"

It was my turn to shake my head, and I sighed with fond exasperation. I loved my friends, and the one thing I knew without a doubt was that whatever they'd discussed—and planned—had been done with love. "There's a surprise now, in addition to the wedding you're planning for me?"

"If you'll excuse us for a minute," Jean said with mock formality as she stood. "This was their idea—I merely aided and abetted."

"Oh, that's all—mere aiding and abetting," I said as I stood, too. "Four-year-olds are always coming up with great ideas that require aiding and abetting. Well, I'll keep your spot on the couch warm for you, then," I told her as I did exactly that, then reached out to Tori for the little one so I could hold him, too, as she kept shaking her head, trying so hard not to laugh too loud and wake the little guy.

"You do that—and now you know you have a purpose in life!" Jean said with a smile as she left the room.

"So . . . you all have Trish and me married and living . . . in your backyard?" I asked Tori while I cuddled Trick, who wasn't at all disturbed by either the special effects on the screen or his sisters yelling while they prepped whatever it was with their mama.

Tori shrugged and laughed. "They're mostly harmless, you know."

"What, your wife and daughters, your plans, or your backyard?" I asked. "That's right, Trick," I said, looking down into the tiny little face. "Your family is . . . interesting."

"Are you sitting?" Anna called from the hallway. "Be sitting, *Tia*!" Daisy said, their voices getting louder as they approached.

"Uh . . . let me get back to you on that—and pass me Trick," Tori said with yet another laugh, and reached out to hold the little guy again. "You're probably gonna need both hands!"

I saw the reflection of the sparklers before they even fully entered the room, and I started laughing with Tori while I handed the little guy back over.

"The song!" Daisy demanded as the party of three waited by the entrance to the living room. "We've got to do the song!"

I shook my head, completely amused and anticipating whatever surprise the Scanlon-Scotts had prepared for me.

"You start it, Daisy," Jean gently urged. "Count it in, like *Tia* Nina taught you."

"Quick, Daisy—they're gonna burn out!"

"Stop rushing me! Okay—one, two, three, four!"

And in they came, the girls marching and singing, and Jean right behind them holding—no, it wasn't a bonfire, it was a cake with sparklers, rapidly fizzing sparks flying from it.

"Happy happy song song, happy happy song song, happy happy song song—so when will you have kids?"

I was laughing so hard, I could barely see the cake as Jean handed it to me.

"Congratulations—it's a girl!" I read out loud through the sparks.

"I'm a flower child, I'm a flower child!" Anna sang out gleefully, clapping her hands while she hopped up and down excitedly.

"Me, too! Me, too—I'm a Daisy!" Daisy hopped around with her.

"I love you guys," I said, smiling, even as I shook my head back and forth.

Oh man, Tori was as much like my sister as Linda was—Jean, too—and all of them together, the love they shared and gave, the support and care that was directed at me . . .

Even little Trick was awake now, but he was actively involved in the bottle Tori had for him, though his eyes were very focused on the dancing lights.

"Quick—blow them out!" Daisy encouraged.

"I will, I will—I'm admiring it!" I told her through a smile I couldn't help because I was so loved, and I so loved them all in return.

"Just so you know—we haven't gotten to that point yet," I reminded them all, then took a deep breath and blew.

"Well . . . I *might* be tempted to admit the sparklers *might* have been my idea," Tori said, throwing me a grin.

"I thought I was the one with the fire fascination," I said, raising an eyebrow and grinning back.

"You put them out—that's different," Tori began. "Lighting one up, though, is—"

"Unit Three-Five Charlie, come in." The radio cut in.

I reached over and clicked the mic. "This is Three-Five Charlie—go!"

"We've got a diff breather on—" The dispatcher gave us the address, and Tori flipped on the sirens, then signaled for the turn.

"Ten-four, dispatch, we're en route," I said while I scribbled down the address and information with my free hand.

One quick ride through lower Manhattan, and three minutes

later we were in one of the clusters of buildings that dotted the east side of the borough.

We called in to dispatch that we'd arrived.

"Got everything?" Tori asked as I pulled the stretcher from the back of the rig.

"Yep." I huffed as I pulled the release and let the wheeled part of the carriage hit the asphalt. "O2 tank is already on the stretcher. I've got masks in my bag."

"Me, too," Tori said, patting the bag that hung over her shoulder.

She grasped the other end of the stretcher, then nodded at me. Together we approached the entrance to the tall building.

This particular apartment setup was one of the many remaining New York City Housing project complexes, more simply known as "the projects." The majority of these had been built between 1945 and 1965, and this complex had been done in the popular tower-in-the-park style, which meant a cluster of tall buildings set within a small and somewhat landscaped grounds that included grass and trees—and occasionally an area set aside with climbing and hanging bars, swings, and slides for children.

But despite the semi-parched lawn and occasional tall shade trees with benches beneath them, no one lingered on the grounds outside the building, not teens, not small children, not even dogs or squirrels, even though school still had another two weeks or so before it started.

Some of these complexes had a police presence; this one did not.

The front entrance to the building had large windows. The slightly frosted overcast of them and larger etched-in initials, lines, and random flotsam and jetsam told me right away that it was bulletproof Plexi, not actual glass that we were attempting to peer through.

That had probably been shattered and replaced who knew

how many years ago.

A call box with buttons on it, the frame bent out of true and covered in marker-drawn, highly stylized lettering, waited for us to hit the right numbers.

I keyed in the apartment number dispatch had given us.

"Who is?" a reedy voice, undeterminably male or female, squawked back through the speaker grid.

"Emergency Medical Services—for Mrs. Corazzo. Can we come in, please?" I said into the box.

We could hear the scramble in the background, a mutter of voices, then some scratching sounds. "Come in, please," the same reedy voice answered, then the box buzzed.

Tori quickly pulled the heavy door before the buzz disappeared and locked us out again, and even quicker maneuvering got us and the stretcher in the door, which closed heavily behind us, then gave a distinct click to let us know it had once again locked.

The very late summer, dog days of August humidity had gathered, baked, and doubled over itself again through the heavy Plexiglas windows, and the smell of old cooking oil rolled within it, heavy enough to make me pause for breath before we even approached the elevator. Tori and I exchanged a glance but said nothing. Buildings in this condition were common, and often, when we had residential patients, they were the poorest of the poor, living in structures and conditions that were even worse than this—and this wasn't wonderful.

At least this one did have an elevator—and a working one at that, as etched and painted with graffiti as it might be.

And small.

As it was seriously tiny, perhaps four feet by four feet max, we had to set the head of the stretcher as upright as possible, then slide the length of it diagonally into the metal box and wedge ourselves into the remaining corners in order to fit. Tori barely had enough room to bend her elbow to hit the button for the floor, and we really, really hoped no one else would need to use this elevator, too—there was absolutely no way they could fit.

If the air in the entry hall had been heavy, humid, and smelly, the air in the elevator was almost stifling. We were silent as we pointed with eyes and chins at the various marks on the walls that indicated violent impacts and bullet holes, and we were careful not to lean against the walls themselves. Right at head height was a reddish-brown swirl in whch you could actually see where fingers had tried to wipe it off.

Oh, but that stain—it was unmistakably dried blood, and the shade of it meant it wasn't more than twenty-four hours old.

Tori and I were wordless, way too warm and confined in a tight space that had seen more than anyone's share of violence while trying hard not to gag on the unique-to-these-sorts-of-spaces odor that the heat exacerbated.

When the single door finally slid open to the right floor, we both gave sighs of relief—until we maneuvered out into the hallway.

The hallway wasn't any better, lined as it was with porcelain-faced tiles that had once been cream or maybe even white but were now weirdly yellowed, cracked, even smashed out in places. They were also covered with the same detritus as the elevator.

And it was narrow, so narrow that the only way down the hallway to the apartment we had to get to was with one of us in front of the stretcher and the other behind.

"Fire exit's all the way on the end," I pointed out to Tori.

"Yeah," she nodded as she hefted her bag over the head of the stretcher. We began to walk towards what we hoped was the right door. "Six flights up—and I'll bet they're just as narrow as this."

"Hmph." I absolutely agreed. But I didn't want to waste too much time talking because that meant breathing in more of the stale, stagnant air.

The very truth of it was that I hated, absolutely *hated* going into certain project buildings, and it wasn't because they were in poor neighborhoods but because of how they were constructed: elevators that were too small, hallways that were too narrow, emergency stairwells that were not only narrow but also windowless—and they had no access to the outside other than the ground floor or the roof. This meant if someone started a fire in one (which was not unheard of), they acted as perfect ovens and chimneys with the fire itself accelerated by the layers and layers of paint that covered the original bare cinderblock.

"Mrs. Corazzo, this is EMS. We're here to help you!" Tori said loudly after she pressed the beat-up doorbell, then knocked.

I could hear the rapid run of footsteps overhead in the hallway above punctuated by shouts. Doors slammed, and faint yelling could be heard, too.

As calm as I appeared while waiting for the door to open, I was doing my best not to ultimately stress out. Gangs ran in and out of this complex. Lord knew we'd been called to this exact location for more than one stabbing, overdose, or shooting incident.

What made the waiting worse for this particular—and, by comparison, nonfrightening call—was knowing that if a gunfight was in the process of breaking out above us, if a chase began, or anything of that sort, if they came to this floor, there was nowhere to go in the hallway or the stairs. There was no room for anyone to duck or hide or even go past each other. And the chances of someone answering a door, letting someone in to hide from whoever was outside shooting—especially when that someone could just shoot through the door—that was highly unlikely. But even if that unlikely thing happened, that someone risked life and limb to provide that shelter, should the aggressor decide to enter, there was again no way out.

On the rare occasions that some of these apartments had a patio, they were closed in either by metal rails or fencing.

All of it, the entire place, was a dead end, a deadly shooting gallery trap. Having seen the results on more than one occasion of exactly that scenario, and having barely escaped out of a similar scene from a friend's home during my childhood, I was not in the least bit happy to be waiting out in the hallway of potential doom, a hallway that stank of rank cooking oil and sweat and the piss of human desperation.

As an important side note, yes, that combination, blended with a complete lack of fresh air exchange, meant that asthma and difficulty breathing were extremely common complaints, especially among the very young and the older residents of these places.

Overhead, the heavy running steps were punctuated by soft *pops*.

"Fireworks have started," I said calmly and quietly to Tori.

"Yeah," she agreed as she glanced over at me. Her mouth was a set line as she buzzed, then knocked again. "It's EMS, Mrs. Corazzo. We can't help if you don't let us in."

I could actually hear the slide of the bolt and its chain along the door.

"You EMS?" the dark eye that appeared at the crack of the door asked us.

"Yes, EMS," I answered with Tori. "You're having trouble breathing?" I asked.

The door opened.

"Hurry, hurry—don't let the air out!" the reedy voice we'd originally heard urged heatedly, and we complied.

The door slammed shut behind us, and while the air wasn't cooler than it was in the hallway, at least it was a bit fresher somehow.

But that was only an illusion because, if the smell outside had been bad, inside it was even worse, and in the bright sunlight that streamed in past the orange flower-patterned sheet on the window, the odor of old grease and older sweat over something that could only be described as uniquely fungal increased.

We were in one largish room, and in the center was a hospital-style bed raised as high as it would go. To our left was what was supposed to be a kitchen painted in old burnt orange and a shiny, shimmery brown that bubbled with texture.

"Yeah, it's my mom," the person who'd let us in said, and I visually took them in as best I could as we approached the bed. I say "them" because it was only the shapeless cotton dress, its pattern faded beyond recognition of shape or color and leaving only faint repeated grayish blobs behind, that gave any indication of actual gender.

And if her hair was lank, hanging to her shoulders in long stringy and clumped lines, her face so colorless and thin—God, was she thin, the outline of not only bones but also the cartilage that capped them, the veins that ran over them, all clearly outlined, body as shapeless as the dress she wore—then her mother was in many ways her opposite.

The woman in the bed easily weighed over three hundred pounds, and her hair seemed short and shocked, sticking up everywhere, complete with thick grease shine. She also wore a worn-to-grayish blob pattern sundress, while her skin color matched the gray in the triangle that was her nose to mouth.

Not the best sign.

"That . . . that's my daughter, Helen," Mrs. Corazzo gasped at us as we approached, and I was already counting her respirations against the sweep hand on my watch. "She's a junkie and took all my inhalers and meds. Sold 'em for a fix because she's a sunnovabitch—even sold the goddamn fan!" Mrs. Corazzo wheezed at us.

Helen hung her head and shuffled to the door, staring at the floor the whole while, mumbling something I couldn't hear clearly.

"We're gonna check you out and get you taken care of," I said to her as I got even closer and reached into the med bag for a pair of gloves and a small bottle of alcohol-based gel sanitizer.

There was nothing, absolutely nothing about this call that was getting any better, and I definitely didn't expect it to. There's a saying that if something smells unbearable, breathe in deeply to stop smelling it. Yeah ... that trick—effective on smelly subways and many other pungent urban situations—simply wasn't going to work here; it was much more likely my or Tori's lungs would give out first.

I wiped my hands with the sanitizer, then surreptitiously wiped a touch of it just at the entrance of each nostril.

It burned, yes, to the point of making my eyes water, but it helped the slightest bit. And now *I* could breathe just a bit more again.

I made eye contact with Tori as I passed it to her and quickly mimed what I'd just done so she'd do it, too.

She flashed me a quick grin as she took it, then did the same thing. "Call backup?" I asked casually as I pulled out a blood pressure cuff.

"Yeah, I'm on it."

She unclipped the radio from her belt, then keyed the call button.

"Dispatch, this is Three-Five Charlie," Tori said. "We're requesting backup—the patient is difficult to move."

"Ten-four, Three-Five Charlie," the dispatching operator answered. "We'll send another unit your way."

"So when did you start feeling ill?" Tori asked, beginning the interview while I ran through the exam.

"Oh, I never feel good," Mrs. Corazzo wheezed. "This just got a little worse, is all."

"No, no, just stay there," I said as soothingly as I could as she tried to shift so I could listen to her chest. "I've got this." I gave her a smile.

I was definitely concerned because her breathing rate was a touch below normal with the distinctive wheeze on exhale, so I put the oxygen mask on her with a good flow. Within seconds, the color around her mouth and nose improved. "So," I began casually, "no inhalers anywhere, then? Just shake your head yes or no," I encouraged her. I wanted her to get the most benefit from the oxygen that she could.

She rolled her eyes gratefully at me and shook her head slightly.

"Okay. And you're feeling better with the oxygen, yeah?" I asked. "That's great, but we'd still like to take you to the hospital."

There was no surprise, given the air quality and condition that Mrs. Corazzo—who, in fact, had not only a history of asthma but also of congestive heart failure, as well as being unable to walk—was having trouble breathing. The only surprise was that she still could breathe at all. But the big concern Tori and I had was how we were going to move her. There was absolutely no way we could move her by ourselves, and we could move some very heavy people—and had.

But Mrs. Corazzo's inability to move, coupled with her shape and weight, was such that even if we managed to get her transferred from the hospital bed to our stretcher, we wouldn't be able to safely close the stretcher undercarriage, bringing the bed part of it to the ground, then lift the whole thing into the ambulance.

It wasn't just the danger of Tori and I making the attempt; it was, more importantly, dangerous, too, for Mrs. Corazzo. God forbid either Tori or I couldn't hold the weight long enough—Mrs. Corazzo could get hurt.

And that was the one thing we really wanted to avoid.

Honestly, at that point, the only thing *I* really wanted to avoid was breathing in anymore, but I took another swift and secret sniff of the sanitizer. *I need to bring mentholated rub,* I reminded myself with a mental eye roll for next time—because there was always going to be a next time.

I pulled the sheet out from under the mattress on the right

side of Mrs. Corazzo and rolled the edge of it while Tori did the same on the left. Between us, we pulled it as taut as we could beneath the patient. We'd use this to help us shift her when aid arrived.

I took the railing down, then after ensuring both arms were down on the stretcher, too, I wheeled it over and lined it up as close to the hospital bed as possible. I'd already taken the head of it down.

"Three-Oh John is en route," the radio sang out.

"This is Three-Five Charlie—thanks, dispatch," Tori answered.

And the buzzer rang just at that second.

"Who is?" Helen asked into the box by the door, where she'd stood since her mother had first revealed to us her issues.

Given the lack of affect to her voice, the way she didn't use full sentences, and even her head-down shuffle, I wondered if Helen might have some cognitive impairment, since her hearing seemed to be just fine.

"EMS, Mrs. Corazzo. Let us in," the box squawked back, and Helen pressed the button that would allow the second responding unit to enter the building.

I admit, I sighed with tremendous internal relief, and Tori glanced over to give me a look I easily read as the same.

"All right, Mrs. Corazzo, they're gonna come up, and we're gonna get you moved. Do you have pajamas or a book or something you want to bring with you, just in case?" I asked her. "You might be there awhile."

Helen shuffled behind us, and she came up to me, holding a small plastic orange box with rounded edges in her hand.

She handed it to her mother.

"The radio? You want me to take the radio?" Mrs. Corazzo asked with difficulty.

Helen nodded.

The doorbell rang, which startled Helen, who ran back

to the door.

"EMS—let us in!" a male voice called.

Helen looked back at us, the expression she wore clearly asking what to do.

"Ah, Helen, let 'em in!" her mother wheezed.

"They're gonna help us out," I encouraged.

Helen nodded, slid the bolt and chain, and peeked through the crack she'd made, just to be certain. Given where we were, I didn't blame her for the caution.

Personally, I couldn't wait to get us all out of there and at least outside where the air would be so much fresher, while our rig itself would be even cooler . . .

"Hey, hey, Grego, Scotty! How's it goin'?"

With his standard saunter, swing to his hip, and conveniently empty-handed as always except for the radio, in came Rich Johnson, a medic with an overinflated sense not only of self but also ability.

Tori caught my eye just as one of his long-suffering partners, Tony Vincent, who, in fact, *did* carry a gear bag—and a portable EKG—walked in just behind him. "Hey, guys, whatcha got?" he asked, waving at each of us in turn.

"Diff breather, asthma history, wheeze on exhale—and out of meds and inhalers."

"Uh-huh, uh-huh," Tony said as he began his own assessment, and I supplied him the paperwork that listed the rest of the information.

"Gonna work her up here?" Rich asked, hands on his hips as he gazed around at everything but the patient.

We all turned to look at him like he was nuts, because he was. Or stupid. Or maybe even both. Though given that he still had a job and such a knack for getting out of work, I was voting for lazy jerk.

"She's having an active attack, and she's got no meds. We're transporting her, and we need assistance in doing so—the transfer to the stretcher, then the stretcher into the ambulance," Tori said mildly.

"We can just nebulize her here," Dick—I mean, Rich—said, wearing an incredulous expression. "Let me just—" he walked over to kitchen area, "—clear this out and—" He tripped over something on the floor or maybe just slipped on the grease that seemed to coat the linoleum. "Oh—fuck!" he exclaimed as gravity claimed him. "Oh! Fuck!" he yelled even louder as he caught himself on the shiny brown wall with a loud *crack-crack-crack*!

In that very same second as the wall caught him, the shiny brown and copper bubbles began to *move*, and it took everything I had to control the shudder of complete and utter revulsion that raced through me.

Because the shiny copper-brown texture on the wall wasn't paint—it was roaches.

"Goddammit!" he cursed quietly while Tony tucked his chin into his chest and tried not to laugh as he joined me on the far side of the stretcher.

I tossed Johnson the sanitizer from my pocket.

"Hospital," he said firmly as he poured the gel out onto his hands. "Right-oh, then."

"You think maybe they got that girl a sandwich?" Tori asked me as we began the return drive from our center of rove and over to the station to finally call an end to this long day.

"What—you mean Helen or whatever? Would take more than a sandwich to help that, no?" I asked as I maneuvered onto the highway that would bring us home, such as it was.

"True—but maybe it would be the start of . . . *something*," she said thoughtfully, then sighed.

"Agreed," I said, then glanced over at her. She was staring in a nonfocused way out the window. "You all right?"

Through my periperal vision, I could see her turn from the window to watch me for a moment. "Yeah . . ." she said quietly. "Just tired, you know?" She stretched her arms over her head, then laced her hands behind her neck. "Some days are longer than others." She closed her eyes.

I really felt what she was saying. "Yeah, they are," I agreed, and sighed with her. "Sometimes they really are—what a cluster of a day."

Because it had been. After the call in the projects, we'd gotten a chest pain, a bicyclist hit by a car—which had actually happened in front of us while we were en route to another call, so we had to cancel and have dispatch send someone else—and then we backed up medics on not one, not two, but three cardiac arrests.

In other words, just another normal day . . .

God, was I tired.

"So," I began as I pulled our rig into the station lot. "Any plans tonight?"

"Actually, yes," Tori answered, and gave me a bright smile. "Jean's in the same battalion as you, so she's going into her three-day swing. And assuming she doesn't get slammed with overtime, and—"she scrambled in her pocket and whipped out her phone to scroll through the screen, "—I've got no texts saying anything other than I love you, so I'm thinking not—" she paused as she pocketed her phone again, "—which means the babies are staying with their aunts and cousins tonight. I took tomorrow as a comp day, so . . ." Her grin became a bright smile. "We have a date planned. How about you?" she asked as I found a spot in the garage. "Any plans for the three-day swing?"

"Maybe . . ." I said slowly as I jumped out of the front cab, then pulled both my personal phone and the bat phone from my pocket. "Don't know yet."

The bat phone was so far blank, no new messages, but my regular phone—

The text had come in a few hours ago—we'd been too busy for me to even take a moment to see it originally delivered.

> Trish: So much for the season being done. We're out in about a half hour or so—they're desperate for jumpers in Alaska. I love you, I miss you, and I hope you're being careful! I'll get in touch as soon as I get back and we'll figure out our next days together. This season has to end soon . . .

> Trish: I love you, Bennie. I love you so fucking much!

"Trish got called out to a fire—in Alaska," I told Tori as I hurriedly texted back. Even with all the gotta-be-on-it stresses of the day, the thought and memory and want of Trish was a constant on my mind and in my blood, and reading the text from her set mine on fire, a burning need to touch and connect with her again in any way I could. And then there was the text that followed.

> Trish: Uh, hey, I hope you don't mind but I put you down as my next of kin. Not that I expect anything to happen but you're the only one that I care about that I know for certain cares about me. You're the one I want to know about it if something actually happens.

> Trish: And I love you.

Reading that—yes, of course, I wanted that, didn't realize I did until I read it, and the words made my heart contract painfully, knowing how much it meant and what it meant about us, about where we were as a couple and where we were headed. It made my chest hurt because I knew just as well as anyone else how dangerous, how necessary that contact information was.

God, I was desperate to reach out and get in touch with her because end-of-season fires could be difficult, even more so than usual, because the hope that it was over, the battle fatigue of it all, the accumulated sleep deprivation and body stresses . . . they took their toll.

I knew there probably wasn't the slightest chance that she'd see my text before she jumped, but if there was a moment, if they got clear quickly—even if it wasn't for hours and hours, I wanted to get that bit of contact in while I still could.

"Christ—when does the season freakin' *end* for you guys?" Tori asked as I followed and typed behind her.

"Yeah—this one's a fucking long one," I said, and I admit, I was probably a bit distracted as I said it. "Happens like that sometimes."

> Bennie: Baby, I'm coming off shift now, and I want you to know I love you, how much I love you and miss you, want you and need you.
>
> Bennie: Be safe, baby, just be safe. And yes, we'll figure that out as soon as we can.
>
> Bennie: And no, I don't mind that at all, in fact I'm touched, I'm honored, I love you. Please be very careful.

"Still, though—raging fire with crazy winds and bears or stifling man-made caves and guns—those are the choices, huh?" Tori said as she opened her locker.

"Well, you did forget to mention the glory that is the New York City cockroach," I reminded her, exaggerating the pronunciation the way most New Yorkers did so that it sounded like "caca-roach." Joking about anything was good—it took my mind off the fact that my Trish was probably already battling a blaze in Alaska, where the territory was so different from the rest of fire country, with water hazards and different fuels, changing wind patterns and—

"Oh yeah, the caca-*roaches*," Tori said with emphasis, interrupting my cascading line of thought. "Can't forget 'em— would like to—and I bet Dickhead is still wiping gross bug guts off his uniform!"

"Johnson," I said with a mock serious tone, doing my best to imitate his delivery. "It's Richard Johnson. It's only Dick sometimes."

"Oh yeah—like *that* makes it so much better!" Tori said, then laughed. "His parents knew what he was like before he was born!"

I laughed, too. "At least he made some friends today."

"Hi, I'm Dick—splat!" Tori slapped her hand on her locker.

"Ugh!" I shuddered at the gross reminder, even while I kept laughing. "You gotta hope he's a better medic than that, at least!"

"Oh God, right?" Tori agreed.

And at that moment, my other phone buzzed for an incoming text. I checked the screen.

> Ryan: All personnel: Advise on
> standby for AK—CALL TO CONFIRM

> Ryan: All personnel: Advise on
> standby for AK—CALL TO CONFIRM

Ryan: All personnel: Advise on
standby for AK—CALL TO CONFIRM

Another Alaska fire, and a call—repeated—just a few hours after Trish went out—they weren't messing around. The forecast for both the weather and the fire had to be dire.

"Welp, looks like I've got plans for the weekend after all," I said to Tori while I texted my reply.

Grego: Available in approx 60 min.
Will call to confirm.

It was funny, I supposed, if you thought about it. I was already back in the mode, planning out what I needed to do: drive home, shower fast, put on my other gear, then either wait for a pickup or drive to whatever airport had been designated either for regular commercial flight or reserved plane. I was mentally rehearsing the jump steps and count, and my hands were on mechanical autopilot as I closed up my locker for the day.

"That fast? What—flying out to California for a hot date?"

I chuckled at that, thinking about it. "Well, it's definitely hot, but it's a fire in Alaska, so yeah, I guess you could say that."

"Hey." Tori touched my shoulder "Is that a good idea? I mean, it's been a busy week and all—your shoulder and back okay?" Her eyes held real concern as she looked at me.

I rounded my shoulder and flexed my back. "I'm good to go—it was just a bruise."

"You know, I absolutely understand wanting to get out and help—heck, if I could do what you do—and had the time"—she shook her head—"I would," Tori began, then gave me a small smile. "But this call, this . . . this is . . ." I watched her mentally grasp for the words. "Bennie, sit this one out," she said finally.

"Let someone else go this time."

I stared at her, just so completely surprised by what she'd said. A seeming million thoughts and feelings ran through my mind, and all of them were layered under an almost shocking numbness because it was unbelievable to hear, unthinkable that she—

"Tori, you know how this goes—they need, they call. Who else does this if we don't?" I asked, letting the emotion that reigned—confusion—show in my face and tone.

Tori didn't try to hide her distress. "You know I know that, it's just ..." She ran her hand through her hair, a sure sign that she was upset, too. "You and Jean—you're making so much progress with your book, and you've got some new possibilities, stores that want to carry your work. Why don't you focus on that—let someone else go this time?" she said gently, and touched my arm. "Just this once." Her eyes pleaded with me. "Just this time."

I was still shocked by the request, yes, but I was touched by her concern, too. And then I realized that Tori didn't know the one thing that I did, the thing that ensured I was going: Trish was out there, in it. And it was bad enough of a fire that she wanted me to know I was listed as her emergency contact.

"Tori . . . Trish texted to let me know she made me her emergency contact—she's out there—and in it," I said simply.

Tori's eyes widened as she took it in. "All right." She nodded, her mouth a straight line, the line I recognized, the clearing of head and self when there was a job to do. "I understand." She nodded again. "So all right, then," she said as she clapped her hands together. "Whattaya say we arrange for dinner or something when you get back, then, okay?" she said with a touch of forced cheer. "Kids miss you, you and Jean can do some work, and we all need to tease you more—and please, bring Trish when she gets here, all right? The kids need to meet their new Tia." She gave me a lopsided grin.

I smiled as best I could back at her, because this was

familiar territory—it relieved the tension of the moment, and I appreciated the real affection, the honest friendship behind every single word.

"You got it," I agreed, and gave her a grin as I hefted my gear bag. "Best be prepared for a make-mine-Marvel marathon—all the kid-appropriate ones."

"That's most of 'em, then," Tori said, then grinned back at me. She hefted her bag over her shoulder. "I'll see you in a few days, then." She held her arms open for a hug.

"You got it," I agreed, then hugged my friend.

"Be careful—don't get burned or anything, 'kay?" she said, and patted my back.

"Always," I promised. "Besides," I said with a bright smile of my own as we released each other, "we've got a movie marathon to plan!"

"We do, and we will!" Tori promised with a laugh. "See ya in a few!" she said and waved.

"You got it!" I waved back.

I was hurried but careful as I made my way home to prep.

I had a fire to get to and a perfectly good plane to jump out of into it.

Because time was, as the saying goes, of the essence, and there wasn't a convenient available commercial flight, this time the pickup was to a smaller airfield in New Jersey—a smaller, semi-commercial plane. The flight out to Alaska was a tense one for me. I kept mentally reviewing the notes I'd left at home for Nana and Linda.

Nana, Linda,

I got called for a fire out in Alaska.

Nana, thank you for keeping my parachute and uniform in such great condition—I love you and I thank you! You are a literal lifesaver.

Linda, as soon as I get back, it's my turn to make something yummy! Text me with your thoughts, but I've got some ideas . . .

And, Nana, yes, I took the small bottle of holy water from your desk—I have it in my pocket right now!

I love you, and as soon as I can, I'll call and let you know how things are going, and yes, Linda, I'll text you as soon as I land.

Love, love, love,
Bennie

That is the best I can do, I thought as I tried to settle back into my seat and the miles sped away between me and them.

Still, I thanked the Universe for the fact that having a designer who was an incredible seamstress for a grandmother meant that my gear was always in fantastic condition. I patted my right chest pocket where the small plastic vial of holy water lived, just on the other side of the resident small drawing pad.

I couldn't really say if I believed in it or not—the holy water, I mean—but Nana did, and that she knew I had it might relieve some of the worry she felt while I was away.

I sighed, then closed my eyes. I needed to try to sleep for as long as I could, knowing full well that I had to get as much of it as I could in now, that even if sleep wasn't a bank you could save in, at least I could bolster what I had, and definitely what I would need, keep it as a little something more to draw from when we hit the ninth hour or more and there was nothing left but the internal fire, the flame within that fought the blaze without.

The ride from the airport to the base where we'd catch the plane into the fire was tense. Romes was there, as was Goldilocks, both sporting stubble that was a day or so old. From what we already knew of the ongoing situation, I was strongly betting that they'd be sporting more than that by the time we were done.

"You know, Alaska has those fucking Kodiak bears—we're gonna have to fuckin' watch for those," Goldilocks muttered as he stood next to me in the ready room while we waited for a briefing and a breakdown on the jump list.

I stared at him a moment as everyone shuffled around. The scents of smoke and dirt, of sweat and coffee filled the room. "More likely to see a black bear than a Kodiak," I said finally, then pointedly stared towards the front of the crowd where two commanding officer types conferred over clipboards.

One wore a cap on his head, a frayed and faded color that might have been a dark blue at some point, and the sewn-on name tag over his chest read "Haywood." The other, his hair dark and peppered with gray, wore the same uniform. I couldn't read his name tag because he had his back to us.

"Do you know the difference between them?" Goldilocks asked eagerly. "Because the Kodiak makes—"

"A shit in the woods, like all bears do," Romes said, closing in behind us. "Here," he said, and handed me a Styrofoam cup filled with coffee. "It's not the stuff you're so good with, but it'll fuel you," he said with a grin.

"Thank you. You are a scholar and a gentleman," I told him with a grin as I took the cup he offered. Because he was right: coffee was necessary, even if it wasn't as good as mine.

"I do my best," he said, and gave a small twitch to his cheek that I knew was a grin. "And hey, Goldilocks?" he asked laconically, turning to him.

"Yeah?" Goldilocks asked eagerly.

"If you see a fucking bear, don't bother trying to figure out what it is—just get out of its fucking way!"

I couldn't help but chuckle, and Goldilocks scowled. "Y'all don't take bears seriously enough," he said, sounding genuinely aggrieved.

"All right, people, here we go," one of the guys in the front half spoke, half yelled over all of us, and volume in the room dropped completely. I could finally see both his face and his name tag. The face had a mustache that was blond and red, in contrast to the dark salt-and-pepper on his head, and the nametag read "Suarez."

"This is what we've got—lightning's still coming down with a pound, so let's get you the update so y'all can get to jumping this sonofabitch," he said into the now crazy-expectant silence. "And for as long as we have the people, we're gonna go with three-man sticks—we need it! Here's the weather report coming in from the wires."

For anyone on a fire line, from the jumpers and the hotshots to the local fire departments and medical crews—if they existed—weather absolutely ruled the world. And in this weather-ruled world, we were expecting and beginning to experience something known as a katabatic wind—wind that blows downhill—and if it arrived, everything about this fire, every single last thing would be exacerbated to magnitudes that should rightfully cow even the bravest and most experienced of us.

Because it's very simple, really. Wind . . . is King. You could have a storm. You could have a mudslide. You could have a fire. You could have a flood. And any single one of those things could be dangerous and terrible.

But add the wind—and what was arduous and dangerous becomes catastrophic.

Because wind is King.

Because wind, mixed with fire and flame, becomes a firestorm. And in a firestorm, nothing, absolutely nothing is safe.

Metal becomes water, sand becomes stone, and all living things become ash.

That—that was what we hoped to prevent. And that's what we were headed towards.

Hell.

And Trish was in it.

It was a foregone conclusion that the response to this blaze was huge. Approximately sixty-five Alaska crew were already on-scene; there were another 170 from the rest of the country with calls still going out for all who could be spared and sent, which was why I and the crew I flew with were here in the first place.

Once the jump orders had been given, Romes, Goldilocks, and I would be the last of two crews to go out until folks were relieved and rested and/or they got more jumpers from the lower forty-eight states.

I didn't know where Trish was, and I didn't ask—there was no time for it.

Besides, if they knew and I got an answer, then it would change my headspace and my response out there, if we weren't near enough to catch up to her crew.

And if they didn't know—and I knew that they didn't know—it would only increase the tension I already held.

I had my marching orders, and I was going to follow them to even better than the best of my ability.

This desperate, with resources stretched hard and thin, the powers that be were digging down to the ground for supplies of all sorts, even and especially our transportation, so much so that I didn't recognize the type of plane we were getting into, but I could tell it was an older and well-used model.

That was the absolute thing about jumper squads—low finances made for excellent mechanics stretching out every last piece of equipment repaired to its best possible condition and kept as usable as possible for as long as it was safe.

I eyed the skin of the plane and patted it as I boarded. I was certain that it had been to more fires in more years than I had actually been alive.

And then each of us in the group found our spot on the floor, hugged our reserve chutes tight, and were up in the Alaska air.

Once again, I was first man, first stick, first to jump, so here I was again, tapping Romes on the shoulder for the mutual gear double-check, along with Goldilocks.

Three-man sticks, like Suarez had said.

We all gave each other the thumbs-up, and then watched the streamers fall out the door and twirl down into the landing area, the always critical observation, the one that gave us a heads up on what to expect once we were out from the relative safety of the plane.

"About a hundred yards drift to the south, bit of a tricky wind," the spotter yelled.

I slid my visor down as I watched the red drift. Oh, but that same trickster wind brought the smell of the fire of hell into my nose . . .

"Are you ready?" the jump supervisor yelled.

"Yeah!" I nodded and gave him a thumbs-up.

"Get in the door!"

I did my final four-point check before I got into position, staring out at what I was determined would be my landing point. I evened my breathing.

Cool, cool, head.

I saw Trish in my mind's eye as I stared out into the fire, marking visually the point about a thousand feet from it that I'd do my damnedest to hit properly.

176

"Watch for the draft!" the supervisor yelled as we banked into position.

I heard. I nodded.

"Get ready!"

Hell was out there. Trish was out there. I didn't know where. All I knew was that I had my reserve chute hugged tightly in my arms, gear stuffed in many pockets, and the dragon's breath in my nostrils as I got ready to jump. I breathed in and out, poised by the door and staring out into the air, waiting for the slap on my shoulder that would shoot me forward.

And then the world shifted.

The plane faltered, then took a sideways lurch that made me stiff-arm the door frame, pushing me back within. God, that was such a fucking sick feeling. The sideways motion continued, and we started to go down, down, fucking down into a whipping spin that made everything just that much worse. Centrifugal force was pinning us to the walls, the doors, each other. The centrifugal force was huge, and we were falling forward, the strength of it pulling me to the deck so hard, so fast, I had one leg hanging out the door, my head pinned to the metal beneath me.

Earth and sky and earth and sky and earth and sky kept spinning before my eyes, and I knew, knew with every racing moment that we would only pick up more speed.

God—we were going down, we were going down, we were going down . . .

Suddenly, the spinning stopped, and we were in a straight-down fall.

I could pull my head off the floor, and like a douse of frigid water over a sleeping head, I knew with chilling clarity: staying with the plane meant I was going to get killed—we were all going to die.

Christ.

I didn't want to die. I didn't want *any* of us to die.

And faces flew through my mind's eye.

177

Nana.

Linda.

And Trish . . . oh, Trish . . .

I had to make a decision and make it now: jump or not. I gathered my body as best I could and gave a hard push out the door, not knowing if I had enough altitude for my chute to open properly—would I even clear the damn tail?

Would it hurt too much if I didn't?

I shoved myself—*hard*.

Jump thousand.

The fuselage and fucking tail flew past my face, and I could barely breathe.

Look thousand.

I had this irrational thought that not breathing would keep me smaller, keep me out of the way of the spinning blades that meant my sharply imminent death.

Reach thousand.

I saw another human ball fall or jump from the plane as I went down in a tumbling spin.

Wait thousand.

The wind was ripping at me and I struggled to stay in position.

Pull thousand.

My canopy opened with a massive jump and jolt that pulled me so fucking hard it felt like a reverse impact, a hit up instead of down.

But it felt like the lines were twisted and taking me with them, and I toggled as if my life depended on it—because it did. I couldn't get full control, and even with the fast and wild movement, I cast my eyes about as best I could, trying to find a clear spot to land as soon as I could get control of this thing.

There was a wide stream, a depth I didn't know.

There was a field of stones.

There was a stand of birch.

And there . . . was the fucking fire.

But no matter what I did, complete control eluded me. My heart was pounding, there was roaring in my head, and I thought I heard someone yell "drogue!"

I had managed to somehow maneuver away from the rocks and the water, just ahead of the birch, and there it was: the clear spot—I had it! I just about had this motherfucker under control.

Then a draft caught me hard, so damn hard, and—

"Aw . . . fuck, fuck, fuck!"

I don't know if I actually said it or not, but once again I knew, as clearly as I knew that staying in the plane had meant certain death, that no matter what I did, I was getting pulled back into the copse of birch.

Goddamn, goddamn, but *goddamn*! It was too fast, too fast, too fast—God.

I hoped to hell I didn't get too hung up.

And then the branches slammed into my back, taking my breath with their impact, beating against my body, and the slam into my right shoulder whipped my arm up and before me with such intense pain that I thought the sun had exploded into my face, and I thought of my father and my mother, falling from the sky, falling into the jungle, and a line of fire cracked under my faceplate, sending a burning line along my cheek.

My mother.

My father.

Nana and Linda, Tori and Jean and the little ones, Daisy and Anna and little baby Trick . . . and Trish.

Oh . . . Trish.

My chest hurt, my *heart* hurt as *I love you* was all I could think, could feel, a burst of energy and emotion sent out into the Universe, a desperate reach to all of those faces that I wanted to know, to really know just how much and just how truly I cared, I loved, loved them all. The next slam exploded through my back and shoulder, a bright lightning strike that ran through me, shaking the arm I couldn't control, a painful forced exhale of the light that ran through me, from me, and I loved everyone so much—I burst.

Chapter 7

The Morning After

OH MY GOD, I was cold.

Seriously motherfucking *cold.*

I had never known such a cold, a biting freeze that made my teeth hurt. There was sound—a high note click-clack of chattering, a low note of rich growling—so loud, so clear, singing counterpoint to each other, surrounding me, crowding so close I felt the pressure of their tones on my skin ... and then I realized it was me: I was growling, my teeth were chattering, and suddenly, I realized I was nauseated, I was swaying, swinging wild like a kid in a breeze.

I thought about moving, but I couldn't move anything, and then again, I didn't want to because just the thought and the tiny movement of my head blossomed into a huge desire to heave, and there was pain, but since it seemed like it was just big white clouds in my head, I didn't even know for sure it belonged to me.

Then the ice grabbed me again, and I shivered uncontrollably with it.

Cold.

So.

Fucking.

Cold.

And now, through the cold and the clouds in my head and the swinging that I really wished would stop, I really wanted coffee—coffee like Linda or Nana or even I had just made, and I bet almost anything that, as soon as I had some, I'd be steady and fine, and the roar over my head, the wind ripping at me and this fucking cold that soaked through me would go away and—

"We got her!" I heard a deep female voice yell over a roar I realized was a chopper at full throttle in the air.

That voice—I knew it.

"Trish."

I thought it, or maybe I said it. I tried to open my eyes against the weight that held them closed, the roar of the chopper, and the wind. "You're all right—you're gonna be okay. I gotcha, you're okay."

I opened my eyes to see deep dark ones staring back at me. I locked onto them.

"I've gotcha, you're all right, you're gonna be okay."

"Yeah?"

She smiled, the corners of her eyes crinkled as she did, and her eyes seemed to grow larger, lighter, luminous. I was cold, but those eyes shone with warmth, with love—God, how I loved looking into them . . .

Trish's eyes, her smile, they were a blooming heat of bright warmth in the frigid cold that encased me, and just seeing them, seeing her made me happy, as if all of me smiled.

"Yeah—I promise," she said. "Let's go!" she yelled over her shoulder, and the sway started again, making me close my eyes.

Impacts never get any softer.

It doesn't matter how often you do something, say something, get a certain type of news, all you can do is best prepare yourself on how to land, how to say it, how to receive it. But the force of it—the impact—that *never* changes.

No matter how you brace yourself, physically or emotionally.

You're still going to get *slammed*.

Thing is, sometimes you don't know just how hard it will be, even if you did everything right, because any one little thing moves out of just the right place, and all bets are off.

Every single last damn one of them.

I'd been dreaming.

Dreaming that Trish and I were still in bed, curled up together in her room back at the base, when the call went out throughout the entire station, a blare through the speakers that outfitted every room.

"Boys and girls, Fairbanks is crying for jumpers—they got pounded by dry lightning, and there's just not enough—there's shit goin' down in Idaho, and the Zulies are needed back home in Montana—and California thanks you, Zulies," the cheerful male voice said, his tone like a happy morning DJ just talking about normal traffic patterns. "Those of you on roster, get on up and come on down to the ready room—you know the drill!" A brief second of white noise filled the air, and then the speakers cut to full silence.

Not even a second later, we could hear my phone going off with the incoming text as we held each other close.

"When's the last time you had a few days off?" Trish asked me as she nuzzled into my neck, lips so soft against my sensitive skin.

"Probably more recently than you did," I said, then brushed her hair from her forehead so I could lay a kiss there.

"You're going, huh?" she asked, then gently twirled her fingers through the strands of hair that lay over my shoulder.

"And you're not?" I asked softly as I pulled her even closer against my side.

She chuckled against me, and I relished the feel of her, warm and vibrant and loving next to me as we indulged in these last few moments before we jumped up to answer the call.

"I kinda have to—they expect it of me here, being that it's

my job and all that," she told me, then accompanied that with a kiss, her fingers light and electric down my chest, down my stomach as the kiss lingered, then grew, her tongue such an amazing and addictive feel and taste in my mouth and—

"All jumpers be on the ramp by 8 a.m. The flight is approximately twenty-five minutes out."

"Oh . . . Christ," Trish muttered as we oh-so-very reluctantly broke off from the gorgeous kiss we were enjoying and the flames of our own we had happily fanned.

"I know," I groaned out in agreement. "We need to figure out when we're going to continue this . . . conversation," I said as we reluctantly separated and got out of bed.

"Shower with me," she invited, and tossed me an oh-so-very-sexy grin over her shoulder. "Let's discuss it there."

I shook my head with a smile as I walked around the bed and towards her. "I like the way you think, baby—you got it," I said as I caught up to her, then took her in my arms for yet another brief but very hungry kiss.

"I think you like so much more than that," she murmured against my mouth as we walked, still embracing, still kissing with joyful awkwardness, to the bathroom and the shower.

"Actually," I said between kisses to her neck and jaw, "I more than like more than that." I reached behind her to turn the shower on. "In fact, I love it, love all of you."

That the water was the perfect temperature should have been my biggest clue that this was a dream, if the first wasn't the fact that I'd never slept in Trish's room at the base, never mind the barracks of the base itself.

And there was a sound I kept hearing, and a scent that was at odds with the rush of water and slip of skin and heat of kiss within my mouth, and I wasn't sure if I was hot or cold or . . .

Crying.

That's what I heard.

I heard crying.

And suddenly, I wasn't dreaming anymore, even though the taste of Trish's tongue still lingered in my mouth and I really wanted to keep feeling the silk of her skin against mine, I suddenly was aware that I was thirsty—no, I was achingly, ravenously *hungry*, and I had a vague memory of moving my head and that causing me nausea, so I carefully tried again and . . .

I opened my eyes to a semi-dark room, everything colored in blues and grays. But still I heard crying, and I decided to sit up to get my bearings.

That caused a wave of dizziness, and I gasped with the sudden sharp pain in my shoulder.

"Oh, Bennie, no!" Linda was suddenly standing before me, gently pressing me back down. "Don't move—what do you need? I'll get it."

I let her guide me back down onto pillows as I blinked up at her, noting her swollen eyes, her lashes still wet and heavy with tears, and the gentle smile she gave me, even as she stroked her fingers gently through my hair.

"Oh . . . your face, *querida*," she said softly, stroking gently over a place on my cheek that I just now realized both burned and itched. "But it's going to heal, and you'll still be as beautiful as ever—it just looks a lot scarier than it is. And everything else—what is it, *mi Benita bonita*?" she asked gently again, using a nickname—pretty Benny—I'd not heard from her nor anyone else in years.

I stared up at my cousin, so much love shining in her eyes, so much worry. The dizzy was gone, and even with the pain that I felt like a cloudy weight in the right side of my neck, running down both the front and back of my shoulder, I was hit by a craving, a need, a desperate, desperate desire for—

"Coffee?" I croaked out, the word almost a whisper through lips and a throat that were much drier than I thought they'd be.

"What, *hermanita*?" She leaned down, smiling at me, tears still shining in her eyes. "What do you need?"

"Coffee," I repeated, this time a bit more clearly, or maybe it was just that Linda's ear was near my mouth. "Please." Because I wanted coffee more than I wanted anything in the world at that moment. It was all I could think about, was where my mind had fixated.

God—I. Needed. Coffee.

"Yes, okay, I'll make sure you get that," Linda agreed, and kissed my forehead. "But you'll have to wait a bit, if you want it the way we like it."

I nodded because I understood. And suddenly, as much as I desperately wanted coffee, I was also now absolutely exhausted. I closed my eyes with the sudden and deep heaviness of it and sighed out.

Linda patted my head, and all I could think was that I'd have coffee soon, and it would all be okay.

The itch and burn and pain in my face kept bugging me, and the more aware of it I became, the more aware I was of the soft murmur of voices somewhere near me.

I reached to scratch, and the bruising ache in my right shoulder bloomed into white light pain, but even as I moved my hand, I heard "No, Bennie, no," and a gentle hand was over mine, holding it down with a careful firmness. "You need to rest your shoulder."

"Nana?" I spoke even before I opened my eyes, but I did, and there she was. "What—why are you here?"

Between the last wake-up and this, I had managed to figure out that, first, I was in a hospital—somewhere—and given the last thing I remembered was a tree had tried to achieve oneness with me, I was pretty certain I was still in Alaska.

Also, I knew I had a cut of some sort on my face that had made Linda cry earlier, but my eyes still worked, and I could wiggle my fingers and toes.

I had no chest pain other than what radiated from my shoulder, and I had no trouble breathing. And since it was only pain that stopped me from moving my right arm too much, and those fingers worked, too, I was pretty certain that I was going to be just fine.

"*Pero, qué cosa me preguntas? Y dónde voy estar, si no es contigo?*"

Yes, I was definitely going to be fine, since I already found myself mentally rolling my eyes at her asking me what sort of thing I was asking her. Though I fully admit, my heart warmed and enlarged hearing her say where else would she be if it wasn't with me?

"*Pero . . . tu trabajo,*" I protested. "Your work!" Because I knew she had that event coming up, and as a result, there was so much on her plate. "*Tienes ese wedding, y—*"

"*Ai, hija, no te preocupes de eso!*" she said firmly. "You no worry—and I bring you something!" she said, and her eyes shone and sparked at me, beautifully dark and bright. "Linda—" she waved over to the corner where I realized I was still hearing low voices from "—*Tráelo.*"

"*Sí*, Nana!" Linda agreed, and separated herself from the corner she'd been standing in. "Just so you know," she said as she neared, "this required some interesting packaging arrangements for Nana to bring here!"

Nana carefully held my hand as I just as carefully sat up to see clearly. Linda opened a silver thermos and put it under my nose.

Oh . . . but that first whiff was heavenly, and I closed my eyes with joy as I inhaled. "Coffee!" I exhaled gratefully. "*Gracias a Dios, y a la madre de Dios, que nos ha dejado llegar a esta hora con nuestro cafecito!*"

"That's right!" Linda said with a laugh. "We definitely thank God and His Mother for letting us get here with coffee!"

Linda poured me a cup while I watched Nana think about

whether she'd smack my shoulder, then decided not to. "Ah, Bennita—just enjoy it," she said, shaking her head at me, even as she rolled her eyes to the ceiling.

I found that if I tucked my arm into my side and just bent from the elbow, I could move my hand without hurting my shoulder, and I balanced the mug Linda had poured for me between my hands in just that way.

"Thank you," I murmured gratefully, then took a sip.

That . . .

That. Was. *Good* . . .

I closed my eyes again, savoring the taste that lingered in my mouth, the warmth in my hands and now my chest.

"Oh, coffee . . . I so missed you," I murmured.

Someone sat on the edge of the bed, and I opened my eyes again.

It was Linda. "So," she began quietly, "what do you remember?"

Nana was still standing next to me, her hand on my shoulder, so I shifted over. "Sit with me?" I asked her, and she did. She rubbed my back, which, until that second, I hadn't realized was sore.

I took another sip from my mug and thought about it before I answered.

A few things struck me in a part of my brain that seemed to always observe: I was in a hospital and as a patient, which was just so very weird; my neck and shoulder ached massively if I lifted my arm the wrong way; and there was a muzziness in my head that I also realized wasn't normal. In fact, the more I thought about it, the more my head hurt, and the more I realized that there was absolutely nothing normal nor right about this— except that my family was here, and I had coffee.

This was good.

God, I loved that coffee . . .

"Hey, Bennie," Linda said softly, returning my attention to

her. "Do you know where you are? Do you know what happened?"

I stared at her, and I could feel myself begin to frown. That pulled at the bandage on the side of my face and made it itch. I was careful as I reached up with my left hand to touch it, gingerly feeling around the edges of the remaining tape.

"This was gauze, I think, the last time I touched it. Now it's just medical tape," I said as I thought and worked my memory.

"Mmhmm," Linda nodded encouragingly. "It's better than it was. What else?"

I stared at her and tried, tried hard to remember.

"I . . . I was working with Tori," I said slowly, staring down at the white waffled blanket that covered me from the waist down. Those blankets were always so blindingly white . . . I focused on the pattern, still playing delicate fingers over the tape on my face. "I got a text from Trish—wait." That caught me short. I gazed up at Linda. "Where's Trish?"

Linda reached over and put her hand on my knee. I could feel the warmth of her palm through the blanket. "She's still out on the fireline," Linda said, her voice still soft. "She'll be here as soon as she can. You were jumping for a fire, Bennie. Do you remember?"

I frowned, trying to think, to remember. I remembered . . . standing just by the open door, doing the last-minute check. "Romes," I said finally. "I was with Romes—and Goldilocks always complains about the damn bears."

"Goldilocks complains about bears?" Linda asked. "Shouldn't the bears be complaining about—"

"*Ai*, Linda, *déjala descansar—eso es para más tarde*," Nana said, and from her tone, I knew she was slightly aggravated.

My head was really starting to hurt—I agreed. We could talk more later because, right now, the pain was really increasing—and I was super tired again. "Yeah," I said as I lay back down, careful in how I leaned on my shoulder. "He's not always wrong, though," I told them as I closed my eyes.

189

"Goldilocks isn't wrong about bears," Linda muttered as I let the fog and the heaviness in my head take over. I snuggled into the pain in my shoulder. "We might be here awhile."

The next time I woke up, it was quiet, and the light in the room was filtered by the curtains on the window.

I was achingly aware—literally—of the pain in my shoulder, the hurt in my head, and the soreness that spread over my entire back. I reached automatically to touch the spot on my face that itched and burned, but I already knew better and put gentle fingers on it instead of scratching. Yes, the tape was still there.

My head suddenly completely cleared—and I remembered. *Every* thing.

I glanced around, getting a better view of where I was, the situation I was in, my bearings in a very unfamiliar landscape.

In my head, I was by the door to the plane, doing a last-minute gear check with Romes and Goldilocks. I could see the thumbs-up we gave each other, feel the reserve chute hugged tightly to my chest.

From my hospital bed, I saw the door to my room was slightly closed, and I could hear the normal hustle and rumble of a working hospital floor: the voices, the rolling carts, the occasional beep of a monitor for fevers or blood pressures or whatever else.

I flexed my left hand and realized I had one of those over-the-finger devices on my index finger. My eyes followed the wire to the monitor that was just over and behind my head on the same side.

Moving like that made my eyes swim, so I let my head rest back against the pillow and mattress again, noticing that I was in an elevated position.

Once again, I was back in the plane, the sickening lurch, the irresistible pull down to the deck, and the pinning of my head to the spinning view of sky and land and sky and land and—

I blinked against the nausea, planted my left hand firmly against the mattress, gathering the blanket and sheet up in my fist as best I could with the monitor on, and took a deep breath, smelling the scent of wax and floor soap, reminding myself as I felt the texture under my hand and the cool air in my nose that I was in the hospital, not in the dying plane that was trying to take me and my fellow jumpers down with it. I forced my eyes open and turned my head towards the window.

Just before it and not too far out of reach from where I lay was one of those typical elevated tables, and I noticed a package on it. Beyond it was a chair, and while I could see the legs stretched out, the table and the package on it obscured the owner's identity.

But I knew the length and stretch of those legs, and I recognized those boots. It felt like my whole body smiled with the recognition, filling me with happy warmth.

"Trish?" I said softly.

Her head popped up, and I smiled as I recognized the still-sleepy smile she gave me. "Hey, you're up," she said as she stood.

"I definitely feel so," I agreed. I watched as she neared, simply appreciating her face, her presence. "I'm really happy to see you," I told her honestly, meaning it so deeply, feeling how much I wanted to see her fill my chest with a gorgeous, heavy warmth.

God, her smile was so damn beautiful, and the shine in her eyes as she gazed on me was so bright, even in the dark of the room.

I reached for her as she neared, wanting to hold her close to me. "Oh, oww . . ." I couldn't help it. My shoulder reminded me something was wrong.

"Oh, baby—don't," she said, and gingerly reached down for me. "It's okay."

I shifted over so she had room and reached for her with my

left arm anyway. "I'm holding you, I don't care about the stupid shoulder," I said, filled with the desire to hold her close. I found a way to move the right side without it hurting, and oh, thank God, I finally had her in my arms.

"Am I hurting you, baby?" she asked as her arms closed around me.

"I'm fine—you're here with me—I'm perfect," I told her. She sighed, a long, low sound of comfort and relief as we settled in together.

"God," she said in a low exhale as I breathed in deeply of her hair, the warm skin of her neck. I nuzzled against her cheek, kissed the line of her jaw. "I'm so damn glad you're okay, Bennie, just so damn glad."

Her lips found mine, or maybe mine found hers—it didn't matter because our kiss was gentle, sensual, desperate. Her fingers dug lightly into my skin, and I welcomed the pressure of them, returned the warmth and the press until her fingertips found the bandage on my cheek. She gently broke our kiss.

"But that was the worst thing I've ever seen," she said, her voice heavy and low as she buried her head against my shoulder. "I really love you," she murmured, then kissed my neck.

I stroked my fingers through her hair, relishing how close she was to me, feeling the silken texture of the strands, the solidity of her shoulders and back. Still, I could feel her tremble slightly against me.

"I really love you, too," I answered. "And yeah, it was a pretty bad fire."

Trish gently shook her head as she pulled it away to look at me. "No, baby, that's not it—you, Bennie. It wasn't just the forced jump and the wind—your reserve didn't deploy right— you got dragged and hung up in the trees."

I stared at her.

And I remembered it, the push and the pull and the drag, the smell in my face, the slam against my body.

"You got caught and hung thirty feet up, we had to cut you down—I don't know how we got the fuckin' airlift out, but we did."

Oh . . . Christ.

I *remembered*.

The plane. What happened to the plane? To the jumpers?

"What happened? To the plane, to the—" I reached for Trish's arm. The sharp movement hurt, but I did it anyway. "To Romes, Goldilocks—everyone? Are they okay?" I felt my heart jump up into my throat, afraid for them as I waited for her answer.

"They're okay, Bennie," she assured me, stroking my arm to soothe me. "They're all okay—pilot, jump crew, all of 'em. Engine flamed out, the pilot managed to regain control after everyone else bailed. Romes got slammed into a snag—broke a leg but he's fine, and Goldilocks—I swear—" She shook her head, then gave me a grin. "He just has some damn luck."

"A bear?" I asked, relieved, so damned relieved that I felt as if a tremendous weight had lifted from my entire body.

I guess in a way, it had.

"Yeah, but not what you think," Trish said, and gave a half laugh. "Out far away enough from a village, not a campsite anywhere, and Goldilocks finds a stuffed bear while we were digging line."

"You're kidding!" I couldn't help smiling at the irony of it.

"Yeah—middle of nowhere, fire coming up the flank, digging line—he goes to get rid of a snag, and right on top of the damn thing is a teddy bear!" Trish was laughing now.

"What did he do?"

"I told him he should put it on something and wear it around his neck for luck—and he did! Pulled a shoelace out, tied it 'round the ragged thing, and I think he's still wearing it!"

The mental image of Goldilocks, complete in his gear and with a teddy bear hanging from a lace around his neck—I started laughing.

"Oh—ow, ow, ow!" I said, still laughing despite the pain in my shoulder and now in my head. I leaned back against my pillow.

"You okay? Can I get you something? Call a nurse?" Trish carefully moved off the bed, her bright laughter now wiped away with concern.

"I'm fine," I assured her. "It's just a little pain."

"Uh-huh," she nodded, but I could see the concern writ large on her face. "Do you know what's going on yet?"

I thought about it as I adjusted myself. "Not really," I admitted, and her hand reached for mine.

I tried to collect myself, gather and examine the pieces of what I knew. My grandmother. My cousin. They'd been here. "Have you seen—"

The door opened, and both Nana and Linda entered the room.

"*Estas despierta!*" Nana said brightly, holding something in her hands.

"Hey—you're up!" Linda echoed, also wearing a smile and bearing a thermos. "You didn't give Trish a hard time, did you?"

"I hope not!" I said, gripping Trish's hand even more tightly.

"She's perfect," Trish said to Linda. "You guys get a break?"

"Break, *ni que* break," said Nana as she neared, opening what I could now see was a small jar.

Actually, I could smell it—and Trish shifted over as Nana neared.

"*Quiero ver*," Nana said with a nod of her chin to my shoulder as she demanded to see, and the scent of the goo that was now on her fingers filled my nostrils, a cross between Tiger Balm, Vicks Vaporub, and who knows whatever other thing.

"Yes, of course you can see," I said, and I tugged at my gown so she could look at my shoulder. Nana began to dab at it with the aromatic ointment.

"*Vas a ver—esto te ayudara*," she assured me.

194

I wasn't sure I agreed with her that I'd see that her cure would help me, but no matter whether it healed or not, at least I'd smell like she'd tried, as the antiseptic hospital smell quickly disappeared into the pungent odor from the ointment.

"Yeah—it'll help—and it'll clear your sinuses, too!" Linda said with a laugh.

"Well, I see you've got a lot of company that cares," said the new person who entered the room. "I'm Dr. Aguta—and don't be scared, I'm not here to gather the dead."

I stared at the woman who held a clipboard and now stood by the foot of the bed, and gave her a puzzled look.

She wasn't terribly tall, though from where I was, everyone was taller than me, at least for the moment, and her hair was a deep black I'd rarely seen, pulled back to reveal a line of silver running from her temple. But what struck me the most was that, despite the serious mien she wore, a smile played in her eyes.

"*Aguta*—that's what it means in Inuit," she explained as she neared. "Actually, I hope to do the opposite, in a way—ferry folks away from that, rather like you do."

She stood on the left side of the bed. "It's nice to see you fully awake, and I'd like to talk with you about—well, you and what we're looking at, here. Do you want your family here, or would you rather they come back later?" She glanced around at everyone, and Trish began to stand.

"Nah, I want them all to stay," I said, and tugged on Trish's hand lightly. "You, too," I told her, and she smiled at me.

"Well, okay, then," Dr. Aguta said, and began to flip through pages. "You've probably worked out by now that you had a slight concussion, yes?" She glanced up at me.

"Yes."

"Which right there means you're gonna need to rest for a while—bright light still hurting your eyes?"

I thought about it for a moment. "Uh . . . I haven't even thought of trying that yet," I answered honestly.

"Head still hurt?"

"Yep."

"All right. Well, that's the starters. Here's the other news, such as it is. The cut on your face needed stitches, but admittedly, I'm a pretty good stitcher, if I do say so myself, and I do, so that shouldn't scar. You'll want to be careful with it for a while, though. You do know how to handle stitches?" Once again, her dark eyes looked into mine.

"Don't scratch, don't wet, let you look at it, put healing goo on it."

"Great. You know, I didn't want to assume. So . . . let's talk about your shoulder."

I shifted it under my grandmother's warm hand—the ointment was a soothing sort of hot as she rubbed circles into my skin.

She stopped.

"I know it's not dislocated," I said, rounding it experimentally. "Certain reaches, certain stretches—they hurt like hell, though."

Dr. Aguta nodded. "Yeah . . . you're right. Not dislocated. The pain, though, is because you seem to have a few torn and strained muscles, and damage to the rotator cuff itself—after swelling goes down, you'll need to make some decisions," she said.

I cocked my head at her.

"Initial X-rays show that the humerus—it's not broken nor dislocated. It seems that the structure surrounding it has been, well, stretched, so the head of the bone is resting a little lower than it should be. You'll notice your right shoulder is a little lower than the left right now."

I nodded as I listened, and Nana just left her palm, warm and loving, cupping the shoulder we were discussing.

"Surgery can tighten that up, bring it back into place."

"Is it necessary?" Linda asked, and I was grateful that she did because I was still catching up to what Dr. Aguta was saying.

196

She turned her attention to Linda. "Well, nothing until the concussion's fully clear—not chances you want to play with. But the head of the bone is lower in the socket, which means it's putting pressure on both the brachial nerve as well as the brachial artery. Do you know what that means?" Dr. Aguta looked right at me.

I stared at her as my brain worked at the simple math of it all. My head was beginning to feel a bit heavy. "I'm right-handed," I said simply. "I have to work."

"She's an artist, too—she draws," Trish added quietly, her fingers curling and gently rubbing against mine. "How will that be affected?"

"Yeah," Linda seconded. "Repairs to that area—will it really fix it, or what's the potential loss here?"

I was so grateful to have them there with me; they were asking the questions I couldn't think of nor find the words for that readily.

Dr. Aguta blew out a breath and nodded slowly, flipping through the pages again before she spoke. "Yeah, yeah, it can help because the way it seems right now, even if it does heal well, one good pull the wrong way and the humerus can drop farther, impinging both the nerve and artery—and obviously threatening use of the entire limb."

She glanced up at me and came closer. Nana's fingers squeezed lightly into my skin. "Surgery," Dr. Aguta began, then took a quick breath. "Surgery will tighten the structure and prevent that from happening—and you can do that in the next two months or so, after a bit more recovery from the concussion itself."

My head was now beginning to ache with the information I was trying to absorb. "Wait—I bumped my head, I hurt my shoulder, but it's not dislocated, but if I go back to work, I can basically pull it out of the socket?"

Dr. Aguta closed the distance between us. "That's a good

balm," she said to my grandmother. "It'll help bring circulation into the damaged muscles." She reached and touched just under my collarbone on the injured side. "This muscle—the pectoralis—is torn," she said, skimming light fingers over it. "Not badly, but still torn. And this—" Her fingers touched into the space where the collarbone met the shoulder. "This is badly pulled. And this—" Her fingers skated over the shoulder, then onto my back over the shoulder blade itself and just under. "This muscle is torn, too."

I winced as she traced because it hurt, and I tried to roll my shoulder again to ease some of the pain when she stepped away. Finally, a thought was able to form itself coherently in my head, words and all. I looked up at Dr. Aguta. "So," I said, thinking each word as I said it to be certain they came out okay, "if I do the surgery, what about range of motion?"

"Good question—and eighty percent. You'd have eighty percent, maybe more, if you're lucky, if therapy goes right."

I could feel my skin chill and tighten across my entire body. I may not have had the words to describe what I knew that meant, but I had the images and the feelings—I knew what the implications were, even if I couldn't speak to them.

And Trish, who had not let go of my hand this entire time, apparently did, too. "She's *right*-handed," she said, a bit more loudly than she'd spoken before. "She's right-handed, and she draws." Trish's voice was strong and firm. "You're talking twenty percent loss ROM, gross motor control. What about the fine motor control? How will that affect her drawing?"

Dr. Aguta stared at me, eyes again dark and her expression sharp and serious. "You're an artist?"

"Not really," I said, since it wasn't something I made my living from.

"Yes, she is," Trish said firmly.

"*Si*," my grandmother seconded, her hand now warm and firm again on my shoulder blade, rubbing out the pain.

I was so surprised at Nana's response, I glanced over at her—and the sharp move made me wince again.

"You've got a choice to make, then," Dr. Aguta said. She folded her hands over the clipboard before her. "And while I realize you have a concussion and it's not the best time to make decisions or even think too much on anything, this is as simple as I can put it."

She glanced down and nodded, then took a breath before focusing on me again. In that moment of silence, I noticed the sun had shifted, and a beam fell through the drawn curtains, over the table that still sat near the window just behind Trish. It angled down over the foot of the bed, wide enough to reach my feet, and ended there.

It left Dr. Aguta and the rest of us still in the shadow.

It seemed to me that I could see every single mote of dust that hung in the air, suspended, and the shadows the beam left by my feet. I felt each individual pad of Nana's palm on my back. I felt the way Linda stood, leaning casually on one hip but stress in her arms as they crossed while her eyes laser focused on Dr. Aguta, her lips tightened. I felt every single one of Trish's fingers curled with mine, could feel the texture of her skin, the shape and the lines, the folds and creases as they pressed against mine.

And despite the fact that the sun didn't shine directly on Dr Aguta, there was still a shine to her inky dark hair; I could make out individual strands, trace how they framed her face and flowed back behind her ear.

But her expression ... Where it had been a friendly, almost bored concern before, now it was devoid of anything other than a seriousness I'd only seen and felt at some of the worst scenes I'd ever been on.

The ones where things weren't going to be okay in the end.

The ones that meant something massive had happened— and lives were going to change, quite possibly forever.

I saw it in her expression, or lack thereof, the "how do I tell this person, as kindly but concisely as possible, that their whole life has already changed, and they don't know it yet?"

That scared me.

Because I knew that I wasn't one hundred percent with the concussion, which meant that I was missing information, and that what I was getting I might not be processing as well as I normally would.

It wasn't until I felt the answering squeeze of Trish's fingers with mine that I realized I'd tightened my grip.

"All right. What is it?"

"The surgery will guarantee that the arm itself doesn't dislocate, shear down, and impinge your nerve and the artery—but it will limit your mobility, and I don't know that you'll be able to draw—manipulate objects, certainly, and write, yes, of course, but draw—" She paused and straightened her shoulders. "That's a very fine sort of motor control. That's likely something you'll have difficulty with."

I nodded as I attempted to absorb it.

"What about the recovery time?"

"Okay." Dr. Aguta seemed to snap back into a less serious mode. Which made sense, I supposed, since we had probably returned to ground that was much more familiar for her. "It'll take about a year for that to get back to normal—but you have to recover from the concussion anyway, so you have several weeks to go before you begin to schedule everything."

"Uh-huh." All I could do was nod.

"What about the torn muscles?" Linda asked. "Do those require repair?"

"There's no evidence to indicate they'll be anything other than painful for a while, so rest is the best medicine here—and that balm doesn't hurt," she added with a nod of her chin towards my grandmother, who still rubbed my shoulder.

My head was beginning to ache, and I found myself blinking at the light shining in that was now becoming too much for my eyes. But something was becoming very clear to me as I gently shrugged myself away from Nana's touch on my shoulder and gave Trish's hand one last squeeze before I let go.

"I have to choose—between my job and the full function of my right hand. That's what you're saying, right?"

Dr. Aguta cocked her head at me. "Well, I was presenting to you more of a timeline. You'll still be able to function and—"

"No." I waved my left hand in negation. "You said that I'd only have about eighty percent range of motion, and fine motor control on this"—I shook my right hand in the air—"won't be one hundred percent. So ... it's my job—my career—or drawing."

"I'm sure that's not what—" Linda started, but Dr. Aguta shook her head.

"No, she's got it, because rehab and recovery alone—even with an ideal outcome—will last about a year, and yes, there will be all sorts of physical therapy to reduce definitive stiffness in the wrist and hand. That sort of long-term limitation—it can have permanent effects."

"That's what I thought," I said, shaking my head. I put my hands in my lap and stared down at them. My head hurt so intensely, and I was in such shock because, no, I wasn't an artist, not by trade nor definition, not the way my Nana was, not the way Trish said—but I loved it, loved drawing, loved creating the world and the stories that I did, with Jean, without Jean—it didn't matter.

Drawing—it kept me company when I was alone, it let me find something funny or interesting, even beautiful sometimes, when I was in between calls during the middle of a long shift or there was downtime after a big blaze.

And ... it was my friend.

Even after everything that had happened, it had never left me, even though, in some ways, I'd left it by not fully investing the way I'd wanted to back during that time when I could have—I should have.

I didn't even realize that tears were running down my lowered face until I watched first one, then another hit the back of my hand.

Without my job, without my career, what was I? Who was I? I was an emergency medical technician, I was a smoke jumper, and I was both good at and proud of what I did—and it wasn't a bad living for me, for Nana, for Linda.

I provided for my family in a way that made me feel like I was, on most days, doing something good for the world.

But there was this other thing, reality, the secret part of me, or maybe just the deeper part of me, I suppose. That part had never really lost that little kid inside, the one who wanted to draw for the X-Men.

"Are you all right? Do you need a pain med?" Dr. Aguta neared.

"I'm okay." I shook my head and wiped my tears. "I could use a tissue, though," I said, and forced a grin over to Linda, who handed me one. "When do I get to go home and make all these life-altering decisions?" I asked as matter-of-factly as I could.

Because I couldn't cry, not right now, not at all. I was going to have to do something, though. I'd figure it out, but not right now because, oh, was my head aching . . .

"You're otherwise all right—I just want to keep you one more night, make sure there's no surprises in your noggin, check your stitches one more time, and if that's all good, I'll clear you to fly, provided you promise to remain hydrated and at least take Tylenol during the flight."

"Oh yeah," I promised while Nana, Linda, and Trish all chorused in with agreements. "Thank you, Doctor."

"You're welcome." She nodded. "And okay, then, I'll see you in the morning," Dr. Aguta said, and turned to leave the room. "Oh, Ms. Grego?" she asked as she reached the door and paused.

"Yes?"

"Thank you for what you do—and you, too," she said,

nodding to Trish. "You save many lives—both now and for tomorrow when you save the land for the future. And that—is a lot to care about."

I didn't know what to say to that, and neither did Trish, as I watched Dr. Aguta leave, then partially close the door behind her.

I was exhausted. I had a lot to think about. And my head, Christ, the pain was so damned sharp—

"*Échate,*" Nana told me, gently shifting while simultaneously guiding me back down against the mattress and pillow.

"Yeah, lie down," Linda said, echoing her.

"You need to rest—I'll see you in a little bit," Trish said as she stood.

I couldn't help but sigh as I rested my head back, because the ache in my head had spread to my neck and to my shoulder.

Nana gently kissed my head. "*Duérmete un pocito,*" she murmured, her mouth against my hair. "*Mañana nos iremos.*"

I hadn't even realized I'd closed my eyes until I could feel Trish near me, so I opened them to see her eyes, dark with love and concern, the same reflected in the curve of her lips so close to mine.

"I love you," she whispered, then gently kissed me.

"I love you, too," I told her, meaning it with everything I was, and I fell asleep.

I was incredibly thirsty, and the first thing I noticed the next time I opened my eyes was that the room was relatively dark. A light shone from the semi-closed bathroom door across from me, and there was another small light over the light switch by the door, but still, through the gap in the curtains, I could see it was night out there.

And once again, someone was sitting in the chair.

I shifted on my side so I could reach for the water on the bedside table, but it was Linda who uncoiled from the chair. "I'll get that for you," she said as she hastened over. "Let's not strain anything new, okay?"

I smiled and thanked her as I took the cup, complete with sippy straw, from her. "Sit with me," I invited, and shifted over so she could.

"How are you doing, *querida?*" she asked, and reached out to gently stroke my face.

"I'm okay," I said, and kissed her hand. "Where's Nana and Trish?"

"Hopefully resting—though probably not," Linda said, then gave a small chuckle. "We'll getcha outta here tomorrow, then home for you—what do you think about that?"

Oh.

Home.

And suddenly, I just wanted to cry. "I want to go home," I said to Linda. "This . . . this is not fun."

Linda slid over and put her arms around me. "Ah, *hermana*, I know, I know . . ." she soothed. "But please, please don't cry, don't think about it right now—it'll hurt you more," she said over my head as she held me closely. "You need to recover from this first—and you'll be home tomorrow to start that."

I knew she was right, but I felt so overwhelmed—my life had just turned on the proverbial dime, and I knew, I knew I shouldn't cry, shouldn't think too much, get too emotional, too anything—I knew what that could do to the concussion, but there was a time limit on when to make decisions, too, and . . . I tried to calm myself down, knowing how important it was to my own recovery process.

I gave Linda an answering hug, then dried my eyes.

"Linda—my job," I said as I rubbed at my face. God, I had stitches in my *face* . . . and for a second, I felt the impact on my face shield, heard the crack and felt the lightning sear my skin, before I was back. "My job—my career. This—" I waved my arm to indicate the hospital, the room, everything, "—is all I know, it's everything I do, the rushing and the crazy, the screaming sirens and the flare of lights—it's all going to hell—it *is* hell. But for a few moments—" I took a breath, and I looked straight into her steady brown eyes. "In those moments, maybe I can make it all right for someone, be an island of sanity in the chaos. And everything's so clear—" I shook my head, thinking about it, then was instantly sorry at the increase in pain when I did so. I spoke through it anyway. "Everything—what I can and can't do, who I can and can't trust."

My head ached, my shoulder was burning with pain, and I put my hand over Linda's while the tears I tried to stop ran down my face anyway. "What—Linda, what am I gonna do?"

Linda curled her fingers through mine and touched my face very gently. "What *we're* gonna do, *querida*. What *we're* gonna do," she corrected, then pulled me back into her.

I let my heavy hurting head rest against her shoulder, and she released her hand, but only to hand me a tissue.

"I've already handled calling both work and the agency for you. The agency is paying for the flight home, and I've already got that handled," she told me as her fingers stroked gently just above my ear. "You'll have to sign a few things when we get home—but that's the first thing we're doing. We're going home, and you're going to rest."

I nodded against her. "I have to make decisions, Linda. The apartment—how are we gonna take care of everything? Nana—she was sick, she needs to rest, you've got school—Linda, this is—"

"Stop, stop, Bennie, stop!" Linda ordered me, and pulling me very close, laid me back down to rest against the bed with her. "We'll be all right—just, please, don't focus on that right now," and I could hear tears in her voice.

I'd closed my eyes again.

"I don't know what to do," I admitted, my head still pressed against her. "I just don't know what to think."

"Hey," she said gently, and she shifted a bit under me. I heard her shifting things, and when she came to rest again, she placed something in my lap. "Why don't you look at whatever this is? Trish brought it earlier."

"Okay, I will," I promised, eyes still closed.

The nature of concussion meant I didn't really know I'd fallen asleep again, but when I woke, Linda was curled next to me the way she usually did, the way we'd been doing since we were small, and the package was still on my lap.

I was clear again, at least for now, and while my head still hurt, it was background and not the overwhelming fierceness that kept taking over my world.

I wriggled quietly and smiled at my sleeping cousin—God, I was so loved, and I loved her back very much, I thought and felt as I pulled the edge of the first box just a bit closer.

I was still just as quiet as I worried the first corner, and I wondered what it could possibly be as I carefully split the tape.

Finally, it was before me, and even in the semi-dark, I could see the large type on the cover—or make that several covers: Trish had given me several pads of high-end drawing and watercolor paper, a name brand that was, honestly, expensive. And with it, beneath it all, was a pack of Bristol boards, the heavy paper used by comic book artists, complete with non-repro blue lines—the blue that cameras and copiers can't pick up—bordering the pages.

"What?" I asked under my breath as I reached for the other, smaller package. I was just . . . I mean, wow, that she'd remembered, that she'd actually gone and hunted down the brand and—

I stared at the new thing my hands had revealed.

It was a tin of specialty pencils, forty-eight colors, that could be used either strictly as they were or gone over with a watercolor brush, creating a whole new dimension of visual possibility and interpretation.

I kept staring, and as I stroked along the aluminum, I realized there was something taped to the back.

I flipped the case over, and there were two things: a note and, under that, an envelope.

I read the note first:

> I was going to give this to you our
> next visit anyway, but since I had
> the opportunity now, I took it—
> and maybe it's good timing!
>
> I love you.
> Trish

I smiled and shook my head. *Oh, Trish,* I thought, *you have no idea just how incredibly sweet you are.* I felt my heart fill with warmth and love for her as I opened the envelope. It held a simple card.

> I got this for you because I think
> this is something you love—and
> I would love to see you do even
> more of it.
> You keep being you—and you
> keep making the world a more
> beautiful place.
>
> Love you so much, baby.
> Trish

It made my heart smile, made my eyes tear and my heart hurt because she had given that to me, because she was talking to a part of me I thought was long gone, a part I only let out to play every now and again, and because now, now—

I didn't know who I was anymore.

Not if I couldn't work.

Not if I had to choose that and the surgery that meant I'd be able to do it or the full use of my right hand.

I couldn't imagine what life would be like if I couldn't draw anymore—and what would I say to Jean, to Tori? That we couldn't make these stories, these worlds live anymore?

But what was I going to do to live? What sort of life did I have before me? If I didn't have my job, I had nothing to offer—anyone. Not my family, not my girlfriend—not myself and not the future.

But if I couldn't draw . . . a part of me would die, a part of me I loved, a part of me I didn't ever want to live without. And all those stories and all those worlds . . . the people and places that lived in my head and my heart—they'd die, too.

I stared at the presents before me, presents Trish had given me in love, in a vote of faith and confidence that was unmistakable. They were lovely, beautiful—all of it was so incredibly thoughtful, and all I could think was that here I had this choice before me.

"Hey, whatcha got there?" Linda asked softly behind me.

"This," I said as I gathered it all in my hands, then turned to hand everything to her.

"Oh," she said, her voice still low. "These . . . these are really expensive, right?"

"Yeah," I said with a nod. "They are." I thought about it a moment. "She probably shouldn't have spent that much. I mean, I don't—I don't . . ." I sighed.

"She got you good stuff because you're good at it, Bennie," Linda said. She stroked my forehead as I settled back again. "You need good tools to do a good job."

"But . . . but that's not my job." I blinked at her.

Linda smiled at me and kept stroking my head. It helped the fuzz within it feel not so bad. "Right now, your only job is to get better—that's all you need to do. We go home, and you get better, okay? That's the plan."

"Okay," I agreed, and tucked myself back in. Still, in the drift, I wondered what this would all mean for me once I did get better, and a grim voice said *if*—if I did.

Chapter 8

We Bring These Gifts

"ALL RIGHT, you go lie down here, and we'll get everything else set up," Linda said as she and Nana helped me through the door, then led me to the sofa.

The sun was shining through the windows, its direct brightness softened by a white sheer, and I was so glad to be home, so damn happy, despite the pain in my head and my shoulder, the full-weight fuzz in my head, and the nausea I'd been holding back and down as far as I could during the ride home, that it didn't matter to me at all that I wasn't going to my room, that I wasn't—

"But Nana, this is her—" spot, her favorite place to sleep, I tried to say, but—

"Just lie down," Nana insisted quietly while Linda hovered next to my steps.

"Yeah. We got this covered," she said as she guided me down, and I was glad she did, because even that small bit of movement made me dizzy, and I was glad for her arm against my back as I put my head against the pillow. I gratefully closed my eyes, then I remembered.

"Trish," I said urgently as I struggled to sit up again and reach for my phone, which was in the jacket Linda now held.

"I'll text her for you. Don't worry," Linda assured me as she guided me back down. "You need to sleep—sleep and heal."

Honestly, I couldn't even nod my agreement, my head was so full and it hurt so damned much. My eyes were already closed when I said "thank you," and I was already half asleep, my back and injured shoulder cradled against the back of the sofa, when Linda curled my fingers around my cell phone.

My first week or so home was mostly that—I slept a lot, I ate every now and again, and I spoke with Trish instead of texting because, first, I missed her and missed her voice, and second, the light of my screen could and would trigger a massive headache.

In the meantime, Nana and Linda recruited Tori and Jean, and somehow among the four of them, they rearranged seemingly every last thing in the apartment, minus the bathroom.

Because another arrangement had been made: Trish was coming, and she was going to "stay for a bit, just until you're all steady."

Because even though I didn't want her to care for me that way, didn't want what felt like would be an uneven relationship in our beginning, she insisted that it was fine—and it turned out that, not only did Nana and Linda expect it of her anyway, Trish had been the one to suggest it in the first place, and the three of them had arranged it together before I'd even left the hospital.

"Agreements made while I was still concussed probably shouldn't count too much," I grumbled as we all finally sat around the newly set-up eating area in the kitchen. "I really hate the idea that she's gonna come here and play nanny or something like that. It's not fair, y'know?"

Honestly, I was scared—because I really did want to see her, so craved the extra time with her, but at the same time, I didn't want a weird sort of caregiver/taker relationship to arise between her and me, and what I really didn't want was to have her relive in any way the pain and pressure that had been the situation with her mother.

"Look, it's not like everyone gets an easy start of things—

and not for anything, think about it, I mean, you guys literally met while learning how to deal with emergency situations and disasters; it's who you *both* are!" Tori said to me while Linda passed us each a plate.

That distracted me for a moment, because especially after the hospital, the food really did all look and, even more importantly, smell good!

"*Es tu novia, por supuesto quiere venir,*" Nana said as she began to serve us.

"Of course Trish wants to be here with you," Linda seconded. "And it's not as if any of us—even you—would expect any less from anyone else."

"Hey—it's not like she's *not* gonna be your babysitter," Jean added as she reached over. "You know this, right? She, like, really loves you—and you were there for her with her mom. You need to let her be there for you for this. That's if—" she said, then took a deep and very obviously grateful inhale of the plate before her. "If you really want things to be equal between you."

"I know, I know," I said, then sighed as I dug into the food before me. She was right, and I knew it. But what about the rest of my family? This was a huge change, on top of another already huge adjustment with my injury and recovery and all of that. "And seriously—you're all okay with this?"

"Right," Linda said in between swallows. "We're all here rearranging everything because we all think this is a bad idea. Sweetie, your concussion is talking again."

I shot her a look but continued eating, anyway. "Four women in one apartment," I said as I picked up my fork again. "Dormitory syndrome, anyone?"

"*Yo no tengo ese problema,*" Nana said with a shrug.

It was true—she didn't have that problem anymore, so we all laughed.

It was done.

The room that had once been a combination study and ready room was now just mine. My gear was in the closet, the computer was on top of the desk, as was the drawing tablet, along with my pencils and pads—both the ones I'd always had, and the ones Trish had given me.

And because this was a new arrangement, and I was going to be sharing this bed with Trish as part of our new . . . evolution. I had a brand-new bed and furniture to go with it, and I'd made sure Trish had had definite input and decision-making in style, placement—everything.

Linda and Nana now shared the room that had been Linda's and mine, while the area that had been the dining room had been converted to a working studio for Nana—which was why we now had a table that fit a friendly six in the kitchen.

Still, that studio now held a new drafting table, Nana's dress forms, the dining table converted for her to cut on, and her well-used sewing machine, while Linda had a corner of the living room that held her books for study and a new computer.

"Another two days, baby," Trish said into my ear through the phone, and I smiled at her voice as well as the reminder. "Two days, and I'm yours!"

No matter what my misgivings in previous days might have been, in this moment I sighed happily because there could be nothing in this world better than that. "Baby, I honestly can't wait—and you're sure, you're really sure that you want to do this?"

Because as happy as I was to see her—to *be* with her—I loved her enough that whatever made her happy, up to and including changing her mind about everything, was fine with me.

Trish's gentle chuckle sounded in my ear. "Are you asking me if I really want to spend time with you? Bennie, there's absolutely nothing I want more! Baby, please don't worry—unless you're having second thoughts?" she asked very gently.

That wasn't it, and I didn't want her to think that at all. "Baby, no—I want to see you, and yes, I do want to be with you. I'm just concerned that it'll—"

"This is not the same as the past," she said, going right to the heart of one of my biggest concerns. Her voice was still very gentle. "This is you and me—and if you want me with you, then yeah, baby, I want to be with you, too. Everything else is everything else."

"But right now, I can't—I mean, I'm not . . ." I sighed.

"Baby, it's all good. If you want me there, and I want to be there with you, and the family is fine with it, then everything is fine."

Her words warmed me, reassured me, and the feeling I kept trying to sit down on, the full of my chest that was my love and longing for her overflowed, and I couldn't help it—I started crying. "I just miss you so damned much," I said as best I could. "And I want to be enough for you, to be able to *do*, you know?"

"Bennie, baby, you're perfect as you are. Oh, baby, please don't cry, because I can't hold you right now and it's tearing me apart—and it's bad for your concussion, baby. Two days, my love, two days and I can hold you, you can hold me, and everything will be all right."

She was right, I knew she was right, and I breathed hard as I tried to calm myself down. "Okay . . . okay," I breathed out. "I love you, Trish. Two more days?" I asked.

"Two more days, baby," she assured me. "But I'm yours forever, anyway."

It was easier than I thought it would be—none of my fears came even close to fruition as we all settled into a new routine.

Admittedly, mine consisted of a lot of sleeping because of my head, with trips three times a week to do some light therapy for my shoulder. Linda's school and work schedules continued the same, and Trish had already picked up a per diem position—interviewed on the phone and everything with a person we'd both known from working for the city—before she'd even arrived, while Nana had her regular work and clients with occasional bigger jobs for special events, such as school recitals, performing bands and choirs, things of that nature, in addition to the usual weddings and formal events.

Life went on pretty much as normal for everyone but me, although this was for now a new normal.

I couldn't read—not that I'd lost the ability, but to even do more than a few sentences at a time could give me a blinding headache.

I couldn't even watch too much television—because the light of it could cause a headache that made me wish I had done anything other than hit my head.

As far as my face was concerned, I'd had my stitches removed, and there was still a faint but definitely healing line. Every night, Trish faithfully rubbed in the ointment Nana gave me specifically to heal the scar. "You, my love, are absolutely gorgeous," she'd tell me when she was done, then kiss me, which I have to admit, did in fact make me feel a bit better about the whole thing.

I'd been to an orthopedist to ensure that not only did my skull have no cracks in it, but also that my neck was stable—despite what seemed to be a pulled ligament that ran from my shoulder to my neck. It was also important to ensure there was nothing that required surgery at this very second for my shoulder—because given that I was still recovering from my concussion, everyone agreed that surgery wouldn't be a good idea for now.

Those same limitations from my head meant I had a very light physical therapy regimen that mostly consisted of crawling my fingers up and down the wall for as high and as low as I could go to prevent stiffness.

But still, the neurologist I was required to visit assured me that everything about this was normal, and that I was "coming along, nicely. Patience, Ms. Grego, and don't stress on it because that will not help anything," he'd told me.

That patience had to extend to everything—including lovemaking. Of course, Trish and I wanted to, and of course we did.

Honestly, learning and discovering how to move around and with each other in ways that wouldn't hurt my shoulder was easy—and definitely very enjoyable—but there were times that coming for me meant that as my body built to that moment, randomly and suddenly so would the pain in my head, and it was a pain so intense that I couldn't bear any light at all, which would hit with simultaneous nausea, or I would simply develop a nearly blinding headache some moments after.

To say that it was frustrating is severely understating. "Baby, it's okay—I don't want to if you can't, love," Trish would say, breathing hard and fast, our bodies pressed and wrapped around each other, tight and eager and oh-so-close with the love and the want and the need.

"That's not fair, baby," I said, and groaned out between kisses and strokes that made me want nothing more than to love her as closely and completely as I possibly could. "I want—I *need*—to love you, to touch you."

And sometimes we would continue from there, sometimes we wouldn't, but only because Trish felt that it was unfair. "Baby, don't worry about it—it'll be okay, and when you're better, I promise—we'll make up for the lost time," she always assured me with a very sexy grin, and an even sexier kiss that sometimes led us to try anyway, and always led to the most gorgeous make-out session.

And God, I loved her so much for being so damned perfect . . .

But I admit, even though I understood that this was a "thing" with injuries of my sort, and despite how genuinely loving Trish was, there were still times I felt terrible about it. The disability— as temporary as I was told it was—left me disappointed with myself, disgusted even, because I couldn't give pleasure to the woman who loved me, who had traveled so far and spent money she'd risked her life to earn, to come be here with me.

Additionally, Linda and Nana handled everything about the home—from cleaning, to shopping, and cooking, which made me feel even worse in those moments when I was fully awake, fully aware, and not in pain.

But still, every day Nana took the time to reassure me that I was in fact helping: Nana had patterns she was working from, and in those moments for me of freedom from pain and clarity, she'd ask me to help her.

"*Necesito tu mano y tus ojos firmes y expertos para hacer esto,*" she'd ask me, somehow magically knowing every single time I was feeling okay enough to do something that would require my "steady hand and expert eyes" as she described them, to help her transfer patterns.

I'd spend hours working with her, tracing forms and shapes in chalk and red pencil back and forth, to and from cloth and paper so she could cut and sew them into such graceful forms. I actually cut many of them for her, according to her instructions, to both speed the work and relieve my Nana from the sometimes heavy work of it—she may have worried about my head, but I worried about the arthritis and soreness in her hands.

The work my Nana did both amazed and mystified me— how she could take these flat geometric shapes and combine them to build something so vividly dimensional.

I was glad to be able to help, that there was something I could actually do that was useful in some way.

So I was grateful that, despite everything, I had a lot: I had complete use of both my hands, I could button and unbutton my own pants, that sort of thing, and I was even more thankful that my family was as wonderful as they were—because whether I liked it or not (and I didn't), I required someone to at least keep an ear or eye out when I took a shower.

Still though, that was an improvement, since at first, I'd needed help putting on a bra, until I got smart and switched to one that closed in the front—that, at least, I could do.

Every morning, before I opened my eyes, I was warm and happy and snuggled up with Trish before she had to get up and get ready for her shift, if she was on that day.

There were mornings while she readied herself that I'd stare at the desk where the computer sat, where the pads and pencils—both the ones Trish had given me and the ones I already had—sat in prominence on top.

I hadn't opened the pencils yet.

I wanted to, wanted to tear the clear plastic that kept it all safely encased, wanted to see the colored shine of the wood, hold it between my fingers . . . but I wasn't ready—not yet.

Not while I still hadn't made a decision with regard to my shoulder.

Because if I had to give it up, I might as well start getting used to it. But every day at some point I'd think about it, trying to somehow mentally feel the future without being able to create the way I did, and I'd find myself crying.

But even though there was just so, so much that stressed and upset me and that we were all dealing with, still I was grateful that every night I fell asleep with the lovely weight and feel of Trish in my arms and the sound of Nana's sewing machine singing softly through the walls. And even though I felt really bad about how much more everyone else was working to help out with everything—since the injury insurance money wasn't nearly as much as my actual income—the sound of the machine was childhood familiar, and the comforting *shrrrr shrrrr shrrrr* would dull my headache and lull me to sleep.

"Look, if you want to pretend there's some sort of magical everything-will-be okay button, you go right ahead. Yeah, uh-huh, uh-huh." I heard Linda's raised voice, clearly angry, which was a very unusual thing to hear as well as to wake up to. Trish had already left for her shift.

"*No me levantes la vos!*" And that was definitely Nana, answering—no, ordering—Linda *not* to raise her voice.

Well, yelling at Nana was *never* allowed, and especially not on my watch. So okay, I was up, pulling on my sweatpants, and despite the bit of dizzy I felt, I walked out.

Linda and Nana never argued—well, hardly ever, anyway—so this was serious. And while I could understand anyone feeling frustration, I didn't want to hear Nana spoken to in that way.

"What do you want us to do?" Linda continued, though her voice was, in fact, lower. "Go to sleep, feed the fantasy, change absolutely fucking *nothing*? We need to—"

"*¡Pero no es el dinero, es su vida!*" Nana spoke over her. "*Tú no tienes que vivir con esa decisión, una cosa que puede ser tan grave.*"

"Okay, I have a concussion—I'm not deaf," I said as I entered from the hallway, only to see Linda standing with her hands on her hips while my grandmother stood on the other side of the table, her hands spread out on the pattern stretched before her.

They both stared at me. "And you need to not speak to Nana that way," I said to Linda. I had fully understood what they'd both said—and since Nana was talking about decisions that could have grave consequences, I knew they were discussing me. "If you've got something to say, why don't you ask me directly?" I challenged, now standing almost midway between them.

Linda shook her head and blew her breath out in obvious

frustration. "Nana, *lo siento—perdóname, por favor*," she said, apologizing to her. "Bennie, I'm sorry—just go rest—I'm sorry." She kept shaking her head. "I've got to go. I gotta get to work, and I've got a practical exam tonight."

She dashed over and gave me a quick kiss on the cheek, then rushed back to hug Nana over the table. "*Disculpa me*, Nana—*yo te amo*," she apologized again, also giving Nana a quick kiss and assuring her of her love, then hurried to the door. Nana gave a nod as she returned the hug and kiss

"You guys—you just do whatever," Linda said as she turned the knob. "But when you decide you want to get real, to *be* real about everything going on"—she huffed out her breath and squared her shoulders—"then you come to me."

Linda shut the door firmly behind her, and I stared at it for a long moment in the silence that followed. I knew I had to do something and do it soon, but I wasn't quite ready yet to give up my—

"*Bennita—necesito tu ayuda*," Nana said, waving a pair of scissors in one hand and waving me over to her with the other.

"Sure," I agreed, and hastened over. Her head was already down and over her work, and she passed me a piece of chalk, using her chin and hands to point to which pattern, which bolt, and which form she wanted.

I laid them all out, each piece over the other, then pinned everything in place. "*Quieres hablar de todo . . . eso?*" I asked her, because if she wanted to talk about all of it, then I did, too.

Because she was my Nana, and I would do anything to make her happy.

"No," she said around a mouthful of pins, which she began to place meticulously through the join and seam lines she had drawn. "*Está llena de miedo, y tiene que—como se dice . . .* deal with it." She glanced up and gave me a grin. "*Y tú*," she continued, "*tú necesitas completar esto!*" She held up the yards of cloth with part of a pattern pinned to it; the rest of the pattern was coming out under my hand. "*No puedo mandar gente a la boda* naked!"

"I'm hurrying, I'm hurrying!" I answered with a laugh, because I appreciated her take on everything: that Linda was scared but needed to deal with it, and because she'd just said I needed to finish the pattern so that she could finish the dress, because she didn't want to send people to the wedding reception naked.

We worked on in a very companionable silence, but I thought about what I'd heard Linda say and what Nana had answered just minutes before, that she—Linda—was afraid but she had to deal with it.

I knew that if I didn't do anything, just left my shoulder the way it was, the theory was that I wouldn't be able to work in the field at all—ever, really. The chance of the bone falling farther, slamming onto the precious nerve and artery was too great, bringing with it the possibility that greater damage could and would happen.

But . . . the doctors could promise only eighty percent function. And it was over a year for post-surgical recovery to find out if I'd lost any more besides that—not to mention how much I'd have to retrain my hand to draw after such a long time inactive. And . . . not being able to do something even as simple as what I was doing now—tracing long lines, careful curves, and oh-so-precise angles—I hated even imagining it. That . . . and Jean and I had been making such great progress with our combined work.

How could I let either of us down? It was the thing that kept everyone sane—well, me, anyway—the hope I had that I wasn't a "lifer," as some of the older medics called anyone who'd done emergency medical work for six or more years, the hope that someday maybe there was something else I could do, something with less death defying and sadness, something that would bring me personally even more joy.

But with my arm the way it was right now—right now—

what would I do, if I couldn't do the job I was so good at, had spent so many years training and invested in?

How would I take care of and contribute to my family? Nana couldn't work forever—and I didn't want her to, or at least to *have* to. And Linda—Linda wasn't going to stay forever. When she was done with school, with her grades—and I was certain her scores would be great—and the resume she already had, she'd have her choice of places across the country, if she wanted them. And sooner or later, she'd be involved with someone, want to start a family, which was good and normal and healthy and wonderful.

But I didn't want to have everything depend on her, especially when it wasn't fair. And then . . . Trish.

She wanted us to move forward as a couple in our relationship—and I wanted that, too. I really did. God, how I wanted everything that implied! And it was so close, I could touch it and taste it—but how could I create that, provide for that? What direction could it go while I wasn't working, not doing my share of—

"*Ai!*" Nana exclaimed, and I saw she was holding her hand.

"*Que paso?*" I rushed over to see for myself what had happened.

Nana just shook her head back and forth, her mouth tightened into a line as she gripped her hand. I saw the drop of red run between her fingers.

"I'll be right back," I told her, and raced back to my room to get my gear bag.

"Is nothing!" she called out to me as I moved. "The scissor—it slip!"

Mentally I rolled my eyes as I brought my bag back to the studio, and a part of my mind laughed to realize that my grandmother was no different from the EMTs and smoke jumpers I worked with. It could have been a chainsaw that slipped, and still she would have said it was nothing. "Let me see," I said, and I already had sterile water popped open to rinse with and a bandage ready to go.

Nana silently showed me. It was a nasty little bite; blood still dripped, but at least it wasn't pouring, and knowing to be careful not to get anything either on the worktable or the nearby bolts, I poured a bit of water on it, then quickly covered it with a bandage.

"*Es feo,*" I told her honestly, because it was ugly, "*pero está bien,*" I assured her, because it was true: it was a nasty slice, but pressure kept it from bleeding anymore, and a quick inspection showed that even that was rapidly slowing, so it wasn't going to need any stitches. Still, though, it ran right over the bends in the joints, which would make it stiff, painful, and tender for the next few days.

Nana let out a heavy and frustrated sigh, then said something I didn't quite catch as I set the bandage and the tape more comfortably.

"I can't do this alone or one-handed—you must finish," Nana said.

She shook her head down at the blank paper that was waiting to be magically transformed, the patterns already laid out and waiting for cutting, next to the bolts of fabric they needed to be carefully attached and transferred to. "There's no time."

"Of course," I agreed instantly, because seeing my Nana so upset and so forlorn hurt my heart—and I would do anything to make her happy again. "What do you need me to do?"

She brightened immediately, and within moments, without another second wasted on concern about her hand, she concisely directed me in exactly what she wanted and needed.

I drew and pinned and cut, she sewed and sewed, directed me, then sewed some more. In between, I would arrange pieces to help cut, then pin them on forms, remove them—carefully— so she could sew them, and place finished parts and pieces.

Hours passed. My back hurt from bending so often, and this

time when my head hurt, I recognized it for something different than usual: it wasn't the concussion—I was *hungry*.

I pressed my hand against my lower back as I straightened up and glanced around the room. Every surface, except for the worktable itself, was covered in pieces that had yet to be attached, grouped together as the outfit each set would become, and—hung perfectly on a standing rack—were some now-complete pieces that hours of magic had put together.

Nana noticed I'd stopped, so she glanced around the room with me, even as she literally kept her foot pressed hard against the pedal that powered the machine she worked so diligently.

"*Gracias, hijita,*" she said quietly, thanking me as she slowed the machine for a few seconds. "*Tú y tus regalos son mi regalo—no te olvides de eso,*" she told me, her eyes dark and fixed on mine as she tried to drive her meaning home. Me and my gifts were gifts to her—and I wasn't to forget that. I nodded that I understood, and Nana gave me a quick smile, then turned her attention and the throttle back up on her machine. "*Ya estoy para terminar—anda mira lo que hay para comer!*" she ordered me with a smile, telling me she was almost done as she shooed me away one-handed to find us something to eat.

I couldn't help but shake my head and smile to myself as I did exactly that, and as I rooted in the refrigerator for the now cold chicken and rice that had been made the night before, it hit me, and hard: I hadn't thought—not once, not a single time—about the job, about what calls might be going on, if there was a fire or disaster raging somewhere that I wasn't in the thick of in one way or another.

And also not once had a memory snapped into my head: a vivid replay of the fire, the jump, the fall.

Not the smell, not the fear, not the pain—not even when I'd reached just a bit too far on the table to round over for a shoulder piece on the fabric that Nana was so painstakingly putting together. In fact, I'd quickly blocked and labeled the pain as a twinge, marking it down as a minor annoyance. I gritted my teeth—and got on with it, dismissing it altogether.

Hours and hours spent drawing, cutting, piecing together, then drawing and cutting again, and all I'd felt was . . .

Contented.

Peaceful.

Because in addition to going back and forth aloud with Nana over what was next and which piece to put where, as well as admiring the shape, and cut, and line of her work, I'd also spent time thinking about the next panels I wanted to draw for the project I shared with Jean, had imagined sketching Trish, the way the sun hit the angle of her face when she was curled up and reading in the corner of my—*our*—room, and thinking about which angle might be the best to start doing a study from.

And as I automatically went through the motions of reheating and serving our plates, it occurred to me with sudden sharpness: I'd had a great day.

What would it be like, I wondered as I portioned the food, *if every day was like this? Is that even possible? Can I somehow make that happen?*

My brain froze on that.

What if . . . ?

Can I do this? Can I spend every day of my life not *running into danger and instead spend it creating worlds and stories and images?*

I felt the world spin and tilt, and I barely noticed as I put the bowls in my hands back down on the counter so I could lean on it, catch my balance as I felt my head spin and buzz.

How would I—could I— even begin to do that? I knew how to draw, sure, and I knew how to use some of the layout software involved, but Jean did most of that because she inserted text and all that . . . could I learn it?

I could, right? I mean, I had a nice and brand-new computer with a great processor for the graphics software I used, and I could always buy the software I didn't have. I could sit there and just figure it out, right?

Hey, if I can figure out entry and exit paths through fires, crushed cars and planes, assist with deployment for tremendous incidents such as floods and hurricanes, earthquakes and firestorms, power outages, and the crazy vagaries, from people with guns to walls covered in cockroaches, I can learn this, I reminded myself. *I can do it.*

But then . . . if I did that . . . what did it make me?

I was who I was, an emergency medical technician, a smoke jumper. I saved people for a living, and I was good at it—really damned good at it.

And it was a necessary job, a vital job, a job that required people like me—people who really cared—to do it.

I had taken an oath to serve my city and its people.

Was I really going to turn my back on that—and on them?

What was I, if I turned my back on all of that?

And much more important: who?

My head was really buzzing now, and the ache in my shoulder reminded me it had been there all along.

And a natural question came with the pain: *what if I can't do rescue anymore, anyway?* I knew, I knew very clearly what the options available to me were as well as the dangers, along with the likely outcomes of each.

I could do the surgery, spend almost a year convalescing, probably lose some of the finer function in my hand—which I supposed wouldn't really matter, not to most rescue personnel, wouldn't mean a thing at all, if I didn't—

Draw.

I sighed, feeling myself deflate with the breath.

Sure, yeah, Jean and I—we sold a couple of books here and there, but that was mostly money for new pencils, new paper, the cost of print itself after a while . . . and then there was the occasional pizza.

What was I thinking? Did I really think I could give up a career that provided me with food, home . . . *identity?*

For what?

I stared at my right hand where it held me up against the counter, then raised it to examine it. There was my palm, with light calluses across the pads just below my fingers from years and years of lifting stretchers, setting and pulling ropes and cables, lines clearly marked across the surface—there the one for life, there the one for love, health, creativity . . .

A triple bracelet of lines crossed the tender inside of the skin of my wrist; my veins pushed up under my skin, unique in their path and blue, carrying blood and oxygen over the tendons that weren't discernible under the palm but powered the fingers that ended them, each joint marked the same way my wrist was.

And my fingers . . . they were long, lean.

They were very visibly and obviously strong.

I'd shaped them with years of working, whether it was handling a pencil or setting a broken bone. I looked at my fingers closely—the shape of the nail beds, the clean cut of my nails, the stretch of tendons to each finger—they belonged to the hands of a worker, an artist, of someone who saved lives, of someone who drew new ones. Hands that had helped pull a baby out of a plane wreck, cuddled her to me gently and safely in the midst of chaos and horror. Hands that had first sketched, then created a world that held a story that my friend had brought forth. The very same hands that had held a fellow smoke jumper's as we ran—fled, really—from a breakaway that had swept our way, pulling and tugging and hauling each other over snags and rocks and away, as far away as possible from a ravening dragon we wouldn't be able to put down for a few more days . . .

This . . . was *my* hand.

It had soothed my grandmother's brow while she'd been ill, had cupped the tiny heads of each and every one of my friends' children when they'd been born. It had held so many others' hands: the young, the old, the sick, and the injured . . . sad, scared.

Felt their pulse.

Steady in my hand.

I had drawn pictures of my family and friends.

I had, with pencil and line of sight and a vision in my head, built worlds and spaceships, real animals and imaginary heroes.

Landscapes, real and envisioned.

All in my hand.

I had held Trish's fingers entwined with mine, stroked her hair, held her close to me, pressed my palm against her chest to feel the beloved beat echo through me.

My hand.

With its four fingers and thumb, each vein doing exactly what it should, channeling over and under and through bone and muscle and tendon, and each of those functioning in concert with the other, allowing me to take care of myself and others, allowing me to build—anything.

Anything I chose.

Whether it was health or life, a lean-to, an image of a superhero, or even—I chuckled to myself—an entire wedding party's outfits.

If I went for the surgery, I would lose all of that for almost a year because of the swelling, the healing, the new physical therapy I'd have to go through—and none of it with the guarantee that I'd get more than eighty percent of it back and no one certain of what that twenty percent loss might be.

And that was assuming everything went perfectly according to plan—no complications on either the surgical side or from the natural vagaries of medicine, biology, and anatomy.

If I didn't go, well, it would be at least another ten months before I could start working with any real weight on the shoulder at all—and no guarantee that the tendons and ligaments would snap back to their original size, and a too-heavy strain before it was ready—if it ever was—meant I could completely dislocate the arm. The damage *that* might cause to the nerve and artery that nestled just within that junction—

There might be no coming back from that.

Ever.

So what was I supposed to choose? *How* was I supposed to choose?

And yet . . . I didn't really think there was a choice here.

I—who prided myself on what I did, who was so independent—had kept me and Nana going when she couldn't work, my way of being family, of saying "thank you" for every single day of our lives, the care and love she'd given to me every single day of *my* life that I could remember, and I had handled it all again, and handily, when Linda had first gotten here and needed to get on her feet.

Ten months to a year or more needing help to wash.

Ten months to a year or more needing help to get dressed.

Ten months to a year or more learning to brush my teeth with my left hand.

Ten months to forever without being able to write.

Ten months to forever without being able to draw.

Right now, so long as I was careful and kept up with the small bits of physical therapy that I could do, I had complete function of my right hand; I could do everything I used to, for the most part, except for lean on that arm with real weight, reach behind me or over my head.

Pain and non-weight-bearing aside, I was almost completely functional.

If I never lifted another stretcher again, even without further physical therapy, I'd eventually be all right: the shoulder itself would be more easily prone to strain and sprain and I'd probably be able to tell weather patterns by it, but still, overall I'd be all right, sooner or later.

Was I really contemplating giving all that up so I could keep running out into rain and fire and gunshots? And roaches . . . *Ugh.* I grimaced at the many memories. *There's always roaches.*

And what was I contemplating giving up my ability to do

art for, really?

Because after the money was made and the bills were paid, what was there to life, anyway?

Being able to enjoy sitting and taking apart a design—the use of color, of line, of flow—in a magazine with my grandmother.

Enjoying laughing with Tori and Jean and the little ones, watching sometimes silly movies and getting inspired, making up stories that created a world, a world that brought something to us—to me, anyway.

Feeling Trish curled up next to me, loving the pressure of her head on my shoulder—the very one that was the cause and source of this question—and knowing that there was no feeling more beautiful than this.

Reading. Thinking. Drawing and putting all those things into colors and lines on paper, bringing it to a two-dimensional life that somehow became so much more than that when I shared it with someone else . . .

But oh . . . I'd had such a good day, I'd felt good and purposeful, so definitively zoned into the moment and the motion with successful results.

The combined strength and skill of my arm and hand.

Was I going to sacrifice one for the other?

If all I did was go to the job—which I did love—with nothing else to do, only able to observe the things my grandmother did, only able to discuss the stories in my head, not share them in the way I loved best, what would be left? Because I'd still have scar tissue and even with a successful surgery with no complications, the shoulder would never be the same, it wouldn't have the same strength it had before, still have an increased fallibility potential.

I loved saving lives—and I was good at it, damned good—but what did it mean if I gave up the joy in mine to continue to do it?

But if I didn't give it up, if I preserved that part of me, then how did I go forward? How did I take care of my family?

Because . . . I'd still have to work, and what would I do? I didn't have a complete formal education, and other than the work I'd just done with my grandmother and the occasional issues I put out with Jean . . .

I had nothing.

No degree.

No knowledge of what the industry might need—or even what it really was.

No experience.

And no idea of how to get any.

I sighed heavily, feeling my whole body bowed down with the weight of it.

"*Que te pasa, hija—te olvidaste?*" Nana asked as she walked in, asking me what was wrong, if I'd forgotten.

I blinked, brought back to the here and now, steaming bowls of food before me, and a pair of hungry stomachs waiting to be fed.

"Nana," I said as I picked the bowls back up, then walked them to the table, "I don't know what to do."

She gave me a sharp and steady glance as we sat down. She waited for me to find my words.

Silence stretched while I stared down at nothing.

"Eat," she reminded me gently in Spanish. "You'll think better."

She was right, so I did. And after the first few swallows, the words and the images, the ideas became easier.

"Nana," I began, "how did you know what you were going to do? Did you always love making other people's clothes? Why that? Are you happy with it? Why did—"

Nana reached over and patted my hand to shush me. "I don't think you want to work in couture or as a seamstress," she said in Spanish. "Why don't you ask me what you really want to know instead?" Her eyes were loving and her hand warm on mine as I arranged the words I wanted to say.

"I don't want to lose my hand, Nana, I don't want to not be me—but if I don't work, what do I do? And if I don't do all of it"—I waved my fork around, trying to somehow encompass the totality of rescue with it—"then who am I? I mean, am I letting us down, letting the city down, my friends? Because how am I gonna work when I don't know a thing about how all of this—"I gestured again, trying to mean everything else that was important, like art and stories, and love and joy, "—even works at all?"

"You mean—should you get the surgery and wait the next ten months or more to go back to work to see if maybe you'll be able to get some of your skill back, or should you spend the next ten months that you have to have off anyway developing a new skill and trying a whole new life path from the very beginning?"

I stared at her because, yes, that was exactly what I meant, and that she'd found the words so easily while I was still struggling to put them together into a sentence—

"And then you're worried about letting everyone down, from your city oath"—she gave me a small smile—"to your friends, and worried if you'll still have anything in common with them, with your friends, with Linda . . . with Trish. Is that everything?" She rubbed my hand gently for a moment. "Take another few bites—it's not as good cold."

I did as she suggested, staring at her all the while, shocked that she could see me, read me, know me so clearly.

But then again, why wouldn't she? She'd been there when my mother gave birth to me, the first to hold me after her, the one to change and care for and feed me while my mother had to work, the person I cried to when—as much as I don't remember all of it—my father first came home and picked me up, a stranger with a brushy face . . . the one who'd had to tell me that my parents were gone and who protected me from everything that could have followed.

Nana, at an age when most people were enjoying their early

maturity, had had to raise a child after losing her own, revisiting every marker and milestone and making me doubly her own as both child and grandchild—and making sure I never, not once felt any loss of love.

Why *wouldn't* she know me so well? The bigger shock would be if she didn't.

"Nana . . . what if I disappoint them? What if I can't do anything with this and I'm useless, unable to have a real career or do all those things, like buy a house and have a retirement plan, support a family, and"—I paused to take a breath—"what if I completely, miserably fail?"

She nodded and glanced down at her plate, then reminded me with a gesture to keep eating. "And . . . what?" she asked.

"What do you mean, 'and what?'"

Nana took a sip from her glass, then took a deep breath. "You fail—at what, really?" she asked in very carefully thought-out and pronounced English. "So you don't have those things right away—nobody does. You are a smart woman, a hard worker, Bennadette. You do what you've always done—you apply yourself, the way you did when you first learned to talk—and you go, you make it happen. Your friends," she said, and paused so she could cut into the food on her plate. "Your friends will still be your friends, your family will still be your family—the difference is you will not ever wonder, 'what if I'd tried?'"

I stared at her.

"That's the failure, *corazón*, you *not* trying. And if you don't take this time—this golden moment of opportunity hidden inside what could have been tragic—then I have failed *you, mi cielo*, failed to teach you what I thought you'd already learned."

I cocked my head at her, wondering what she meant.

"Not that life is short—you know this—but that we waste it if we don't use our gifts. And you have many: the gift that you survived, the gift you have of your heart, your talent—and now, this precious time to take a chance."

I could feel the lump form in my throat, even as my eyes began to sting as they filled. "You think so, Nana?" I asked. "You think that this is—"

"*Veneno que no mata, engorda*," Nana told me, her voice serious and low. "*Es tu tiempo, por fin.*"

I nodded as I digested both the meal and her words. Poison that doesn't kill fattens, or rather, that which doesn't kill one makes one stronger. And that it was my time, finally.

"But what if I lose what I've already built? I spent so much time, Nana, risked so much—and all that experience, it goes to waste?"

"*Hijita*," Nana said so gently, "you—you jump out of planes and into fires. What are you, of all people in the world, afraid of?"

I glanced down at the table as I thought about it, trying to find the words before I faced the question Nana had placed before me. "I'm afraid . . ." I began, then took a breath. I started again. "I'm afraid . . . that I don't have a parachute."

Nana nodded and put her hand over mine. "But that already happened—you fell from the sky," she reminded me as she rubbed the back of my hand. Her eyes, loving and dark, shone on me, and I realized, as I looked into them, that they held unshed tears. "And lived."

I was stunned with the enormity of what she'd just pointed out to me, and not just metaphorically, either.

God, it really did hit me so hard.

Nana . . . was right.

I'd jumped out of a plane—an out-of-control plane, right into a katabatic wind, too close and too wild to be able to let my parachute function fully—and survived. Anything else would be so much less dangerous than that.

My heart pounded, and I could feel my chest expand with the possibilities of what that might mean, its potential . . . my future.

"So," I began as I thought and felt about what she'd said, "you're telling me I should jump again?" I asked.

"You're not seriously thinking about not having the surgery, are you?" Linda said loudly, walking into the kitchen. "*Hola*, Nana," she said, and leaned down to give her a kiss. "I mean, yeah, you've got a bit more recovery concussion-wise to go, sure, but seriously—you've been doing this for years. What the hell else do you think you're gonna do?" she asked as she served herself from the pot that was still on the stove. "Sell coloring books at the comic book store with your friend? Because that pays you, like, what," she hazarded as she pulled out a seat and sat with us, "thirty bucks a month?"

"*Pero no es tu cuerpo, ni tu vida,*" Nana said with heat and strength in her voice. "*No es tu decisión!*"

"She's my family—you're my family. It's the future we all have to think about!" Linda answered just as heatedly.

God, the stress of this was beginning to make my head ache with a fullness that I'd not had all day. I rubbed at my temples to try to ease it.

"And what are you going to tell your crew, your friends?" Linda continued. "You're dropping out of a good career with a definite track to it so you can play like what's his name who ran away to Tahiti to paint the natives? And how is *that* going to go over with your superhero girlfriend?"

Superheroes.

For whatever reason, that stuck in my head. Among so many other things, that was something Trish and I had in common. And suddenly, I realized Nana was right. I'd jumped out of a plane with a failed parachute—and lived. There was nothing left to be afraid of.

"You know what?" I said as I stood, then whipped my phone out of my back pocket. "I'm just gonna call and ask her!"

"Oh, for fuck's sake!" Linda said with exasperation. "Just sit down and eat—talk this through with me."

"Nope," I said, and began keying in my message.

> Bennie: Baby, I miss you! Let me know
> if you have time to talk when you
> come in tonight. I love you. I love you
> so damn much!

> Trish: My love! I miss YOU!!! Yes,
> please—I LOVE talking with you! I'm
> off shift in 5 minutes, and I'm all yours,
> okay, well I'm ALWAYS all yours, but in
> 5 minutes I'm outta here and home in
> half an hour. YES, let's definitely talk!

> Bennie: Yes, love. Counting down,
> starting now!

I couldn't help but smile as I read, then answered the text from the woman who really was my superhero girlfriend. I glanced up to see both Nana and Linda watching me.

"You're right," I said seriously to Linda as I walked my dish to the sink. "She *is* a superhero—so I think she can handle this." I walked around her, then paused by Nana to give her a good-night hug.

Nana's eyes were shining on me warm and bright, and I felt my chest expand with not only how much I loved her but how much she loved me, too.

"Besides," I said as I bent down to hug my beloved grandmother, "I already jumped out of a plane without a parachute."

"*Me debes veinte dólares,*" Linda said with a laugh behind me.

"*Sí,*" my grandmother agreed as she hugged me. "I send it via CashNow App."

"Waitaminute," I said, wanting to be sure I understood, and it wasn't just the still-healing concussion playing games with my head—literally.

"You guys had a bet I'd call my girlfriend?"

Linda laughed again, and even my grandmother chuckled.

"No, dope—we had a bet on when you'd decide to finally do the right thing by yourself and be your own superhero. Nana thought it might take you until scheduling the surgery and said we should go slower, and I said if we rip the bandage off, you could start your new life sooner rather than later."

"Oh," I said as I absorbed that. "I was wondering why you were being so . . . so . . ."

"Aggressive?" Linda said helpfully as Nana held me tighter for a moment.

"Hard spicy," I said finally. Because it was true—Linda could be sharp, but this had been getting close to actually nasty—and that was unusual, to say the least.

"I figured something a little different might jog your brain into working it out a bit faster."

"That's maybe a dangerous thing to do with my concussion and all that," I reminded her. "What if that had backfired?"

"We had . . . what you say, backup," Nana told me with a smile in her voice.

"What?" my head was beginning to spin with the complexity of their plan. *Or maybe this time it's really the concussion*, my brain reminded me.

"Backup, my love," Trish said, walking into the now-full kitchen. "I'm your backup."

"Oh, thank fucking God!" was the very first thing Trish said after we'd kissed and hugged hello, she'd showered from her shift, and we'd sat down to discuss. "Baby—you know I love you for who you are, not what you do, don't you?" she asked as she pulled me into her for a very warm embrace. "And who you are, the art—that's a part of you. It would be horrible if God or the Universe or whatever you want to call it spared your life and you wasted that gift." She kissed my cheek.

"I don't—I don't want to disappoint anyone, especially myself," I admitted. "I mean, what if nothing comes of it, and I wasted time and opportunity to move farther within the service and all that?"

Trish shifted to gaze at me, her eyes warm, dark, and shining on mine in the low light of our room. "Bennie . . . sweetheart," she began, then glanced down and took a breath. When she raised her eyes back to mine, I saw there were tears in hers. "Baby . . . you could have been killed, not just in the usual 'I'm an EMT, and it's part of the job' thing, but from a fucked-up plane malfunction with a bad jump that messed up your parachute—baby, it's a fucking miracle that you're even alive, that, that . . ." Trish was crying in earnest now. "Baby, all you ended up with is a concussion that will heal, a shoulder that won't let you lift for now, and a scar on your face that's already fading and will ultimately disappear—and I am so grateful for that. If you never do it again, I don't care. I'm just so fucking glad that you're okay."

I held her close, my eyes running as freely as hers while she spoke, and as she did, I could smell the smoke from the fire, feel the wind whipping against my face and the useless strain of the toggles in my hand as I'd tumbled.

And the pain.

And the whiteout wash.

And the love that had taken me with it.

And suddenly I knew, knew Trish was right, felt to my very core a tearing sorrow and fear that this, this moment of Trish in my arms, held loved and close to me, and me to her, sharing each other's breath and feeling the beat of her heart against mine—this could have all been lost. As solid and real and as perfect as we were in each other's arms, it was sacred and rare and ephemeral, and it could have been wiped out by a tree limb placed a different way, a gust gone different, a deeper cut than the one my face had received.

And Trish—Trish had put her life on the line for me that day, too.

Yes, she'd been part of the entire response to begin with, but she was the one who'd climbed the tree and directed the crew, all to get me down from the height I'd gotten horribly caught up in, her position precarious, and the massive fire bearing down.

So this gift, this gift of life, of ability, of the potential—yeah, I wasn't going to waste it. Because what if—*what if*—I could actually make a dream come true? What if I could do that and bring her with me?

I had a chance—a chance to live, a chance to love, a chance to try with the love and the wholehearted support of people who really and truly cared about me.

And sure, that chance might be a small one, but my chances of having survived what had happened, of having survived it and being as able as I still was—those chances had been even smaller. And yet—it had happened.

Anything was possible.

"It's okay, Trish, baby," I whispered, holding her even closer as she cried against me. "I'm okay, and that's never going to happen again—I promise," I swore as I kissed her head and her cheeks and the delicate skin over her closed eyes, the taste of her tears full on my lips. "I'm going to try this—I'm scared, but I'm going to try. I'm more scared of losing this part of me than I am of anything else," I told her honestly. "I'm not going to waste the chance you risked your life to give me."

Trish wriggled a little so she could look at me, and she wiped at her eyes. "Baby, you fell from the sky and survived. You're not just gonna try—you're gonna fly!" The smile she gave me was a shine that lit her face, her eyes, all of her, and in the face of that light, of the love she shone on me, all I could do was sigh as I felt myself fall even deeper in love with her, and I could only answer her with a kiss that spoke everything I was thinking and, more importantly, feeling.

The kiss deepened, became taste, became touch until we were tangled together, skin bare and sliding, silken and soft, and the desire we'd held at aching bay now the demand we both followed close, then closer still, the love and the want and the burning need, until . . .

"Baby . . ." Trish whispered, love and need and desire in her voice and her touch and her body. "Are you sure? We don't have to, we can—"

"Yes," I answered her with the same heat pouring over and through me, the slip and taste of her lips and tongue against mine, the feel of her body, the pure beauty of touch between us the only thing I needed, wanted, holding me fast and safe and loved before the unknown future that lay before me. "Yes," I said again, "because I love you, because you love me, because I've missed you, baby, I've really fucking *missed* you."

"Me, too, baby," she murmured against my skin, the heat of her mouth and her body and her touch the fire I wanted and needed and ached to get lost within. "I've missed you so fucking much . . ."

No pain.

No doubt.

No fear.

Because Trish was right. We didn't just jump.

We flew.

Chapter 9

It Only Took Two Years, a Lot of Work, and Maybe a Prayer

"MAN, THIS looks just like something out of Star Wars!" Linda said, her voice unnecessarily loud and close to my ear as she glanced around the high columns, the dramatic-view terraces, and the people—or rather, the beings: elves and orcs, robots, mermaids, superheroes—with and without capes—space ninjas, and soldiers. And those were just the identifiables within visual range because the crowds before us, behind us, and around us were huge.

"*Es porque lo filmaron aquí*," Nana told her.

I glanced over at her. "I didn't think you'd know this place inspired one of their sets," I said to her, genuinely surprised that she knew that.

"*Es obvio*," she said with a smile and a slight shrug.

"Is this where we're supposed to be?" Trish asked from next to me, her eyes poring over the printouts she held while my phone buzzed an alert.

I grabbed it out to read:

> Scanlon-Scott: Don't move—we sorta
> see you! Be there in like a minute!

"We're good, we're good," I assured Trish over the din of thousands of aliens and heroes and troopers from all over the multiverse. "They're going to meet us here."

"*Tia!*"

I don't know how I heard that little voice above all the rest, but sure enough, I did, and I automatically turned to see Daisy, dressed all in red with a band about her head, with her sister's hand in hers on one side (dressed identically but in navy blue) and her barely walking brother's held tightly in the other (dressed in yellow), streaking towards us.

I knelt down so I could be at their height when they threw themselves into my arms, Tori and Jean just behind them.

"Annie-Banannie! Daisy! Trick!" I exclaimed as I hugged them all, happy to see them, and gave them each a kiss.

"It's Jack!" Daisy corrected me. "Because trick or treat and Halloween and he's a little punkin'!" she explained earnestly. "Jack, see?"

I laughed because I did. "Yes, sweetheart, Jack—I forgot!"

"Jack!" he nodded affirmatively, then popped his thumb into his mouth.

"All right, we're all here—are we all ready?" Tori asked as she simultaneously picked up her toddler, deftly replaced his thumb with a sippy cup, and passed the papers she'd had in her hand over to Jean.

"As ready as we're gonna be, I guess," I said as we gave each other hugs all around.

"All right, then," Jean said. "Everyone's got passes and all that stuff?"

Nana waved impatiently towards the gate we were all supposed to go to. "*Vamos, ya!*"

"We're going, we're going!" I laughed and assured her.

"You ready for this?" Trish asked me as she grasped my hand.

I squared my shoulders and took a deep breath as I entwined my fingers with hers. "No. Absolutely not."

"So," she began, then kissed my cheek. "You're fine, then," she said and smiled at me.

I held my wife's hand, and simply enjoyed looking at her for a moment while I took a settling breath. With her hand in mine and her smiling at me like that, well honestly, how could I not be?

"I am," I agreed, smiling back.

And into the massing throng we went.

San Diego Comic Con was an event like no other—except for maybe New York Comic Con—in sheer size alone. With an attendance of over one hundred thousand people, not including exhibitors, panelists, and performers, it was a fast-formed city of creatives and creative fans jammed into one huge convention center for four days.

It was great to be in San Diego, and this time something *wasn't* on fire: our title, *Hex*, had grown a loyal following and people were talking about it in different places.

As a result, Jean and I had been invited to participate on a panel about women, diversity, and—yep, of all things—gay women not just making comics but actually starring in them, like they did in our story.

So yes, of course we were there—the whole family: Linda and Nana because they'd never been to California, ever; Trish because she was my wife and not only did I refuse to be without her, this moment couldn't have happened without her; Jean and Tori with their kids because how could they go to Comic Con and not bring them; and me because, yes, I was half of the creative team behind the title.

While Jean and I reviewed notes and points, trying our best to make sure we were ready for whatever questions might possibly come up, our now-combined family made their way into the room where the presentation would be.

It was probably one of the best feelings in the world to be sitting next to my friend and creative partner, asking and answering questions, and always, always able to see—right there in the very front row, seated as close to parallel with us as possible—the people we loved most and who loved us, too.

People asked questions, we answered, and through it all, every single time I glanced their way, I could see the smile Nana wore, the grin and occasional head nod Linda gave, the light that was Trish shining my way while Tori smiled broadly at Jean, and the three little ones doing their best not to wriggle.

There were photos—so many photos—taken with readers and fans, and a video of the event, plus there were people to talk with after, and all of it rushed because the group that had proposed and sponsored the panel had also scheduled us to perform a portfolio review right after, as well as to sit at their assigned table to sign books for those who might want them.

Still, even with all the rush and the people, there was one person and one person only I wanted to see, just as soon as I could descend from the stage.

"You did great—you both were awesome!" Trish exclaimed, hugging me enthusiastically after we kissed.

"That wasn't so bad," I said with a smile, feeling as if I'd just done something—well, if not important, then at least good.

"Do you need help carrying books? Your shoulder okay?" she asked me as we gathered together by the hall exit to make our way to the next stop.

"They've already got some there," I reminded her. I rotated my shoulder experimentally just to check how I was doing. "And my shoulder's feeling okay."

"All right, baby," she agreed. "But let someone carry stuff for you if it twinges, okay?"

"Yes, my love," I agreed as we made our way through the maze of people and booths.

"So okay—I'm kidnapping Nana, your wives, and the kids," Linda informed me and Jean with a big smile as we arrived at the required booth. "There's a preview screening we have to go to!"

"Sure, sure, take them," Jean said with a laugh. "But be sure to bring them back safely!"

"Yes'm!" Linda saluted her. "Safety is my middle name!"

"Really? I always thought it was Mercedes!" I said.

Annie put her hands on her hips and stared up at Linda. "We are not kids!" she announced, a scowl across her face that made her adorable.

"No?" Linda asked and knelt down to hear her better. "Then what are you?"

"We are super ninja warrior princesses!" Daisy told her, then gave a twirl to illustrate.

"And a prince," Annie corrected, then gave a twirl of her own. "And we are *all* from outta space!"

Trick, who was now punkin' prince Jack, wriggled in Tori's arms until she let him down to give a twirl of his own, and I couldn't help it—I laughed.

"Oh, they are all so very definitely your wife and kids," I told Jean as Linda, Tori, and Nana herded them all together, then disappeared among the steam punks, space aliens, and probably quite a few other warrior ninja royalty from "outta space."

"And I'm very proud of that," Jean said, and smiled back at me. "Seriously proud!"

We took our seats behind our name cards, and it seemed like there was instantly a line of people waiting to be talked with, portable devices with and without printed materials, and so many drawing pads to look at . . .

"So I don't have anything for you to look at, but I do have someone for you to meet," a voice I knew said as I was bent over signing an inside flap to a copy of the print—yes, the actual print—of a first-run first issue of *Hex*.

245

"Robbie!" I said with real joy as I glanced up to see our friend, supporter, and even in many ways business mentor, from JHU. "You're here!"

"Heya, Robbie—nice to see ya!" Jean said next to me.

"Well, yah, duh, of course—we have a shop set up—which you guys are gonna come visit, maybe hang out and sign a few things?"

"Yeah, we can do that, right?" I glanced over at Jean to make certain we were on the same page.

"Oh, definitely," she agreed with a nod and a smile. "You're always so awesome to us!"

Robbie blushed. "Yeah, well, you know it's good stuff," he said, staring down at the table, pink dots bright on his cheeks. "So, uh, I have a friend who wants to meet you," he said, regaining his composure, and he turned sideways to let the person who'd been standing behind him come to the fore. "Hey, Buddy? This is Bennie Grego and Jean Scanlon-Scott. Bennie, Jean? This is Buddy!" Robbie announced with a pleased smile as we each reached over to shake hands.

"Oh wow—I'm really glad to meet you two!" Buddy exclaimed. "Your work is really a bright spot, different and exciting, makes ya think and is fun, all at the same time, y'know?" he said enthusiastically as he shook our hands.

I wondered why he looked so familiar even as I felt myself blush, the heat rushing all the way up to my ears. Jean had pink spots on her cheeks, too.

"Thanks," I said, not so sure of what else there was to say. I decided I must have seen him at the store from time to time, hence the familiarity.

"We're really glad you enjoy it," Jean told him.

"Oh man, yeah!" Buddy continued. "You guys—you're really pushing the boundaries of all-around storytelling genre—even with the look of it all! How do you do it?" he asked in the same excited rush. "Jean writes and you draw it, or do you guys work

246

it together, or what? I mean, it's all so organic!"

Jean grinned as she glanced at me before answering. "Actually, we both have input into all of it. Sometimes Bennie will come up with a story idea or we'll flesh out one of mine together, we both come up with interesting phrasing, and the story itself is something in the end we both worked on, even if I do more of the writing part."

"Right," I agreed. "And we talk about how we both see it, from the world to the characters, and sometimes Jean will pass me a sketch of what she envisions—then the next thing you know, it's all together, the art and the words, even if I do more of the drawing part itself."

"Yeah," Jean seconded. "I'll do more writing and she'll do more drawing, but it's always the thing we made together that ends up out there."

"Yeah, that's just awesome. The work is seamless," he told us. "So here—"he laid a pile of our collection on the table, "—if you guys would sign these for me, please?"

"For you or for . . . ?" I asked as I pulled the first book down and opened the cover, and tried not to be astounded that someone really liked our work as much as he did.

"Oh, they're for me—Buddy."

I passed the book over to Jean as I finished and reached for the next.

"So, uh . . . Robbie tells me you both worked for Emergency Medical Services, and you used to jump out of perfectly good airplanes and into fires, Bennie, huh? I bet you both have good stories to tell!"

Robbie began to laugh. "Oh my God," he said between laughs. "You should tell him about that time with the guy we had in the store, the one who thought he'd been invaded by— what was it? Micromutants that were taking over his body, and the cure was in some episode of—"

Jean burst out laughing, and so did I, with the memory. "Oh

247

my God—you remember that?" I asked.

"God, wasn't that like one of the few times we worked together?" Jean asked me with a smile. "Oh man, he was definitely special!"

"Didn't you guys end up wrapping him up in a thermal blanket or something, you know, that thing with the foil?" Robbie asked.

"Christ—yes!" I said, trying to speak between laughs. "We convinced him that it would suffocate the buggers already in there—"

"Yeah, and—and prevent the new ones from beaming in!" Jean finished.

"Oh God, and then you offered him a balloon," I gestured at Robbie, "and he freaked out!"

"Because he thought that was the ship they'd traveled over in!" Jean finished. "Yeah, that was one for the books, all right!"

We were all howling with laughter at this point, and even Buddy joined in as a line began to grow behind them.

"So hey, just in case," Buddy said as he stuck his hand into his pocket, then pulled out his wallet. "I'm working on a new project—maybe you guys could come up with something for it?" he asked as he handed us each a business card. "I have to go— gotta be at an interview in, like, five minutes," he told us as he gathered his things. "So email or call me or whatever, yeah?"

"Sure," I agreed as I glanced at his name, number, and email on the card. I slipped it into my back pocket.

"Yes," Jean said as she did the same.

"All righty. And thanks for signing these!" he said, holding his books up. "You coming, Robbie?"

"Uh, yeah, sure!" he said to Buddy as he began to walk away. "So you two are gonna stop by the store booth later, right?"

"Uh-huh!" I assured him. "We'll see you later!"

Robbie stepped away, and the next person handed me their folder full of work. As I opened the envelope, Trish suddenly stood behind me. She put her hands on my shoulders and leaned down to kiss the top of my head. "What was that all about, baby?" she asked into my ear, her lips soft against its ridge.

I turned my head so I could kiss her because I loved the feel of her lips on mine, and the kiss became its own beautiful thing, until I could hear clapping.

"Beautiful, guys!" Jean said, part of the clapping crowd.

Trish and I both laughed as we gently ended the kiss. "More—later?" I asked her softly.

"More—definitely!" she agreed, then kissed the top of my nose.

"So what was what about?" I asked her as I spread the contents of the envelope out on the table before me.

"You guys were talking with Buddy Frey—what did he want?"

I reached into my pocket and handed her the card he'd given me. "Oh, he's a guy from the shop. He's working on something new. Probably wants me and Jean to look at his comic or something," I said as I paged through the drawings before me.

They weren't bad, I thought as I looked. In fact, this kid had some talent—but there wasn't a story here, just a random collection of images and—

"Baby—are you serious?" Trish asked, and it was her tone that made me look up at her.

"Well, that's what I'm guessing," I answered. "Why?"

Trish wore a bemused expression as she shook her head at me. Even Jean looked up.

"What?" she asked.

Trish focused on the card again for a long moment as we both waited for her answer. Finally, she put it into her shirt pocket, then put a hand on each of our shoulders.

"Guys," she said.

And we waited.

"Guys . . . this is a big deal. Do you know who Buddy Frey is?"

I had no idea. I looked at Jean, who gave me the same "I dunno" expression. "No," I said simply, looking back up at my wife. "He's a guy from the shop."

Trish crouched down between us.

"Guys," she said again. "This . . . is a big. Deal. Like, a really. Big. Deal."

We both stared at her, waiting for an explanation.

"You know that show, the one about the aliens running an underground freedom ring from the whole selling-beings-for-body-parts thing?"

I looked at Trish, then at Jean, who furrowed her brow at me.

"Yeah . . ." I said slowly. "But I haven't had time to watch it much or anything."

"Tori's talked about it," Jean said, "but we've been so busy with deadline for this, there's not been time. So . . . what about it?"

"Yeah," I seconded. "What's that got to do with—oh . . ." I said as a clue finally hit me. "Oh . . ." I said again as I realized why he'd seemed so familiar.

"Oh!" Jean exclaimed as I blushed, because neither of us had recognized him, and now I was embarrassed that I hadn't known, and boy, was I dumb and—

"Christ, Bennie—what do you think? Maybe that new storyline we were talking about or something? I mean, we could get a synopsis together real quick. We already were discussing what we want it to look like," she said excitedly. "Oh hey!" she said as Jack wriggled his way under the table and threw himself into her lap.

"So, whattaya think?" she asked as he tucked his head against her shoulder and his ninja sisters came running around to our side of the table, Tori, Nana, and Linda right behind them. "Hey, baby," Jean said, and reached for the kiss Tori was already bending to give her.

I smiled as I waited—they were awesome together. "You know," I said as I thought about it and Tori wrapped an arm around Jean, "origin stories—they're kinda the best, y'know?"

Jean nodded thoughtfully. "Yeah, absolutely—past is prologue and all that."

"Well, I've got a favorite story," Trish said with a smile as she stood closer to me and I put my arm around her waist.

We all gazed up at her expectantly. "In my favorite story, an angel falls from the sky and thinks she'll die, but she doesn't— she becomes a whole new sort of hero instead." She smiled, then leaned down and kissed me again.

"Hey—I know that one!" I heard Jean say. "That would work. The only thing is, what would we call it?"

Once more, the kiss gently ended, and I peeked around my wife to my friends—my family—with a smile of my own. This question was one I finally had an answer to.

"Oh man, I got that—that's easy!" I told Jean, and I smiled broadly. "We're gonna call it 'Fire Fall.'"

Acknowledgments

Thank you so much, Salem—it's truly wonderful and an honor to be working with you and everyone at Bywater Books.

And to my love, my light, my life—Kris. I adore you. I love you all the lots, always. Thank you.

About the Author

Former Managing Editor for *The Advocate*, artist, musician, and author JD Glass is an American Library Association Stonewall Award and Lambda Literary Award finalist for her novel *Punk Like Me*, and a Lambda Literary Award finalist for *Red Light*, with that and other titles earning an IBPA Ben Franklin Award, Rainbow Reads Award, and Golden Crown Literary Society short lists and awards.

A recipient of Columbia College Chicago's Faculty Recognition Award, and Columbia Scholar Award, Glass' visual work was selected for Chicago Manifest Art Showcase, InArt Gallery Virtual Exhibit, ISee Pixels exhibit, and OnBigDrawingsII Virtual Exhibit.

Glass is also the writer and executive producer for the short film rom-com *Her Curve*, as well as the upcoming feature, and for the series *Punk Like Me–the B Sides*, currently in production.

Follow her at:
Twitter | @JDGlass
Instagram | @JDGlass_Story_Artist
Facebook | www.facebook.com/jdglass2/
Website | http://www.dresenglass.com/

Bywater Books believes that all people have the right to read or not read what they want—and that we are all entitled to make those choices ourselves. But to ensure these freedoms, books and information must remain accessible. Any effort to eliminate or restrict these rights stands in opposition to freedom of choice.

Please join with us by opposing book bans and censorship of the LGBTQ+ and BIPOC communities.

At Bywater Books, we are all stories.

For more information about Bywater Books, our authors, and our titles, please visit our website.

https://bywaterbooks.com